reason to lie to her.

"Would you?" she asked.

He fought the urge to grab her and crush her against him. He never remembered wanting a woman this way in his life. But Patience was no ordinary woman. She was James's daughter.

"No, I won't," he said, hoping the pain he felt wasn't apparent in his voice.

"Why?" She stepped closer. "I wouldn't mind," she admitted, ducking her head shyly.

The timorous movement surprised him. He'd never seen Patience any way but forceful and commanding. Her sudden reticence also aroused in him deep feelings of protectiveness and a surge of defensiveness. She was innocent. And she was his responsibility.

"I don't know what is happening between us, Patience. But it can't continue. I'm—jaded. Hell, I'm more than that. I have a reputation as a rogue, and it's a name I've well earned. You're naive about such things."

"I wouldn't be so naive if you kissed me."

Other *Leisure* and *Love Spell* Books by Marti Jones:

BLIND FORTUNE
STARDUST TIME
A LOVE THROUGH TIME
DREAMWEAVER
TIME'S HEALING HEART

MARTI JONES

LEISURE BOOKS NEW YORK CITY

A LEISURE BOOK®

April 1996

Published by

Dorchester Publishing Co., Inc.
276 Fifth Avenue
New York, NY 10001

Printed in the United States of America.

To my aunt, Martha Knutz—a wonderful woman I am proud to have been named after.

Alluring
Adversary

Prologue

Mobile, Alabama: March 1845

His business finally concluded, Reese Ashburn looked forward to two days of carousing. He smiled as he contemplated a long night of whiskey and cards. And maybe he'd find a cute little doxy to fill the hours after that. He even considered forgoing the first two ventures in favor of the last.

The carriage rolled to a stop outside The King's Inn, a seedy-looking tavern on the docks of Mobile Bay. Reese chuckled. King, indeed. No king would be caught dead anywhere near the place, much less in it. Hell, he suspected even the Mississippi River rats wouldn't sully themselves inside those walls.

It was just the place for him and James, though. He laughed. It was no secret among Mobile's upper crust that Reese Ashburn liked his whiskey neat, his women loose, and his taverns shady.

He swung down from the carriage before Joseph could assist him. Thwarted in his duties, the slave stepped aside awkwardly as Reese closed the door.

"Shall I wait, sir?" he asked.

"No need, Joseph. James and I will find other transportation when we're finished here."

"Yes, sir," Joseph said, climbing back onto his perch. He glanced around, frowned, and turned back to his master.

"Go ahead, Joseph."

With another uneasy look and a disturbed frown, Joseph clucked to the horses and pulled away, leaving Reese standing alone on the darkened street.

Reese looked through the tavern's dirty window. Through the smut he could see packed tables and the blurred outline of a serving wench moving around the room. As he stepped forward to go inside, he heard another carriage draw up behind him. He turned to see an elaborate conveyance pulled by a matching set of grays.

As the liveried driver pulled to a stop, Reese grinned and shook his head. The driver jumped to the ground and opened the door with a flourish.

"Reese, old man," a hearty voice boomed from the interior of the carriage. "I see you've beaten me to the festivities. Hope you haven't been tossed out already?"

A portly man stepped onto the street next to Reese. Dressed in a canary-yellow coat, green silk cravat, and paisley cummerbund, the stout man looked as if a tailor's scrap heap had fallen on him.

Reese's eyes bulged and he guffawed loudly.

"Egad, man, what have you poured yourself into this time?" he bellowed between laughs. "You look like a fop."

James Bentley poked his thumbs into the pockets of his coat and rocked back on his heels, making his extended waist protrude more than usual.

"You like it, eh?" he said proudly. "I'll give you the name of my tailor. Perhaps he can do something about your drab wardrobe."

"Thanks, no," Reese told him firmly. "Christ, I thought we wanted to keep a low profile down here."

He swept his hand in the direction of the fog-enshrouded docks. The smell of weathered wood mixed with the stench of rotting fish. Reese rubbed his knuckle under his nose and thought maybe his choice of a tavern was a bit too seedy this time.

"Nonsense," James exclaimed, slapping Reese on the back with enough force to make him cough. "We want the common folk to sit up and take notice. What good is money if you can't flaunt it? We'll have them dancing attendance in no time."

"Slitting our throats is more likely," Reese joked.

"Bah! You're acting like an old woman. Let's go in. We'll raise the roof off the place."

Reese eyed the ramshackle building. "That shouldn't be too difficult. Just make sure I'm out before the thing comes down."

James laughed loudly and together they entered the tavern.

Reese took another sip of whiskey and let his eyes drift from the cards in his hand to the serving girl bending over the table. Her bosom nearly fell from the ruffled edge of her bodice, and she watched him eye the creamy half-moons of flesh.

Her head tipped toward the stairs invitingly, and she smiled. Reese folded his cards and threw them into the center of the table. He gathered up his winnings, bade farewell to the other men at the table, and followed the girl to the stairs amid loud protests from the players.

At the bottom she turned toward him, pressing her breasts against his arm and giving him a better look at her features.

"Two bits for an hour, or six for the whole night," she whispered, her liquor-scented breath brushing his cheek.

Reese swept his gaze down the front of her whiskey-stained dress. Suddenly she didn't seem as enticing as she had from across the card table. Her eyes no longer seemed bright, but hard and cold. Her face showed signs of age and heavy drink. Powder gathered in the fine creases lining her mouth.

"I'll take the hour."

She looked disappointed but nodded. Reese pressed her elbow, and she started up the stairs ahead of him.

"Reese." James's voice stopped Reese on the third step. "Wait up."

Reese smiled apologetically at the woman, who cut James a withering glance.

"The chap downstairs has agreed to take us to a private gaming house. That is, if you're finished here." He tipped his head toward the woman waiting on the stairs.

Reese looked back at the woman and nodded. "Yeah, I'm finished."

"Well, come on then," James said, leading the way.

Reese turned back to the woman and nodded his head in farewell. She sneered at him and he chuckled, tossing her a coin to soothe her disappointment.

"I suppose I should thank you for your timing, James," Reese told his friend as they stepped out onto the street. "I think you've saved me from something I wouldn't have enjoyed anyhow."

"I thought as much when I saw the girl. Don't know why you bother with the likes of her when you have Rita, warm and ready for you any time."

"Same reason I drink whiskey, ale, and brandy. Variety, old man, variety."

"Ah, there's the fellow now," James said, motioning to a shadowy figure standing several feet from the tavern door. "Let's go."

The night air was cold and damp so close to the docks, and Reese wished he'd kept his coat on. Thrusting his hands into his trouser pockets, he strode along beside James. Their escort stayed several paces ahead.

The street darkened as they left the lively tavern behind, and Reese realized he'd never even met the man he was following. James had exchanged a few words with him in the tavern, but that was the extent of it. Reese hoped they weren't going far, since they were expected to walk.

Caution finally penetrated the fog of intoxication surrounding Reese's brain and he pulled up. Calling to the man ahead, he asked what establishment they were headed to.

"Up ahead," the figure called back. Then he turned into a narrow alley Reese hadn't noticed in the darkness and mist. Reese clutched James's arm.

"I don't like the smell of this, friend. What say we just go back to the tavern?"

"Ah, having second thoughts about that wench? I told you, Rita is ten times more woman. Besides," he said, walking ahead, "this is high stakes."

He laughed in anticipation of fattening his pockets, and Reese had no choice but to fall in behind him. He tried to shake his apprehension, but it took a firm hold. A shudder swept along his spine.

Halfway down the blackened alley, their guide suddenly broke and ran. James stopped, confused, but Reese suffered no such doubts.

"It's a trap!" he yelled, clutching James's arm and dragging the bemused man back the way they'd come.

Out of the mist ahead of them stepped two dark shadows. Reese's feet crunched to a stop on the graveled dirt. James stumbled drunkenly, and Reese had to support his friend as they whirled to run the other way. Two more shadows emerged, and Reese realized that, drunk or sober, they were going to have to fight their way out of the alley.

He bitterly regretted not insisting that they return to the tavern when they had the chance. He could usually hold his own in a fair fight, but James was another matter. The man was heavier and no longer young. What if Reese couldn't get them out of this? If only he hadn't drunk so much, he'd have seen the danger sooner.

James tried to shake off the numbing effects of the liquor and chuckled at Reese. "Well, here we go, old friend. What say we show these bastards what for?"

"I say we offer them our purses and call it a lesson richly bought." Reese nervously eyed the men as they inched closer, tightening the circle around them.

He reached for his wallet with one hand, holding the other up for the men to see. The nearest one swung, catching Reese on the chin with a glancing blow. James supported him, preventing him from falling, and Reese swore. Back to back now, the two crouched, ready for the fight.

All at once, the four thieves lunged. Reese sent the first one to the dirt with a hard punch. He heard James chuckle behind him, followed by the sound of bone meeting flesh. The second man landed a sharp right to Reese's lip, and the rusty tang of blood filled his mouth.

With a roar he lunged, his head meeting his opponent's diaphragm and knocking the wind out of him. He turned to see how James was faring. The first man grabbed him from behind, spun him around and landed a solid punch against Reese's jaw, knocking him back into the wall of the building behind him.

Reese responded with several blows in succession, and the man went down once more. He heard a grunt beside him and turned to see James sink to his knees. The dim light of the moon glinted off the handle of a knife protruding from James's chest. Reese cried out, but the sound was covered by the crack of a metal object making contact with his skull.

His knees buckled. The sights and sounds of the alley whirled around him. James's blood seeped down the front of his canary-yellow coat as blackness enshrouded Reese.

Chapter One

Three months later

The incessant banging brought Rita Mallory out of a deep sleep. She muttered an oath as she slid out of the bed and covered her nakedness with a silk wrapper. Combing her tangled auburn hair with her fingers, she padded softly to the front door.

Pink streaks of dawn filtered through the front windows as she drew back the latch. She opened the door and plopped her hands on her shapely hips, shaking her head at the sight.

"God," she muttered, her gaze raking the mess of a man before her, "you look like bloody hell."

Reese propped himself against the doorframe and raked his hands through his matted hair. His rumpled clothes were soiled and torn in places, his regal features distorted by cuts and bruises and enhanced by the pink scar on his cheek. His fists were bloodied and battered.

Rita moved forward and grasped him around the waist. Reese dangled his arm over her shoulder in an attempt to remain standing. Shuffling his feet, he let her half drag him into the bedroom. At the side of the four-poster bed, she released him, and his body slumped across the mattress. She lifted his legs onto the bed and removed his boots.

"What have you done to yourself now?" she asked, her usually soft voice harsh with disgust. She unfastened his trousers and yanked them down and off, wrinkling her nose and tossing them into the far corner of the room. "You look like something that crawled out of the gutter. Smell like it too," she added as she peeled away his shirt. "I shouldn't even have let you in here."

Reese chuckled, a deep, drunken sound, as he lay immobile on the bed.

"You'd never turn me away, Rita. Who'd pay for all this?"

The lovely face froze above him. Rita's movements stiffened as she jerked the delicate coverlet out from under him.

"Huh," she snorted. "There's plenty more men where you came from."

"Ah, that's where you're wrong, Rita girl. There are none like me," he said bitterly. "This kind of debauchery takes practice to perfect."

Rita looked surprised. "You actually sound

ashamed of your behavior. Is that remorse I hear in your voice?"

"Hell, no," he bellowed, causing Rita to jump. "I haven't had this much fun by listening to my conscience."

"You haven't got a conscience any longer."

Reese ran his hand down over his mouth and sighed loudly. "I never had one."

"Yes, you did. Before James died, you were rowdy and wild, but you were never a drunken sot."

Reese didn't want to hear the truth spoken out loud, so he waved away her words. "Wrong. I was just exactly what I am now. The only difference is that I'm not so pretty now."

"Horseshit!" Rita said. "You're feeling sorry for yourself. You have ever since James died. Do you think I don't know what you're feeling? I know how your mind works. You can't face the fact that James is dead, so you stay drunk. When you're not drunk, you feel guilty for taking him to that tavern in the first place, so you drink even more. And you do all this rabble-rousing because you feel guilty that you couldn't prevent his death."

"I need a drink." Reese pointedly ignored Rita's words.

"The last thing you need is a drink."

"No, the last thing I need is to sit here and listen to your nagging. You've turned into a fishwife."

Reese could see his words had struck a sensitive spot in Rita, but he refused to apologize. He'd come here to get some rest, clean clothes, and maybe to relieve his body's needs. He hadn't come here for a sermon.

"Find me something to drink, and a bath."

"I will not give you any more liquor," she said firmly. "And if you want a bath, you can get it yourself."

She turned to leave, but the liquor hadn't slowed Reese's reflexes. He caught her arm and turned her back to the bed. With a yank, he tumbled her down on top of him. "Don't forget who you're talking to, Rita girl," he growled into her face. "You might find yourself back on the waterfront peddling your wares to every stinking, toothless sailor who takes a liking to you."

"Don't, Reese," she said, pushing his hand away from her breast, exposed by the now-gaping robe. "You're drunk and upset."

"And you're a whore. It's about time you started acting like one."

"How dare you speak to me that way," she choked out, her voice unsteady. "You disgust me."

She tried to rise, but he held her tight. Finally, she gave up and met his hard stare with a look filled with anger and hurt. "Fine, what is it you desire?" she said stiffly, tears filling her eyes.

Reese tried to harden himself to Rita's pain, but he couldn't. Shame filled him. She didn't deserve to be punished because he sought to punish himself. Oh, God, why was it so hard? Why couldn't he accept that James was dead and go on living?

"Just go," he whispered, closing his eyes as though bored. He sank back against the pillows on the bed. "Go and let me sleep."

Rita swiped away tears and turned toward the door. She hesitated, then turned back.

"I almost forgot," she said, sniffing. "Joseph has been here looking for you. He said if I saw you I should tell you that you're needed at Bonne Chance."

"Hah." Reese laughed, a lonely, bitter sound. "That'll be the day."

Rita, probably sensing another round of self-pity, shook her head. "Reese," she said, turning toward the door again, "you're killing yourself. And your death won't bring James back." Without another word, she left the room.

Reese stirred in the bed just as the sun began to go down. He sat up gingerly, a throbbing in his head making him wince. His mouth was dry and tasted foul. Pouring water from a pitcher beside the bed into a glass, he drank thirstily, wishing it were something stronger. Testing his legs, he pulled himself to a standing position with the help of the large post at the foot of the bed. He leaned against it a moment before staggering to the bedroom door.

"Rita!" he shouted, immediately regretting it when pain split his head. He looked around, but only the empty house greeted him.

"Damn," he groaned, stumbling past the table and chairs to the fireplace in the corner. He stirred the embers of a fire to life and took the tin coffee pot out to the pump on the back porch. He couldn't remember being sober at all the last three months, and the idea held no appeal for him now.

But knowing Rita, she probably hadn't left any liquor in the house.

Reese filled the pot and went back to the house to make the coffee. It was no easy task under the best of circumstances, and in his present condition he barely managed. After burning himself twice trying to set the pot on the wire rack, he nearly scalded the thick brew. He gagged on his first sip, then swallowed the coffee with a grimace. It tasted like the black mud at the bottom of the bay. He forced himself to take another sip, then another.

After he'd drunk half the pot, he began to feel more like himself. Rummaging through the larder, he found bread, cheese, and a bit of smoked pork, which he ate hungrily. He couldn't remember the last meal he'd had.

He wished Rita would come back so he could apologize. One thing about his drunken binges—no matter how hard he tried, they never obliterated his memories. Remembering the harsh things he'd said to Rita made his head ache even more fiercely. God, she was such a sweet thing, he had no right to take his pain out on her. His guilt over James's death was something he'd have to learn to live with. Somehow.

Reese found a metal hip tub in the pantry and filled it with water. The process taxed muscles that hadn't done anything more strenuous than lift a glass in the last three months. He sank into the cold water, gasping as it washed over his naked body. He wished he'd taken the time to heat the water, but the effort had seemed too great.

He soaked the grime and dried blood from his body, then scraped away the scraggly beard that had grown out of neglect, carefully avoiding the cuts and scrapes. He stared in the mirror in amazement at his battered face. It was a wonder he'd survived such a beating. His nose had a distinctive bump protruding from it. Reese wondered if it was possible to have a broken nose and not know it. He ran his finger along the protrusion and felt the misalignment. Apparently so.

Setting the mirror aside, he rose from the tub and padded barefoot back to the bed, still wishing Rita would return. He'd never treated her so harshly before, and she didn't deserve it. She was right. He'd spent three months feeling sorry for himself, and it hadn't done him or James any good. It was time to quit.

Suddenly he stopped, the icy water dripping from his body. Maybe it was time he did something that would help James—and himself. He'd given the authorities enough time to find James's killers. Now it was his turn. He'd never forget James, or his part in his friend's death, but if he could see that justice was done, maybe he could begin to put it behind him.

In the chiffonier he found a stack of his clothes, freshly laundered. There was no sign of the ones he'd been wearing the previous day. No doubt they'd been beyond repair. He pulled on a pair of black trousers and a snowy shirt. He donned clean socks and tried to polish his boots as best he could.

Rita wasn't coming back, he knew. She'd stay

gone until he left. He didn't blame her. She'd emptied his pockets onto the smooth surface of a dressing table and he collected enough money to get home on. The rest he left for her with a note of apology. He wondered if that would be enough this time.

Reese drew back on his reins, slowing his mount to a stop on the long, tree-lined drive leading to Bonne Chance.

The overhanging branches of the moss-covered cedars formed a canopy of cool shade and dappled sunlight. He felt the familiar knot of loneliness grip him as the house came into view. Was it any wonder he stayed away from Bonne Chance as much as possible? His father's presence was permanently etched onto every inch of the two-and-a-half-story mansion, from the Doric columns across the front to the upper and lower galleries.

He could almost see his mother standing at the railing, waiting for his father to return at the end of the day. The knot tightened painfully.

The freshly painted black shutters gleamed in the afternoon sunlight, reminding him that his presence had never been needed to ensure that Bonne Chance would be cared for. Even after a three-month absence, Reese couldn't find so much as a blade of grass out of place. The knowledge stung.

His gaze swept the fields lined with steadily working slaves. Outside a storage shed, several small black girls sat atop a pile of last year's cotton, their tiny fingers preparing it for ginning so it could be made into homespun for the slave's clothing.

As he approached, a young boy ran around the side of the house to take his horse. He nodded to Reese, but disappeared without a word. Reese strode onto the veranda, surprised someone hadn't at least come to open the door in welcome.

In the hall he removed his hat, nodding his head toward the sound of raised voices drifting from the parlor. He tossed his hat onto the parson's bench to his left and followed the noise.

At the parlor door he stopped, propping himself against the frame for a moment to stare in amazement. The sight which greeted him brought a smile to his swollen lips, and he grimaced as the tightness reminded him of his injuries.

Content to watch the tableau a while longer, he surveyed the players. Cooper Hutchins, his overseer, he'd spotted immediately. The man was yelling and waving his arms at a petite blonde. Ma Jewel, the housekeeper since he'd grown too old to need her nursing, was standing between the two, shifting from side to side as though to keep the pair from coming to blows.

Reese didn't recognize the young woman arguing with Cooper. As he studied her golden ringlets and porcelain-perfect features, he knew that was a face he'd never have forgotten. He decided he'd seen and heard enough.

"Cease!"

The three froze, stunned by his order. Reese almost laughed out loud at the sight. "Would someone like to tell me what is going on here?" he asked.

No one spoke or moved for several seconds. Suddenly they all started to talk at once, and in no time Cooper and the blonde were face to face again, Ma Jewel futilely trying to keep her massive body between them.

"I said *cease!*" Reese shouted again, rattling the frosted globes in the gilded bronze chandelier. The humor of the situation had quickly deserted him. He waited until the room grew silent once more. "Now. One at a time."

No one spoke. They each looked from Reese to one another and back again. Finally, Reese motioned to Ma Jewel.

"I can't help it, Misser Reese," she said defensively. "These two been goin' at it like this for near 'bout two weeks now. I done told 'em I can't get nothin' done for havin' to break up their fits."

Cooper Hutchins shot Ma Jewel a hard look, obviously displeased with her tattling. She tipped her chins up and sniffed, too irritated with the man to care that she'd betrayed him.

Cooper quickly stepped forward. "It ain't my fault, Mr. Reese. This girly would try the patience of Job, she would. I've tried to be civil, but there's no talking sense to her."

Reese stared from his flustered overseer to the tiny woman glaring at him. She looked like a doll with her moppet curls and huge, shining blue eyes. The pink ruffled dress she wore seemed juvenile, but it couldn't hide the womanly curves of her figure. Unbidden, the thought came to him that her appearance hid a passionate nature.

Shaking off his wild thoughts, Reese studied the matter at hand. "Well, since you seem to have completely disrupted my household, I think an introduction is in order."

Stepping forward, Reese pasted on his most charming smile and bent low over her hand. "Reese Ashburn at your service." His lips met air as the girl jerked her hand out of his grasp.

"Save your Southern hospitality for some empty-headed twit, Mr. Ashburn. It won't work on me."

Reese quirked an eyebrow at the girl. Had that rude retort actually come from those full, pouty lips? It hardly seemed possible.

"That's what I've been tryin' to tell you, Misser Reese," Ma Jewel said. "Ever' time the girl opens her mouth, she cuts someone to ribbons."

"And she opens it all the time," Cooper cut in, shooting another angry look at the blonde.

Reese saw the situation quickly deteriorating again and held up his hand for silence. He wanted to know who the hell this girl was and why she'd upset his household, but it was obvious he wasn't going to get any answers while these three were close enough to trade blows. "Please, Cooper, go back to work. I'll settle things here."

The overseer hesitated as though he wanted to say something more, then nodded. "Yes, sir, Mr. Reese. But you got to tell that girl to stay away from my people. She's tried to get them stirred up, and today she snatched a hoe from one of them and throwed it at me. Them slaves are likely to get ambitious. If they start getting ideas, I'm going to have to resign. I'm just too old for that kind of trouble."

Reese eyed the beauty before him and wondered if Cooper was losing his mind. Shaking his head, he said, "I'll handle everything, Cooper. You can go now."

The overseer nodded and mumbled and left the room. As soon as Reese heard the outer door close behind Cooper, he turned to Ma Jewel. "You may go too, Ma Jewel."

"But Misser Reese, you don't know this girl. She can . . ."

"It's all right. Please leave us now."

Ma Jewel cast a worried frown at Reese and the blonde before leaving the room.

Reese turned back to the girl and narrowed his eyes. "Who are you and what are you doing in my house?"

"Do you mean my father didn't tell you about me? You don't have any idea who I am?" She smiled chillingly. "No, I can see by the look on your face that you don't."

She shook her head, and Reese felt a finger of foreboding creep along his neck. He took another good look at the girl and shook his head. "You have me at a disadvantage, I'm afraid."

"Then let me introduce myself, Mr. Ashburn. I'm Patience Bentley. Your ward."

The name registered first. This was James's little girl? Reese almost laughed at the term. Patience Bentley was no one's little girl. She might be petite, but she was obviously a full-grown woman.

Suddenly the second part of what she said hit him.

"My what!"

"Ward, Mr. Ashburn." She smiled sweetly, as though enjoying his shock. "You've inherited me for the next six years, or until I marry. And I have no intention of doing that."

Reese's mind spun. What the hell was she talking about? There must be some mistake. James would never name him guardian of his daughter. Would he? No, of course not. James knew him too well to make such a blunder.

"Impossible. There's been some mistake."

"Oh, no. I assure you, it's true. His will named you executor of his estate and guardian of his daughter, me. If there had been any way to get around this asinine situation, I assure you I would have found it before I'd have stood still for being shipped to this backwoods swamp."

Again Reese blinked in surprise. The girl certainly had a mouth on her, he thought. "Swamp? You think Bonne Chance is a swamp?"

"What would you call it? The mosquitos are as big as birds, and they swarm like locusts every time you go outside. And the bugs"—she shuddered—"you have roaches the size of cats here. It's revolting."

Reese couldn't keep the smile from his lips. "I'm sorry to hear you've been bothered by insects, Miss Bentley. But I assure you, Bonne Chance is no swamp. We have forty thousand acres and nearly a hundred slaves. We raise cotton and peanuts and enough food to feed everyone who lives here."

She waved her hand in the air. "No matter. The deed is done and I'm here now. I admit I was disturbed at first, but I can see now that there is a silver lining in all things. It's just harder to find in some places than in others."

Reese was still whirling from the notion of becoming a guardian. He eyed the side table across the room with the French crystal liqueur set and the cut-glass whiskey and wine decanters. He really could use a drink.

"Well," he said, fending off the desire for liquid sustenance. "I'm happy to see you've settled in. I'm sure you'll accept our way of life in no time."

Patience Bentley let out a sound like a snort, and Reese turned his full attention back to the woman staring at him. Disgust clearly outlined her baby-blue eyes and delicate features.

"I have no intention of accepting your uncivilized ways, Mr. Ashburn. I intend to change them."

"Change them?" Reese repeated. "In what way?"

"Someone must preach the word of reform to all you flesh peddlers. And let these poor unfortunate people know that their bondage is an atrocity many good citizens of this country are seeking to end."

Reese rocked from the impact of her words. He eyed the liquor and thought, to hell with it. Striding across the room, he poured a glass half full of whiskey and downed it in one gulp.

He blinked to clear his eyes and his mind. The

full significance of what she'd said sank in, and he clasped a hand to his forehead. What in the name of heaven was James thinking?

"My God, you're an abolitionist!"

Chapter Two

Reese saw the first real smile cross Patience Bentley's face. Her expression only served to disquiet him more.

"That is exactly what I am, Mr. Ashburn, and I have always been proud to admit it."

"I wouldn't be so quick to tell that to folks around here if I were you, Miss Bentley. You're not in New York anymore."

"Boston."

"Excuse me?"

"I am from Boston, Mr. Ashburn. I would have thought my father would have at least mentioned that fact."

"We didn't talk about you very much," Reese hedged. Except for telling Reese he had a daughter somewhere by his deceased wife, James hadn't mentioned the girl at all. Reese kept that bit of information to himself, but he could see by Patience's solemn look she already knew.

"I see. Well, it hardly matters now, does it?" Patience tried to keep her voice strong and steady. It was difficult. How could her father have done this to her? They'd never been close. He traveled far too much to have established any permanent bond with her. Even now, death had not brought about the aching pain of separation it should have. But to have robbed her of all she held dear at the same time was nearly more than she could bear.

She thought of Trudy and felt tears sting the backs of her eyes. In his will her father had pensioned the housekeeper off as though she were no more than a common servant, instead of the person who'd looked after Patience her whole life. Since her mother's death, Trudy had been nanny, nurse, and sometimes surrogate parent to Patience. If she'd been able to bring Trudy along, maybe this exile would have been at least tolerable.

"I'm sorry," Reese said, seeing the sudden tears come to Patience's eyes. "It must have been difficult losing your father and having to leave your home at the same time."

Patience had nearly forgotten the man's presence. She tipped her chin up and glared at him. "Don't concern yourself, Mr. Ashburn. As I've already told you, I have come to the conclusion that my father did me a favor sending me here. I might have spent my life merely debating this most important issue amongst people whose views parallel my own. This way I'm able to fight the war against slavery on the front lines."

Reese desperately wanted another drink, but he fought the urge. He had the feeling he was going to need a clear head to deal with Patience Bentley.

"That's impossible, Miss Bentley. And I forbid it. Stay away from my overseer and his workers."

"I am not one of your slaves, Mr. Ashburn. You can't forbid me anything. I'm here now, and I fully intend to instigate change wherever possible."

"Are you threatening to incite a slave uprising, Miss Bentley?" Reese asked, stiffening now in outrage.

Patience stared at the anger on Reese Ashburn's face. For some reason she couldn't understand, she sought to reassure him. "Of course not. Everyone knows the slave uprisings didn't benefit anyone. But I intend to talk with your neighbors about their practices and to assure your slaves that there are people willing to fight for them and for their freedom."

"I'll never allow it," he assured her.

"You have no choice in the matter," she told him frankly.

"This is my home, Miss Bentley. I'm the law here."

"I refuse to be silenced. What do you propose to do about that?" she challenged.

"If necessary, I'll lock you in your room until you come to your senses," he threatened.

Patience merely laughed. "Really, Mr. Ashburn. Is that the best you can come up with? That ridiculous threat didn't work when I was five, and it isn't likely to work now."

"Oh, I assure you it will work," he told her, stepping forward until she had to crane her neck to look into his face. His height and size were intimidating, but Patience had justice on her side. She refused to be cowed.

"You see, Miss Bentley, this isn't Boston. Folks around here aren't going to stand for any rebellious abolitionist prattle. In fact, there are clubs—societies they're called—that specialize in shutting up trouble-making slaves and free-thinking whites who threaten to destroy their way of life. They will never allow you to preach reform around here. And I would lock you up rather than see you fall into their hands."

Patience had heard stories of such mobs, hanging and burning runaway slaves under cover of night and then disappearing without a trace. She shivered to think she might actually be living amongst such vile creatures. Still, she would not shrink from her beliefs just because they might make her unpopular. She'd never done so before, and she would not do so now.

"I'll take my chances," she said, turning away from his determined stare.

"No, you won't. I'm responsible for you. What kind of guardian would I be to let you do something that might endanger your life?"

Patience whirled, tossing her curls over her shoulder. "I am an adult, Mr. Ashburn. Capable of making my own decisions. Your concern is misplaced, to say the least. My father never took an interest in my life while he was alive, and the fact that he sent me here without so much as a word beforehand proves how little regard he had for me. Nothing you say or do is going to make up for his not being a proper father. And as I have lived these past nineteen years without one, I think your paternal affectations are a little belated."

"Very nice speech, Miss Bentley. And perhaps your command of a large vocabulary tends to inhibit the more civilized Northern men you are used to dealing with," he said, purposely trying to put her pert little nose out of joint with his own long-winded diatribe. "But the fact remains unchanged. If I am to be your guardian for the next six years, you will do what I say. Starting now."

He passed her without a glance, set his glass on the low table in front of the settee, and strode to the door. Looking back over his shoulder he added, "Don't try me on this, Patience. I assure you, I will win."

Patience heard his boot heels striking the floor of the hall, then heading up the stairs. She stood rooted in place until the noise faded into silence. Longing to stamp her foot or perform some similar childish action, she resisted the temptation. No, she'd not reward his arrogance with such a display.

Reese Ashburn was a rogue and a scoundrel if the tales the housemaids told were any indication. His injuries, in various states of healing on his face, seemed to substantiate their stories. She had no idea why her father would choose such a man for her guardian, but as she told Reese Ashburn, it no longer mattered.

She crossed to the courting set in the corner of

the room and sank down on one of the twin rosewood swivel chairs. The low stool in the center was reserved for a chaperone, giving the piece its name. Patience ran her finger over the circular table inlaid with marble birds and felt her ire grow. All the room's beautiful furnishings, from the Egyptian marble fireplace to the rich jade brocade draperies, were bought at the cost of human bondage.

How could Reese Ashburn expect her to live in such a place without trying to further the freedom movement? How could she spend a day in luxury while others toiled in slavery?

A trickle of perspiration crept down her back, and she went to the window hoping for a whisper of a breeze. She honestly didn't understand how anyone could live in such a climate. The heat threatened to choke the breath from her lungs. The air, when it deemed to move, was as thick as pea soup and sticky with humidity.

The nights were worse. Not even the thick mosquito nets could keep out the buzzing, whirring insects that besieged her room when the sun went down. They kept her awake, a prisoner beneath the heavy netting of her bed.

She'd walked along the bay several times seeking a breeze, but the slow, hot wafts of air couldn't compare to the crisp wind that came in off Boston Harbor.

She pushed the tedious curls away from her face and sighed. For all her big talk in front of Reese Ashburn, she wasn't certain she could last another day here. If the heat and humidity didn't kill her, the loneliness and boredom would. She longed for Boston with an ache that surpassed homesickness.

A sound roused her from her daydreams, and she turned to see one of the housemaids, a girl by the name of Dolly, refilling the whiskey decanter Reese Ashburn had used. She smiled at Patience. It took the girl some effort to return the gesture, but over the past two weeks the slaves had come to expect greetings and conversation from her.

She passed a comment or two with the girl, then Dolly slipped out, taking Reese's empty glass. Patience immediately chastised herself for missing an opportunity to speak to the girl, especially since her guardian had forbidden her to bother Cooper Hutchins or his workers.

Renewing her vow to seek change without cease, she decided to go in search of Ma Jewel. Now there was a woman Patience felt sure she could do some good for. Obviously the old nurse had influence, and she'd been at Bonne Chance for a long time. She'd know the best way for Patience to go about helping the slaves.

Leaving the manor house by the back door, Patience crossed the yard to the log kitchen set back about twenty yards. She entered, expecting to see the ample figure of Ma Jewel bent over the cookstove. Instead, her gaze swept the room, stopping with a jolt at the rough-hewn table.

"Hello," Reese said, rising from his chair as if she'd come across him in the formal dining room. Irritation still lined his craggy features, but Patience could see he meant to be polite. Even if it killed him.

He pulled out the other chair and motioned her forward. "Won't you join me?"

Patience briefly considered turning around and leaving without a word, but she changed her mind. She might do well to make Reese Ashburn think she'd decided to accept his ultimatum if she hoped to be allowed to continue to roam about unhindered.

With a slight smile, she nodded. She brushed past him to sit and wasn't surprised when he slid her chair effortlessly under the table. The gesture was so smooth that she couldn't help thinking manners were inbred in Southern men. Of course, the men of her acquaintance would have held her chair, but Reese Ashburn did it as though he were born to it. No doubt that was why he made her feel welcome now, so soon after their heated argument.

"Care for a beignet?"

Patience eyed the plate of holeless donuts in the center of the table. "What?"

"Beignets," he said, pushing the plate over to her. He stood and went to the shelves, returning with a small plate and cup. He collected another napkin and set them before Patience on the table.

"It's a French pastry. Ma Jewel keeps them on hand when I'm here because she knows they're my favorite. My mother loved them. She was French, you know."

"No, I didn't," she said, truly interested now.

Except for the gossip she'd heard, she knew next

to nothing about this man she'd be living with. It couldn't hurt to size up her adversary.

Reese took his seat and poured milk into Patience's glass. "Yes, she named the plantation after she and father married. Bonne Chance means good luck. She said every time someone said the name, they'd be wishing us well."

Patience couldn't help smiling. She took one of the powdery treats from the plate and bit into it. "Very good," she said, as soon as she'd chewed the donut. She dabbed the excess powdered sugar from her lips with her napkin and sipped her milk.

"I don't know that it's true, though," Reese said, sipping his milk with a faraway expression in his eyes. He seemed sad suddenly, and Patience lost interest in the food.

"What do you mean?"

He set his glass aside and tipped his head. "Nothing really. I was just thinking that you can't put much stock in a name."

Patience thought of her own Puritan name and had to agree. No doubt she'd been a disappointment to anyone who'd thought she'd live up to her title.

Sweat beaded on the bridge of her nose, and she lifted the back of her hand to dab it away.

"My apologies, Miss Bentley," Reese said, rising and laying his hands on her chair back. "It can get stifling in here. Shall we take a walk?"

The still air outside seemed almost bearable after the heated interior of the kitchen, and Patience lifted the curls off her neck in an effort to dry the dampness there.

"You'll acclimate in no time," Reese said, noting the way tendrils of hair clung to her nape. He admired the smooth white line of her throat as she stood poised to catch the feeble breeze.

"I seriously doubt that, Mr. Ashburn," she told him, dropping her arms when she caught him staring. "It's a wonder to me how anyone survives in such tropical surroundings."

"Shall we walk along the drive? The trees create a cool haven there."

Patience turned to him and saw the pride in his eyes as he looked out over the grounds. She followed his gaze, but all she saw were the fields of young cotton plants tended by slaves and the immaculate green lawn produced by hours of forced labor.

"Perhaps we should forego the walk, Mr. Ashburn."

He turned his attention back to Patience and frowned. "Of course, if that's what you want."

She nodded. "I'll see you at dinner then," she said, stepping away. "Thank you for the treat. And for the offer to walk."

She took a step and Reese Ashburn's voice stopped her. "Tell me, Miss Bentley, is it the heat or the company you are trying to avoid?"

Impressed by his candor, Patience decided to answer truthfully. "The company."

He quirked an eyebrow, and she found herself hurrying to explain. "I could not walk along these perfectly manicured grounds without commenting on the state of the people who tend them."

"And I would tell you that my slaves are well

cared for, and we would quickly become embroiled in another impossible debate," he finished for her.

Patience nodded.

Reese's gaze dropped to his boots and then out over the acres and acres of cotton and peanut plants just beginning to bud. "Just as well we don't then," he conceded. "It is a futile argument."

Patience's temper rose to the surface with the speed of the heat lightning she'd witnessed nearly every evening over the bay. "Reform is a fact which you will have to acknowledge sooner or later, Mr. Ashburn."

"And I suppose you will be at the forefront of the movement when it comes?"

"Do not doubt it."

He nodded and stared hard into her eyes. Finally, when she thought she'd have to lower her gaze or turn away completely, he looked away again.

"Just as long as you do not try to start the movement here on Bonne Chance, Miss Bentley. I meant what I said. Stay away from Cooper Hutchins and the workers. And do not let me hear you preaching reform to my slaves."

"Or else?"

"Or else, you'll be sorry you ever came south of the Mason-Dixon line, Miss Bentley. No matter who your father was."

He turned and walked away without another glance in Patience's direction. He crossed the lawn and headed down the drive, his hands in his pockets as though he were out for a casual stroll.

The sight made her blood boil, and Patience longed to shout at his retreating back. She was already sorry she'd come south. Sorrier than Reese Ashburn would ever know.

Chapter Three

Reese spooned the creamy chicken into his mouth and covertly watched Patience across the table. She dabbed her lips with the linen napkin and sipped water daintily from the crystal goblet. Again he admired her porcelain beauty, amazed anew at the contradiction between her looks and her personality.

The piece of chicken lodged in his throat, nearly strangling him, and he felt much the way he had when he'd read the letter from James's attorney that afternoon.

What a predicament! The terms of the will were pretty much set in stone. And it seemed there was no way out. Unless he simply refused to accept responsibility for her, in which case she'd become a ward of the state.

Of course he couldn't do that. Not after James

had entrusted the girl to him.

But curse the old man and his godawful habit of taking serious matters too lightly! In the past Reese had enjoyed James's sense of fun and adventure. But now he regretted his friend's lack of responsibility, for surely any capable man would never have named Reese guardian of his child.

He looked over at Patience Bentley, his ward, and frowned, rephrasing his thoughts. The woman before him would never be mistaken for a child. Her lips and eyes beckoned a man with their seductive pouts and glances. And the curve of bosom revealed by her low-cut emerald gown . . .

The young serving girl, Gay, appeared at his side to refill his plate with more rice, peas, and turnips. She refilled his water glass, then stepped around the table. Reese saw Patience whisper something in the girl's ear, causing her to nearly drop the water pitcher. Gay flushed and stumbled back to her place in the shadowed corner of the dining room.

Reese's eyebrow quirked, but Patience only smiled sweetly and finished the meal in silence.

"Miss Bentley and I will take our coffee in the parlor, Gay," Reese told the girl. "After you've set up the tray, you may go. We'll serve ourselves."

"Yessir," Gay said, disappearing through the nearby door.

Reese placed his own napkin beside his plate and rose. He went around and pulled Patience's chair out, then followed her to the parlor.

In the parlor, Reese saw that the coffee service had been delivered and Gay was already gone. He was glad, since he had no intention of waiting another minute before confronting Patience.

"What did you say to Gay?" The silver coffeepot rattled against the tray as he waited for an answer.

Patience busied herself filling their cups, prolonging the silence. She could see Reese was angry. She knew her answer would not improve his disposition.

"That isn't any of your business," she hedged.

"When are you going to understand? Everything that happens at Bonne Chance is my business, from the last horse in the stall to the smallest cotton plant."

"To the last slave," she declared, her voice rising with her anger.

"The very last," he confirmed.

Patience sat back on the settee and leisurely sipped her coffee. Reese paced to the fireplace and propped his booted foot on the hearth. His loud sigh broke the stillness, and he leaned on the mantel, not facing her.

"What did you say to her?"

Patience replaced her cup on the low table and bolstered her courage for the explosion she knew would follow her answer.

"I asked her if she'd care to join us for dinner."

Reese whipped around, his eyes dark with fury. "Why in the name of heaven would you do that?"

"You know why."

"No, I don't. Did you hope to upset the girl? Because I can assure you, you did."

"You know that was not my intention."

"I know nothing when it comes to you and your wild ideas."

"My ideas are not wild. They happen to be far more civilized than your views on human bondage," she defended herself heatedly.

"Tell me, Patience," he said, drawing out the syllables of her name as if to remind himself of their meaning. "Did you have servants in Boston?"

She smiled as though she'd anticipated this line of questioning and was prepared. "Yes, we did."

"Ah." He nodded, running his fingers over his lips thoughtfully. "And would you have invited them to sit at your table?"

"They were being paid to do a job. They would not have accepted an offer to join me for a meal."

"Nevertheless, would you have asked them to while they were serving you?"

"Of course not; they were working. It would have been inappropriate." She conceded the point too easily, and Reese suspected he hadn't unbalanced her at all.

"Precisely my point," he said. "It was inappropriate of you to invite Gay to join us for dinner."

"I disagree. Unlike my servants, she wasn't being paid to do a job."

"She was doing her job, as surely as any servant."

"I repeat, she wasn't being paid."

"Wrong," Reese said, pushing away from the fireplace. He went to the whiskey decanter and poured himself a drink, sipping slowly.

"I provide food, clothing, and lodging for every man, woman, and child on the plantation. They lack for nothing. Is that not the same as pay?"

"You know it's not. I admit the invitation might

have seemed extreme, but I only thought to make you see these people as something more than fixtures in your home. They are human beings. And they aren't hired, they're bought."

"I have never considered my slaves as fixtures," he told her. "And I provide for them. No one on Bonne Chance has ever gone hungry. Nor have they ever been forced to sleep outside in the rain or the cold. Can you say the same for your servants?"

"We always paid our servants well," she said, bristling.

"But was it enough?" He took another sip and set his glass down. "I've been to Boston, Patience. I've seen the slums and shanties the immigrant servants are forced to live in. I've seen hungry children pillaging the garbage for food. Can you be certain that what you paid your servants was enough to provide for all their needs? Did you ever ask?"

Patience was silent for a moment, her perfect features marred by a frown between her golden brows. Her fire only added to her beauty, Reese thought, eyeing the becoming pink flush on her cheeks and the sparks of candlelight reflected in her eyes. Her mother must have been gorgeous. No wonder James chose to travel after her death rather than face the memories in their Boston townhouse. Reese understood the depth of his friend's loneliness better now.

"You're being obstinate," Patience said, her voice no longer strong with conviction.

"And you're being narrow-minded," he replied,

returning to the subject at hand. He'd have to be careful around Patience Bentley. Her looks might make a man want to protect and care for her, but no doubt she'd lash him to death with her tongue if he tried. "Why is it so terrible for these people to live here? They work for me, and in exchange I see that all their needs are met. Can you say the same?"

"You are missing the point, on purpose no doubt."

"The point? What is the point, Patience?"

"My servants, all servants, can choose whom they work for and where they live."

"Can they? I don't think so. The immigrants are financially enslaved as surely as if they were legally bound to the areas in which they live. They are no more free to escape their situation than are my slaves. Or do you think they live in squalor because they like it? Admit it, Patience, the North has its own embarrassments which need to be seen to before you come down here trying to tell us how to run our lives."

"But those people have one thing your slaves will never have," she cried, balling her fists in front of her. "They have their freedom."

Reese faced her, and Patience wondered when he'd gotten so close. She could smell the whiskey he'd drunk and the tonic he'd used to smooth his hair down. Her eyes met his, and she couldn't look away. He really was an attractive man, even with the scar and the abrasions on his face. Her heartbeat sped up and she had to swallow a lump in her throat at his nearness.

"Do you think that freedom fills their children's empty stomachs or warms their bare feet in winter? Do you think for a minute those mothers wouldn't trade places with Ma Jewel or Gay when the temperature drops and they have no coal? Do you think, Patience," he asked her, taking her shoulders and drawing her to him, "that they would choose to watch their children die of starvation and disease if they were free to do anything about it?"

He leaned over her, his eyes meeting hers. He continued to hold her gaze, forcing her to acknowledge his words. She stared back for a long moment, then looked away.

"That does not excuse slavery. You are muddling the issue." Patience turned away and wondered how she'd ever been attracted to such a pig-headed man.

Reese turned her back to face him and said, "This is an issue which has always been muddled. No debate is ever clear-cut, Patience, or there'd be nothing to discuss. All I'm asking is that you open your eyes and your mind to a way of life different from your own. You have admitted you have no personal experience with our ways."

Patience tried to ignore the warmth caused by his touch. She stepped out of his grasp. "I don't need to experience slavery firsthand to know it's wrong," she countered, regaining her thoughts and emotions now that he'd released her. She drew several deep breaths to steady her racing heartbeat. "I've never seen anyone murdered, but I know that murder is wrong." She turned away from his disturbing stare. Putting distance between them hadn't helped nearly enough. She could still feel the imprint of his hands on her arms, warming her blood.

"That is hardly a fair comparison, and you know it."

"Perhaps not, but what you're asking is impossible. I will never change my views."

"I'm not asking that you abandon your beliefs. Only that you observe, *quietly*," he stressed, narrowing his eyes in warning, "before you stir up trouble."

Patience shook her head, causing her curls to bounce. "It would be a waste of time."

"Well, we've agreed that time is one thing you have. Unless my attorney can find a chink in the armor of your father's will—"

"He won't," she cut in, saving him the trouble of traveling that already worn path. "I pretty much beat that subject to death with my father's lawyers before I gave in and came here."

"Well, then. You've informed me that you intend to stay at Bonne Chance until you reach your majority. That means we'll be living together for six years, right? What difference can a few weeks make?"

Patience suspected that Reese Ashburn was a master manipulator. No doubt he could charm the birds out of the trees if he were of a mind. She determined that his wiles would have no effect on her. But it wouldn't hurt to use his request as a means of getting some things she desperately wanted. With a short nod, she said, "On one condition."

"I can't wait to hear this. It should be monumental," he replied sarcastically.

"Not at all. It's a small request." She saw his eyebrow quirk once more and added, "Honest."

Reese nodded hesitantly.

"It's about the slave, Nancy, whom Mr. Hutchins and I were discussing earlier."

"You mean the one whose hoe you took and threw at Hutchins?"

"I did not throw it at him. I tossed it on the ground."

"At his feet?"

Patience saw the corner of his mouth tip up, and she resisted the urge to defend herself. "The woman is pregnant," she said boldly, noting the way his eyes widened with surprise. "At least six months. And Mr. Hutchins had her hoeing the field where the new peanut crop is to go. She should not be out in the heat doing that kind of labor in her condition."

Reese fought his shock and amazement. Patience Bentley was full of surprises. Not only did she discuss the unmentionable, she did it with zeal. He almost wished he could oblige her in this. It did seem cruel to work the woman in the fields, but Reese had allowed Cooper full control for years. He couldn't question Cooper's authority now without good reason.

"I'm sorry, Patience. I do not interfere with Cooper's decisions. He is the overseer, and as such he has control of the slaves. He knows which of them are suitable for which jobs and he assigns them accordingly. I trust his judgment."

Patience felt her anger rise again. She couldn't believe this man could be so cruel. Bonne Chance was his plantation—it was up to him to correct the injustices she'd encountered. Starting with Nancy.

"Would you allow your wife to labor in the fields if she were within weeks of her confinement, Mr. Ashburn?"

"I'm not married," he said, smiling irritatingly at her.

Patience planted her hands on her hips and tried to appear larger than her five-foot, two-inch height. But still Reese Ashburn towered over her.

"You're being obstinate again. It is no wonder you have remained unattached for so many years." She watched with pleasure as her barb hit home. So, the man was vain in addition to his many other faults. "Your marital status is not the subject of this discussion. *If* you were married, would you allow it?"

"No," he conceded, still smarting from her remark about his age.

Patience blinked, taken off balance for a moment by his easy admission. However, she quickly regained her composure and forged ahead.

"Then talk to Mr. Hutchins. Have him reassign Nancy until she delivers and has had time to recover."

"And in exchange you will agree to keep quiet about reform and not disturb the slaves while they are working?"

Patience shook her head and smiled. "In exchange I will agree to observe for a time before I make any more suggestions."

She could tell that her compromise was less than Reese Ashburn had hoped for. He studied her as if he couldn't identify her species. Finally, when she was certain he would refuse, he nodded.

"That will have to do for the time being, I suppose. I'll speak with Cooper in the morning."

"He'll have Nancy in the fields at daybreak. If you spoke with him tonight, you'd be able to sleep late in the morning. You must be tired from your trip." She pasted on her most angelic expression and stared up at him.

Reese surprised her further by throwing his head back and laughing. "All right, you win. I will speak with Cooper tonight and suggest he reassign Nancy for a while. Are you happy?"

"No," she told him with a toss of her golden curls. "But it's a start."

As Reese strode across the yard in the direction of Cooper Hutchins's cabin, he couldn't help the twinge of admiration he felt for Patience Bentley. No matter how misguided the girl was, she certainly had guts.

However, he felt certain he'd live to regret that fact before it was over. With her Northern views and abolitionist beliefs, she was a disaster in the making.

The only plan he'd come up with after studying the problem for the better part of the day was to marry his ward off as fast as possible. That would mean putting off his plan to find James's killers until the subject of Patience Bentley was settled. He couldn't very well proceed with his investigation until he'd rid himself of her, since she'd no doubt interfere in that as well.

Of course, marrying her off presented problems of its own. Who in their right mind would take on a mouthy, trouble-making abolitionist like Patience Bentley? No matter that she was beautiful and her lips put a man in mind of long, slow kisses . . . and more.

That same mouth would have every Southern man of his acquaintance running for the woods. No gentleman would want Patience for his wife. Not after she started in with her preaching.

The only hope was to get her engaged before she had a chance to scare off all the young men.

Yes, that was it, Reese thought. He'd just have to let her beauty attract a beau and hope he could keep her quiet long enough to secure the deal.

Patience watched Reese walk out of the parlor. He was a fine figure of a man, even if he did have a skull as thick as aged oak. She quickly brushed off the aberrant thoughts, knowing now was not the time to consider romance. Especially with a barbaric slaveholder.

She listened to the front door slam shut behind him and wanted to exclaim her triumph. She'd won the first battle. And even if the war was far from over, it was a good start.

Besides, she'd only spent one day with Reese Ashburn. If she'd gained this small victory after less than twelve hours, what couldn't she accomplish in six years!

She giggled with glee. Why, she might even bring Reese Ashburn over to her side in the fight against slavery before their time together came to a close.

Chapter Four

Patience found Ma Jewel with her head poked in the door of the larder as she searched a lower bin. Patience stood for a moment and waited, listening to the tuneless song the black woman hummed.

Every time she'd seen Ma Jewel, the woman had been cheerful and pleasant. When she'd tried to draw her into a discussion about the horrors of slavery, Ma Jewel only smiled indulgently and shook her graying head.

Backing from the larder, the old woman turned, her arms full of sweet potatoes. She saw Patience and smiled warily.

"What kin I do for you, sugar?" she said, rolling the potatoes into a big pot set on the scarred work table. She picked up a knife and tested its edge with her thumb. "You looking for a bite ta eat?"

Patience couldn't help smiling. She knew that

Ma Jewel didn't like her much. She hadn't given the woman much reason to become endeared of her since her arrival. But still, she never let on by word or deed that Patience was less than welcome.

"No, thank you," Patience said. "I thought maybe we could talk a minute."

The light dimmed in the ebony eyes, but Ma only nodded. "If that's what you want," she said, motioning to a chair. "I've got ta peel these tatoes, but you can sit and chat with me while I do it."

Patience pulled out a chair and sank into it as Ma picked up the first potato. She wasn't sure where to start. There were so many things she wanted to ask the woman. Had Ma known Patience's father? Had he ever mentioned her? Why was Reese Ashburn such a rakehell? What made him into the kind of man he was?

All of those thoughts seemed too personal, though. She'd be opening her soul to the slave if she asked them. Instead, she tried to remember her goal—and the small victory she'd achieved that day.

"Reese agreed to remove Nancy from the fields until after she has her baby."

Ma tossed the peeled vegetable into the pot and took up another. "Um, hum," she murmured, nodding her head.

"Well, isn't that good? I mean she won't be out in the hot sun, working so hard now." She hurried on, unsure why she felt disappointed by the woman's less than enthusiastic reaction.

"I mean, she was so awkward and uncomfortable. Now she can rest a bit."

"Yessum," Ma agreed. "I reckon that's so."

Frustrated, Patience picked up a potato and twirled it in her hands. "You don't sound too happy about what I've done."

Ma kept skinning the vegetable, her eyes on her work. "Didn't know you was lookin' for praise."

Patience huffed. "Of course I'm not looking for praise, Ma. I'm trying to help. I thought you'd be on my side. I assumed you'd agree with me on this."

Ma looked up, finally meeting Patience's wide eyes. She frowned, studying the girl, then set her work aside. "Tryin' to help where you see wrongs needin' to be righted is a noble thing. But maybe you need to consider your reasons for stormin' in here stirring up a tempest o' trouble."

"I want to see you all free," Patience cried, clutching the potato tight.

Ma just shook her head. "Girl, you cain't know what you are doin'. You're such a young thing, with your high ideals. But you from the North, and that's a whole 'nother world."

"North or South, you're a human being with feelings and rights, just like any other. I know if you had the choice, you'd want to be free. Anyone would."

Patience couldn't keep the indignation from her voice. "Ma Jewel, you're enslaved here. You can't even leave without permission."

She reached forward and took the knife from Ma's hands, clutching them in her own. "You have the right to live your life any way you want to, Ma. You should be allowed to choose."

Ma smiled and patted Patience's hand as she took up the knife once more and slipped it beneath the rust-skinned potato. "Like you, you mean?"

Patience stood up so quickly that the chair tottered behind her. She gasped, feeling as though she'd been attacked by the woman. "That's not the same thing at all," she cried. "I'm not a slave here, I'm a—a guest."

"But you can't go. And that's what we're really talkin' about, isn't it?"

Patience didn't know what to say. She could leave if she wanted to—of course she could. But what good would it do? She had no place to go, no one to turn to.

"I just don't understand why my father sent me here," she said, sinking into her chair once more. "My English grandfather was a baron. If my father had been born first, he'd have held the title. Instead, because of a scandal when he was barely out of short pants, he was sent to America. He had to know how it feels to be banished from the only home you've ever known, yet that's exactly what he did to me."

Ma didn't answer, and Patience regretted her emotional slip. She drew her hurt inside once more and wrapped it beneath the mantle of the cool, self-assured exterior she'd worn since her arrival.

Without looking up, Ma spoke. "I'm jest recommending you look in your heart, ask yourself what's drivin' you. Seems to me you've got a lot ta look at in your own life."

Patience didn't know what to say to that. She

thought she knew how to make the slaves' plight better, but Ma obviously didn't agree. Her father thought she'd be better off with Reese Ashburn, and was he ever wrong! And yet how could she give up now?

"I'm sorry, Ma Jewel. But I can't simply accept things the way you seem to. It's wrong—everything in my heart tells me so. And I must be true to myself."

"You are a stubborn child, jest like Misser Reese."

Patience thought she heard the old slave chuckle beneath her breath.

"Yep, I can see there's gonna be fireworks 'round here 'fore too long."

Instead of being insulted by the woman's prediction, Patience felt proud. She wanted to stir up Reese Ashburn's well-structured, albeit heathenistic life.

"I look forward to it," she said, rising to leave the kitchen. Ma's chuckles followed her, their knowing rasp stealing some of her anticipation.

Reese surveyed the work in the fields. Was it his imagination or did Cooper Hutchins seem jumpy? The man had been overseeing the plantation for as long as Reese could remember, and he'd always done it expertly. So why did he seem so unstrung?

Reese thought about the scene in the parlor with Patience Bentley. Could one little slip of a girl have so unsettled the old man? Were her endeavors giving the slaves ideas, as Cooper predicted? Could the old man handle those kinds of problems on his own?

For the first time in years, Reese took a good look at the old overseer. Cooper had aged before his eyes, but Reese hadn't taken the time to notice until now. He must be in his sixties, Reese thought, doing some quick mental addition. Most of the other plantation owners had young, strong men in such consequential positions.

He'd thought Cooper a competent overseer, but the truth was Reese wasn't around much. And now, with Patience Bentley harassing him, the old man had a lot on his plate. All Reese wanted to do was get back to Mobile. But could he leave the plantation in Cooper's hands with the same confidence he always had?

It wouldn't hurt to stick around for a few days, just to be sure everything worked out. He owed it to James to see that his daughter was settled into her new life here, even if he thought the man crazy for making such an outrageous stipulation without even consulting Reese.

And he owed it to his father to check up on the plantation and make sure Cooper was still capable of running the place. Bonne Chance had been his father's pride and his mother's joy. And, even though he hadn't been a very efficient successor, they'd entrusted it to him.

Mobile called, and he longed to answer the summons. But this once he felt as though he might be needed here. Strange, but the idea didn't annoy him. In fact, he found a certain measure of self-satisfaction in finally being able to offer something of himself to his home.

As long as it wasn't for too long, he thought. He had to get back to Mobile soon. Before leaving Rita's, he'd decided it was past time for him to do something about finding James's killers. The police had had long enough, with no apparent leads.

Sharp, stabbing pain hit him fresh. Why James? He had a daughter, a business. Even with his rakehell ways, he'd managed to build something of a life for himself. Reese had done nothing with his life. And yet, he'd been saved. But for what? What could he ever do to make up for being the one spared?

He removed his hat and wiped sweat from his brow with the back of his hand. Across the way he saw a small figure in a flouncy pink dress strolling toward the fields where Cooper was working the slaves.

"Little hellion," he whispered, replacing his hat. He'd told Patience to stay away from the overseer. He might not be able to do anything about finding James's murderer for a while, but there was something right now that demanded his immediate attention.

He shook his head, dreading the encounter to come, and started across the tree-lined drive toward the fiesty troublemaker.

With long, quick strides, he managed to intercept Patience before she reached the cluster of workers. He stepped in front of her, enjoying the look of frustrated ire that she wore.

"Where do you think you're going?" he asked,

his fists going to his hips. His long legs were spread in a wide stance, his intent to block her path evident.

"I was just looking around," she said, smiling sweetly. "That isn't against the rules, is it? After all, if I'm going to be stuck here, I'd at least like to learn a little more about the place."

"Would you?" Arching his eyebrow, he stared down at her. "I thought you considered us a bunch of barbarians."

"Without a doubt," she quipped. "But it never hurts to know one's adversary."

"Clever conclusion," he said, nodding his head. "Do you ride?"

"Ride?"

"I'll be happy to show you around Bonne Chance, but we'll have to go on horseback. You do ride?"

"Of course."

"You did say you wanted to see everything?"

She turned her head to look over the fields dotted with glistening black bodies bent in labor.

Reese watched her eyes scan the newly turned acreage. What thoughts were spinning through that pretty head? Her crystal eyes looked pained, but curious. The bobbing curls flung over one shoulder added a softness that he felt certain he would never be the beneficiary of.

"Yes—yes, I *would* like to see everything," she told him, her pointed chin tipping up.

His admiration grew. For some reason he had expected her to demure. Maybe it was her appearance that continually kept him off balance.

She looked like a fragile Dresden doll, the type of woman a man had to protect from all the elements. But in contrast to her looks, Reese also saw a tough, intrepid core to her being.

Thankfully, he'd never been attracted to that type of woman. Not that he could ever think of James's daughter as a potential conquest. The citizens of Mobile might think him without the barest scruples, and in light of the past months, they'd have every right. But Reese wasn't totally without conscience. God help him, he sometimes wished he were. It would make life simpler.

He'd made an art of throwing conventions to the wind and taking great pleasure in the outrage he usually caused. But in truth, it had started as an act of rebellion years ago when he'd felt slighted.

His mother and father had never needed anyone but each other, so great was their love. Bonne Chance had Cooper Hutchins to tend it. The slaves, though most cajoled and catered to the little master, had their own families. Reese had sought debauchery as a way to gain the attention he hadn't known had been lacking in his life. Soon, though, it became a way of life. As much a part of him as his looks and heritage.

Until the night of James's death, he had to admit he'd enjoyed himself plenty. Now the nightlife lacked the appeal it had once held. Every drink reminded him of the last one he'd shared with his friend. Every whore looked like the one he'd left to go with James on their ill-fated outing. Every game of cards left the foul taste of bile in his mouth, as his gut told him James's life had been sacrificed in a frivolous search for the hollow pleasure of a good hand.

Still, he'd lived that kind of life too long to brush it off like lint from his frockcoat. It was the only life he knew. The only thing, in his thirty-odd years, that he'd done with any measure of success.

But being a proficient rakehell didn't lend itself to being a young woman's guardian. He almost smiled as he thought what the citizens of Mobile would say when they learned his latest vocation.

"Mr. Ashburn?"

Reese snapped out of his ponderings, facing the delicate beauty staring up at him impatiently. Lord, what had ever possessed James to give the girl such an unsuitable name? It seemed almost facetious.

"Come along then," he snapped, heading for the stables. It would be a trying morning, spent with the argumentative little firebrand. But at least if he kept her beneath his own watchful eye, she couldn't be off doing mischief to Cooper and the workers.

God help him, if he didn't know better, he'd swear James had returned from the dead to punish him. For what could be worse than six years spent with an insufferable chit like Patience Bentley?

Chapter Five

One of them would not live to see Patience Bentley's twenty-fifth birthday, Reese thought as he clenched his fists. His jaw ached from gnashing his teeth in frustrated anger. His face flamed crimson with suppressed rage. Beside him, bristling with high dudgeon, rode his supremely impertinent ward.

"Shanties," she said, sniffing dramatically.

"You consider those houses shanties?" Reese surveyed the row of slave quarters where Patience had reined to a stop. He would not allow her to rile him again. She'd criticized the lack of a school for the slaves and nearly burst the buttons on her high-necked jacket when he explained why Bonne Chance had a midwife instead of a real infirmary.

No, he would not let her provoke his temper again.

"Well, if you consider those cabins to be shanties, it's probably a good thing you never visited the tenements of your Irish servants," he told her briskly, pressing his heels to his horse's flanks. The roan shot forward, and he led the way toward one of the small houses.

He pulled to a stop as a pack of excited children rushed at him. Digging in the pocket of his coat, he withdrew several pieces of rock candy wrapped in cheesecloth. The black eyes lit with pleasure as the children snatched the offering and loped around the corner of the building to divvy up their booty.

"Gonna give those young'uns the bellyache," a voice called out. A tall, slim black woman sidled out of the house, a grin on her bronze face. She propped long, broad hands on non-existent hips. "Mista Reese, what you doin' here? You lose your way or somethin'?"

Reese chuckled as he slid down from the saddle. He paused, as though studying the woman, and shook his head. "You're getting fat, Tishia," he joked, clucking his tongue.

The skinny slave slapped playfully at his arm. "Mind your tongue, you little pup. I brought you into this world and don't think I cain't take you out if I get a notion."

Reese grabbed the woman and spun her in a wide circle. She pushed and huffed all the while, but her generous grin only stretched wider.

"Yes, ma'am," he said. "I believe you would, too."

Patience had tired of waiting to be introduced

and climbed down from her horse unassisted. Tishia saw the young miss working to keep her dignity as she dismounted, and she shoved her heavy palm into Reese's back.

"You lose your manners as well as your money in town?" she chastised.

He spun around, chagrined to have forgotten Patience for the moment. He stepped forward to assist her, but she ignored him, gathering her long riding skirt and hooking the loop on her hem to the button at her waist.

"Hello," she said, mustering her bruised dignity. "I'm Patience Bentley." She held out her hand, and the slave eyed it for a moment before enfolding it in her larger one.

"Yep, I know. Wondered when you'd get around to our piece of ground."

Patience beamed suddenly, her mussed state suddenly forgotten. "You've heard of me?"

She hadn't made it as far as the quarters, mostly due to Cooper Hutchins's interference. The knowledge that her efforts had preceded her filled her with a certain pride.

Tishia chortled loudly. "Heard of you? Child, Nancy ain't shut up yapping all mornin'."

"Oh," Patience cooed, her face filled with self-satisfaction. "I'm so glad she's pleased."

"Pleased? Well, I wouldn't say that exactly."

Reese and the woman exchanged knowing glances, and he shrugged helplessly.

Patience froze, her fingers tucked in the folds of her skirt. Her blue eyes slowly lifted to the faces of the two people watching her. "She wasn't pleased?"

"Child, because of you, Cooper put her in the sugar house. A simpler job, and she can sit all right. But Nancy purely despises the smell of cane."

Patience stared from Reese to the slender slave. Her smooth brow puckered in consternation, and color rose in her pale cheeks. "I don't understand. I thought I was helping."

The duo just stared at her, neither speaking. She placed her hand against her cheek. "I just assumed . . ."

"That you knew what was best for her?" Reese pushed his tongue against the side of his teeth to keep from pushing his advantage.

"Yes," she whispered, her eyes widening in dismay.

Reese could see she was upset by her blunder. And he knew she was sincere in her endeavors to help his slaves. Although he should have enjoyed her discomfiture, he found himself softening. "You were only trying to help, Patience. Don't worry about it."

"But I didn't help at all. I've made things worse for Nancy, haven't I? You and Ma were right."

Neither Reese nor Tishia spoke. Reese wished he could tell Patience she'd done the right thing, but the fact remained that she'd jumped to unfounded conclusions, just the way he'd warned. Yes, she had rightly pointed out that a pregnant woman shouldn't be on her feet all day, but she hadn't bothered to check and see what Nancy preferred. Or even if the woman wanted her intervention. He didn't like seeing Patience suffer, but perhaps after this she'd stop her ill-founded sermonizing without knowing what she was talking about.

"Maybe now you'll listen to me when I tell you to stay out of the way. If you'd like something to keep you busy, I'm sure Ma Jewel would be happy to help you arrange a tea, or even an afternoon soirée."

Patience blinked, her fingers smoothing the frown from her brow. She looked up at Reese, confusion lining her face. "What? What did you say?"

"A soirée, or maybe a tea. The neighbors on either side of us have daughters about your age. I'm sure you'd find them very entertaining."

Suddenly the distraction cleared from her eyes, and her full lips turned down sharply. "I am not here to be entertained, Mr. Ashburn. And don't think for a moment that this one little problem is going to stop my efforts on behalf of the slaves. No, no—this is a minor setback, but I see now I was too hasty in formulating my plan."

"Patience . . ."

"I should have waited until I'd spoken to Nancy, found out what she wanted."

"Patience . . ." Reese's voice took on a warning tone. He stepped toward her, his head shaking as he waved a hand in front of her.

"Yes, that was a tactical error," she continued, seeming not to hear his admonition. "After all, the whole purpose of my intercession was to free these people to make their own choices. Oh my, yes. I can see I've made a grave mistake. But no matter—we must live and learn. I'll just have to start again."

"Now see here," Reese started, taking a brisk step toward her. "You can't just—"

"I'm ready to see the rest of the plantation," she interrupted, her lambent eyes now bright with renewed enthusiasm. She seemed not to have heard his warning at all.

He blinked in surprise. "What? Now? But you just said . . ."

Damn it all, she was turning him into a bumbling idiot. Behind him he could hear Tishia chuckling with glee, and he growled a low remonstration. Tishia snuffled behind her hand, and heat suffused his neck.

"Yes, right now. Obviously I've got a lot to learn before I can further my efforts on behalf of these poor, oppressed people."

"Now, that's just about enough," he bellowed, his fists once again clenching at his sides. She couldn't be serious.

"You offered to show me around Bonne Chance, Mr. Ashburn. Are you going back on your word?" She cut him a look of immense disappointment and shook her head, her sausage curls bobbing. "Oh, my, you aren't a liar as well as a rakehell, are you?"

Tishia lost the battle with her mirth and she spun about and rushed back into the cabin, a softly smothered chortle following her.

Reese bristled with fury, barely resisting the urge to club the little twit over the head. God, how would he ever survive six years of this hell? Curse James's bad judgment.

Patience stared expectantly up at her reluctant guardian, waiting for him to explode. She could see the anger he tried, and failed, to contain. So, she'd hit a nerve. Like most men of her acquaintance, even the disreputable ones, Reese Ashburn couldn't tolerate an affront to his honor—although she suspected that he had little, if any, of that distinguished characteristic.

"Are you going to show me around the rest of your plantation, Mr. Ashburn? Or are you going to renege?"

He knew he was being manipulated, but for the life of him Reese could not bring himself to go back on his word—even though, Lord help him, he knew he would live to regret his decision.

"No, Miss Bentley. I'm not going to confirm your low opinion of me by withdrawing my offer. Even though I'm quite sure I'll be sorry later."

She rewarded him with a beaming smile, and Reese felt a quick, unexpected kick of desire at the sight. He found himself wishing her admiration were genuine.

Cursing, he shook his head in disgust. Heaven help him if he should fall prey to her comely smile, for surely it hid a razor-sharp tongue and a mind set on bedeviling him.

With a grunt, he waved her toward their horses. Obviously pleased with what she perceived as another victory, she sashayed ahead of him. He offered her a hand up onto her mount, and she settled herself, back rigid, in preparation for her tour.

Reese dragged himself into the saddle, jaw set and teeth clamped tight. He must be a lunatic, agreeing to escort Patience around the place. She was nothing but a problem in petticoats. And he was a damned fool for not locking her in her room as he'd threatened.

An hour later, Reese felt better about his capitulation. Patience seemed truly interested in the workings of the plantation, and despite her earlier blunder she hadn't spent her time sulking. She asked intelligent questions and seemed to understand even the most complex operations. She'd even made a few surprisingly astute observations, which had Reese reevaluating his adversary. Despite her frail looks and delicate beauty, Patience Bentley possessed wisdom and prudence surpassing her years.

He'd also found an added bonus to their excursion. As long as Patience was with him, she couldn't harass Cooper or inflame the workers. He told himself he would have to spend a great deal of time with her to keep her occupied and away from his overseer.

He tried to feel displeasure at the thought. But the truth was, after they'd gotten past that first battle of wills, he'd found her company almost pleasant.

They paused atop a small rise overlooking the main body of the plantation, and Reese eyed the lowering sun in the distance.

"We should get back," he said, drawing Patience from her contemplation of the setting sun painting flaming hues across the sprawling acreage. "Ma Jewel will have supper waiting."

For a moment he thought she hadn't heard him. Her eyes shone as she watched the sun's descent. He followed her gaze and knew she'd been momentarily transfixed by the picturesque sunset.

He couldn't blame her. It was a stunning sight—one, he realized with regret, he'd never taken the time to enjoy before. The blazing bronze and scarlet across the rich jade and rusty orange of the tilled fields sent a sharp pang of self-reproach through him.

His parents had loved Bonne Chance. They'd always taken time to appreciate the land and its glories. More than once they'd tried to draw him into the workings of the place. But Bonne Chance had never held the fascination for him that it had for his parents. He'd thought of this as their home—their foremost concern, after one another.

For most of his life he'd resented Bonne Chance and its place in his parents' hearts. And so he'd never found the joy here they'd wanted him to. In fact, he'd spent years avoiding the place, harboring the bitterness he'd felt at playing second best to a plot of ground.

For the first time he really looked at the patchwork of fields, the neat, defined rows of tiny cottages, the carefully charted setting of main house and outbuildings. The rhythm of the design held his focus for a moment, and he suddenly understood the attention that had gone into the layout.

What he had thought a random grouping of structures was actually a true example of harmony and balance. Everything from the position of the smokehouse in regard to the kitchen to the bamboo hedges flanking the gardens had been carefully contrived for symmetry.

And yet, he'd never thought of it as anything but a burden to be passed off to his trustworthy overseer. Until now.

Good Lord, he thought with a shiver of dismay. He was getting absolutely maudlin. He shook off the odd feelings of contrition and groaned deep in his throat. He really needed to get back to town before he found himself considering something really foolish. Like staying on here indefinitely.

"Patience?"

Turning to face him, he saw that her eyes were damp. Was she crying, or had the sun's rays stung her eyes?

"Yes, I'm ready," she said, a suspicious huskiness in her voice.

Reese told himself he'd been acting like a real jackass. Patience had recently lost the only parent she'd ever known. And whether or not they'd been close, that must have been a blow to her. Instead of showing her kindness and compassion, he'd been doing battle with the girl at every turn.

No matter that she seemed to enjoy annoying him, he should have shown her the kindness due his best friend's only child. No doubt James would lament his choice of guardian if he could see Reese's recent behavior.

Chagrined, he offered Patience a benevolent smile. Instead of returning the gesture as he might have expected, she scowled at him with mistrust.

So much for beneficence, he thought. "Come along," he said, reining his horse in the direction of the stables.

"I was thinking," she said, drawing alongside him.

"God help us," he muttered.

"What?"

"Nothing," he said, shaking his head. "You were about to say?"

"I thought—if you wouldn't mind, that is—I might like to start an infirmary for the slaves. I realize I was a bit judgmental earlier, but please hear me out. I'm sure in the past a midwife with minimal medical knowledge was sufficient, but so much more can be done with proper facilities. I think an infirmary would be very beneficial to the workers, and in turn, to you."

"Patience, why do I feel I'm about to be manipulated into another of your schemes?"

"Me?" she cried, clasping her hand to her breast. "Why, I could never dupe such a worldly-wise man as yourself."

Reese had to laugh aloud at that. "Oh, you are an expert in the art of maneuvering. Don't sell yourself short, especially since I'm not about to fall prey to your innocent act after being masticated by you twice in as many days."

She cut him a searing look, then huffed in frustration. "Oh, all right. So I'm not very good at subtlety. I thought perhaps I'd try a more civil tactic since you've been good enough to show me around today."

"Better the viper you see than the one you don't," he murmured.

"What is that supposed to mean?" she asked, clearly affronted at his contrariness.

"Only that I'd just as soon see the attack coming than be struck from behind."

"What a horrid thing to say."

Reese sighed and shook his head. "You're right. I'm sorry. And after I'd just decided to try to be more amicable myself."

"You did?" Her voice rose on a hopeful note. Then she frowned, her eyes narrowing. "Why?"

Again he chuckled. "I have no idea. But I'm sure I'll live to regret that decision along with every other I've made in regard to you."

"You know, if I were to establish an infirmary, I could learn a great deal about these people and their circumstances. Who knows, I might even begin to agree with you about the whole institution."

"Oh, ho, I just bet," he said, laughing dryly.

"All right, so maybe I still wouldn't like this Southern tradition of bondage," she admitted. "But you said yourself you wanted me to observe the practice closely before drawing any conclusions. And since I've volunteered at the hospital in Boston for the last three years, this is one area I *do* know about."

She had him there, he thought. And wasn't it just like a woman to use his own words against him? He'd enjoyed a fine appreciation of females for too long not to acknowledge that Patience

Bentley was far more than just a pretty face. She was astute and clever in her machinations, and his initial attraction returned, accompanied by a grudging admiration as she revealed yet another praiseworthy talent.

"All right," he finally conceded. "You may take action to start an infirmary."

She eyed him warily. "Do you mean it? You have no objections?"

"Plenty. But I'm willing to put them aside in the spirit of compromise—a concept I feel certain we will both spend a great deal of time pursuing during our extensive association."

She graced him with a brief, conciliatory smile. He could see she was congratulating herself on yet another victory. Reese didn't mind; he was silently rejoicing in his own hard-won triumph.

He hadn't agreed to Patience's proposal strictly for her benefit. He had ulterior motives of his own. An infirmary would take a great deal of her time and energy. She would be much too busy to cause Cooper further problems with the workers. If he could keep her interested in the project long enough, the overseer might be able to get the planting done before she turned her attentions back to the matter of his slaves.

Chapter Six

"This will do nicely, I'm sure," Patience said, eyeing the old abandoned shed. "With a little work, that is."

Reese had thought she'd bristle at the offer of the ramshackle building for her infirmary. He gave it another close look. The wood had weathered badly, warping and peeling in places. The two small windows needed cleaning, and one was broken. The door hung askew, one hinge missing the pin.

He'd gotten a perverse pleasure from his suggestion, certain she'd consider the only empty building on the place totally unsuitable. Now, watching her carefully peruse the structure for its possibilities, he felt shame. Had he actually been looking forward to another round of verbal battle with the chit?

Shaking his head, he came to the certain conclusion that he would have to leave soon for Mobile. He was in desperate need of entertainment if he'd been anticipating a skirmish with Patience for amusement.

"Now that I see it up close, I'm not so sure," he said, scanning his memory for another place that might be better.

"Oh, no," she warned, blue fire blazing in her eyes. "You agreed. You can't back out now. I won't let you."

"Settle down. I wasn't trying to back out of anything. I just think this place is too run-down."

"So we'll fix it up."

"*We?* Oh, no. This is your brainchild." Waving his hand toward the lopsided door, he cocked his head. "And you certainly have your work cut out for you."

"You're not going to help me? But it needs a lot of heavy work."

"I could order one of the female slaves to help you. I can't spare any of the men—it's planting time."

Now, he thought, the moment of truth. Would she run screaming from the ramshackle building, worried about getting a splinter or muddying her hands, or would she agree to accept slave labor? He felt a sly grin slip over his face, despite his resolve to be nicer.

"Never mind. I'll handle it myself," she said firmly, planting her hands on her hips. A flicker of doubt flashed briefly across her eyes, momentarily diminishing the fire of zeal. "I'm not afraid of a little work." She turned to him, her features set in determination. "Anything worth having is worth working for. And this is certainly a worthy goal."

She brushed her hands on her lemon-yellow day dress with tiers of ruffles and a crisp band of standing lace at the neckline. A frown creased her brow.

"Not exactly work clothes," he observed. "I don't suppose you brought something more suitable to manual labor?" He couldn't resist baiting her. She might be appalled by slavery, but he'd bet she'd never scrubbed a floor or window in her life.

Yes, this idea to let her start an infirmary was working out better than he'd thought.

"No matter, I'll find something. I don't suppose you'd help with the carpentry? Fix the door, the window?"

He clucked disappointedly. "I'd love to, really," he said, without much enthusiasm. "But I've decided to look over the accounts while I'm here. I'm going to be very busy."

"Yes," she murmured. "At least until the work here is finished, at any rate."

"What was that?" he asked, leaning closer.

She glanced up and smiled, that sexy little grin that sent frissons of desire through his gut and warning bells of alarm through his brain.

"I said, you're very diligent. No doubt that's why this place seemingly runs itself while you're away."

Reese just bet that was what she'd said. No matter, he'd have the last laugh when she came crying because she'd gotten a splinter or, God forbid, had a callous on her baby-soft hands. "I'll leave you to your endeavor, then. Ma Jewel has the keys to the new shed."

"The new shed?" She blinked, her focus slowly turning from the work ahead of her to Reese's statement. She frowned at the light, cheerful expresson he wore.

"Yes, that's where you'll find the tools you'll need. A hammer, some nails . . . mousetraps."

Her cheeks paled beneath the shade of her barrel bonnet, and he fought to suppress his grin.

"See you later," he muttered, sticking his hands in his pockets and whistling a jaunty tune as he strolled toward the house.

From his vantage point on the high stool of the plantation desk in what had been Cooper Hutchins's office for more than thirty years, Reese could see the tall, narrow window of the old shed.

She might be stubborn, but Patience Bentley had mettle. He'd spent his morning looking over the account books and watching her progress on the building. She'd swept and scrubbed every inch of the interior, battling cobwebs and resident blackbirds. She'd dragged out old shelving and rolled out rotten barrels. She even surprised him with her ingenuity when she used a heavy nail as a hinge-pin to fix the door.

He felt a grin tip the corners of his mouth as she swung the door back and forth with pride. After a quick nod of satisfaction, she propped it open with a barrel and began to pile rubbage in the empty keg.

"Stubborn little minx," he said, shaking his head with a combination of admiration and irritation. She hadn't been deterred by the dirt—or the work. She didn't even seem to mind that her clothes would be ruined by day's end. Wearing a once white shirtwaist, of linen unless he missed his guess, and a dark green skirt, she attacked her duties with enthusiasm.

He was finding it more difficult to keep his mind on his task. Even now a stack of bills awaited him in his study. After three months of merrymaking it was, presumably, time to pay the piper.

"And an immoderate warbler she is, too," he sighed, turning back to the accounts. Such drudgery didn't come naturally for him, and it took an immense effort to keep his mind on the figures in the ledger rather than the one outside his window.

If only it weren't such a nice form, he thought. Why had James never mentioned how comely Patience had become? Though not the best father by far, Reese knew the older man loved his child and visited her regularly three or four times a year to make certain she fared well.

And yet he'd never mentioned her astonishing blue eyes, or the locks of golden hair she wore artfully coiffed over one shoulder. Nor had the older man ever commented on her intelligence, which bedeviled Reese but also forced him to acknowledge her as more than a brainless belle. No dainty debutante was buried beneath Patience Bentley's burgeoning bosom.

"A hell-raising malcontent, maybe," he mumbled, thumbing the pages before him with little interest. Curse bills and budgets, he thought grumpily. Not one for manual labor himself, he'd still rather be outside than stuck in the dim, dingy office. Even if he had to work a few blisters on his own hands, at least he wouldn't be bored. No, he conceded with a measure of humor, the one thing he could bank on was that Patience Bentley would never bore him. Infuriate, irritate, even enrage, but never bore.

His hands rested on the thick pages of the ledger, but his eyes strayed once more to the window—and the woman beyond.

"Drinking your breakfast this morning?" Patience observed sarcastically as she swept into Reese's study. She bypassed him with a disapproving sniff and went to his desk, where she scribbled something on a sheet of paper.

Reese eyed her stiff back with disgust and checked his pocket watch. "It's after noon," he told her dryly. "A perfectly respectable hour to have a drink."

"Yes, but a wretched hour to awake," she shot back, letting him know she wasn't fooled by his pressed clothes and close shave. He'd only been up a short time.

Rather than defend himself further, he went on the offensive. "What are you doing rummaging around my desk? For that matter, who gave you permission to come into my study? This is a man's domain and should be respected as such by women."

"Hah," she snorted derisively. "I'd wager I've

spent more time in here than you have. Besides, all that men's-place-women's-place business is nonsense." She made one last entry on the page and stood to face him. His eyes narrowed and his lips thinned. "What?" she asked, certain she'd said something to cause the dire expression.

"Don't tell me you're an advocate of women's suffrage as well as an abolitionist?" he asked with horror.

She cocked her head to one side and bit her lower lip. "Well, since you mentioned it, I suppose I am. In fact, there's a woman in New York who I feel is going to be making an issue of that very subject soon. I met her at a reform meeting just a month ago. Her name is Susan Anth—"

"Stop," Reese ordered, putting a hand to his forehead. "I didn't mean to imply I cared," he snapped brusquely. "Just tell me what you're doing in my study bedeviling me. I thought I gave you enough to keep you busy for days."

She quirked an eyebrow at his unintentional admission, but decided not to goad him further. "I'm making a list of supplies we'll need for the infirmary. I left it on your desk so you'd be sure to see it when you came in here to finish whatever it was you were doing until the wee hours of this morning."

He gave her his full attention for the first time, and another frown creased his brow. "What were you doing, spying on me?" He eyed her closely from head to toe and curled his lip. "And what the hell have you done to yourself?"

She ignored the insulting comment about her

appearance in favor of addressing the accusation. "I don't spy," she stated flatly. "I came down last night for some warm milk." Not for anything would she admit she'd also been looking for some salve for the blisters on her hands. "I noticed the light on, and I heard noises. I assumed you were in here drinking yourself into a stupor. Was I right?" she asked sweetly.

"No, you were not right," he growled. "I was in here working. And you still haven't explained your appearance."

She glanced down at the rough blue workshirt she wore, tails out, over a black homespun skirt. Her sleeves were rolled to her elbows and an old pair of gardening gloves were sticking out of her skirt pocket.

"Well, as you so kindly pointed out yesterday, my clothes were woefully inadequate for the work I was doing. So I borrowed some."

"From where?"

"The rag bag," she told him, confirming his worst suspicions. "You know, I can say one thing for you. Your slaves must be well clothed. Why, these still have quite a bit of wear left in them."

"They look ridiculous. And what have you done to your hair?"

She reached up and patted the triangle kerchief covering her pinned-up locks. "It took me an hour to get the dirt and cobwebs out of my hair last night. I didn't want to go through that again."

"This is absurd. Forget that old shed. I'll have Cooper set the men to constructing a new building as soon as the planting is done."

She looked horrified. "Oh, no. I'm almost finished now. Besides, I don't want to wait that long."

"Another example of the unsuitability of your name."

"Why, because I don't lie about in bed until noon, then spend my time pursuing foolish and unhealthy pleasures?" She eyed his half-empty glass with disdain.

"Look, an abolitionist and an advocate of suffrage are quite bad enough. If you start talking temperance, I promise I'll gag you with that appalling rag you have tied on your head."

"Such brutality, and yet you claim to be humane."

"You haven't seen brutal yet. Just continue to torment me while I'm battling this headache."

"Continue to toss down that stuff first thing in the morning, and you'll be forever battling that particular headache," she told him, nodding toward his tumbler.

Reese scowled and lifted the liquor to his lips, finishing it in one gulp. He smiled amiably and poured another helping from the sidebar.

Patience refused to rise to his bait. But she couldn't help the heavy sigh of disgust she expelled. "We need additional supplies for the infirmary as soon as possible," she said, motioning toward her growing list. "When can you send someone for them?"

"I can't. You'll have to make do with whatever they've been using."

She paused on her way to the door and turned around slowly. "They've been existing on very little. You said I could start this clinic. I need certain things before I can open it to the slaves."

She felt her hopes shriveling, but she lifted her chin. She would not let him see how much she'd been counting on him keeping his word. Why had she put any faith into his promise? He'd shown what a reprobate and a degenerate he could be. He'd made no effort to hide his disregard for her idea. He'd even inadvertantly admitted he was only humoring her to keep her occupied and out of the way. But, darn it, she'd thought he would at least pretend to be cooperative.

"You agreed to let me do this," she reminded him, hating the pleading tone she heard in her voice.

"And you shall," he said, waving his hand to forestall the tirade he felt sure was coming. "But as I've told you repeatedly, it is planting time. I can't spare a single man for the time being. As soon as I return to Mobile, I'll have everything you need delivered."

"You're returning to town?" She paused, wondering why that thought should bring her even a twinge of regret. She should be rejoicing. She would rejoice, she told herself firmly, the minute he was gone. And if she missed their bantering and his company, it would only be because of the loneliness she felt in this wretched place. Irritating and infuriating as he was, at least he kept her mind off the loss of her home and father.

"Yes, indeed," he told her with feeling. "As soon as I settle a few details. Never was much for country living," he said, his eyes gleaming with some remembered pleasure. "I like a more lively atmosphere."

"Like visiting dock-side saloons in the dead of night," she whispered.

"Yes, exactly . . ."

He stopped mid-sentence, her words soaking through the liquor clouding his mind. Looking at her face, he saw the flesh pale below the red kerchief. Her once milky skin turned ashen, and he rushed forward.

Shaking off his hand, Patience made for the door. He grasped her arm and spun her around.

"Let me go," she demanded weakly.

"I'm sorry, Patience. I wasn't thinking. I didn't mean it."

"Didn't you? Don't you think I've seen the bills piled up on the tray in the hall? Don't you think I've heard the servants talk about how you and my father behaved? I foolishly thought my father's death might affect you for the better. But you haven't changed at all. If anything, I think you must be worse than before. Obviously my father's death meant nothing to you, except the loss of a drinking companion."

He yanked his hand away from her arm and stepped back. She'd struck him a blow as surely as if she'd punched him in the stomach. For a moment he couldn't get his breath to respond. She took advantage of his silence.

"I can't imagine what my father was thinking, sending me here. I can't envision a more contemptible place except perhaps hell. And you couldn't be a worse guardian."

Reese could see the pain, the intense sorrow she tried to hide with her anger. But the viciousness of her attack stunned him, and he reacted without careful consideration.

Clutching her shoulders, he spun her around and pulled her against his chest. Breathing onto her cheek as he spoke, he whispered, "You're wrong. I can be far, far worse than I have been. Just continue to provoke me, and I'll show you the true meaning of hell."

Chapter Seven

Reese drank until he resembled the dissolute rogue Patience had accused him of being. He paced the study for some time after she left, then returned to his desk. He ignored repeated knocks on his door and Ma Jewel when she called to him. He refused to leave the study, even for dinner.

No matter how he tried to concentrate on business, his mind continued to whirl with thoughts of Patience Bentley. Even the alcohol he drank couldn't cloud the vision of her he carried in his head.

Again he wondered why James had chosen to make him Patience's ward. The question continued to plague him. James knew him better than anyone, knew what a worthless scoundrel he'd been for better than a decade. The old man had been privy to all of Reese's private demons.

So why hadn't he hidden his daughter away somewhere she would never come into contact with Reese or his way of life? Why had her father cast her into the very heart of the debauchery that had taken his life?

The more Reese chased the elusive answer, the worse his head pounded.

He tried to focus on the account ledgers he'd brought up from Cooper Hutchins's office the previous day. For some reason he couldn't get the columns to balance, despite the fact that he'd always had a talent for figures. He found unexplained deductions listed, yet he couldn't seem to find their corresponding charges anywhere in the ledgers. And the profits over the last months weren't anywhere near what he'd have anticipated, if he'd taken the time to think about such things.

With a curse, he wondered why he even bothered. He should have just handed all his bills over to Cooper and let him pay them, the way he'd always done. What perverse sense of regret made him want to hide the evidence of his profligacy, yet didn't nettle him enough actually to make him consider giving up the immoral pleasures?

Simple pride, no doubt. He knew by the number of bills that had accumulated that he'd enjoyed himself more than he'd realized at the time. Not able to remember all of the debts, he hoped to piece together a sort of itinerary of the last three months based on the receipts.

Knowing he couldn't remember all of his ventures troubled him a great deal more than he would have thought. As disreputable as he'd been in the past, he couldn't say he'd ever been stewed to the point of oblivion. As unruly as he and James had acted at times, he knew he'd sunk to a new low since his friend's death.

All the more reason why Patience Bentley should not be here, he thought. If James had understood the level of Reese's weakness, he surely would not have made such a grievous error in judgment.

Once more he wondered why James had chosen him—and what he could do now to rectify his friend's mistake. When no explanation immediately presented itself, he again searched the bottom of the whiskey bottle, as if hoping to find the answer written there.

Finally, sometime after dark, he sank onto the sofa, his legs draped across the arm, and fell into a deep sleep.

The door to the study clicked open, but Reese didn't stir. Patience tiptoed in, her candle barely illuminating the darkness of the shuttered room. She could see Reese's form slumped over the small sofa like an abandoned ragdoll. His head was tipped at an awkward angle, and she knew he'd have a crick in his neck by morning. His legs dangled above the floor, his boots still on.

It seemed her apology would have to wait for morning. He was obviously in no condition to hear it now.

She shook her head and set aside the candle she carried. As much as she would love to just turn and go, she knew she couldn't leave him where he was for the remainder of the night—although, if the slaves' reaction to her suggestion to approach him were any indication, she'd probably regret her benevolence. Still, she felt somewhat responsible for his condition, so she went ahead.

Shaking his shoulder gained no response, so she softly called his name.

"Reese? You really should get up and go to bed. Reese," she whispered near his ear. "You can't sleep here. You'll regret it in the morning, I assure you."

He snuffled softly and shifted. Patience felt encouraged by the small reaction, and she shook him once more.

"Reese? I'm sorry about what I said earlier—I didn't mean it. It's really late. You should go to bed."

"Bed," he mumbled, flinging one arm over his face.

"Yes, that's right. I'll help you if you like," she said, prepared to assist him up the stairs.

She wasn't prepared for the clasp of his arms, or the quick roll that had her pinned beneath him on the Aubusson rug on the floor. He settled his weight atop her, his leg shifting between her thighs.

Patience gasped for air, both from shock and from his weight pressing on her lungs. She tried to cry out, but only a small squeak sounded in the dark stillness of the study.

"Rita, girl," her attacker mumbled, his words slurred and alcohol heavy. "Yes, yes. Bedding is just what I need."

His hand expertly found her breast beneath the

low neckline of her gown, and he squeezed it roughly.

This time Patience did cry out, but it only seemed to enflame his ardor. She wiggled, and he groaned huskily as he pushed himself tighter against her.

"Don't," she begged, pushing at his chest with ineffectual fists. "Please, stop."

"No, I won't stop, Rita girl. We can go all night if that's what you want."

Patience thought she would die of the shame. Her face flamed, and she felt hot tears sting her eyes. He wasn't actually hurting her, only her pride. She called herself a fool for getting herself into this position. It didn't help matters that he didn't even know who she was. He'd called her by another woman's name!

In desperation, she reached up and pulled his hair. At first, he seemed to enjoy her actions, and his caresses grew bolder. Frightened beyond caution, she yanked as hard as she could.

"What the hell," he cursed, grabbing her hands and pinning them at her sides.

Patience took the opportunity to push her advantage. But without her hands she'd have to get his attention some other way. She leaned up and grasped his lip between her teeth, biting down hard on the soft flesh.

Reese cursed again and grabbed a handful of her hair, dragging her mouth away from his. She tasted blood on her tongue and felt horror at what she'd done.

"Mr. Ashburn, get off me," she ground out,

bucking beneath him more fiercely.

His eyes opened for a moment, and she thought she saw a brief flash of lucidity. Then it was gone, but he'd rolled to the side enough so that she could wriggle out from beneath him.

"What are you doing here?" he grumbled, scraping a hand down his face.

"I came to apologize for our argument earlier. I was feeling sorry for myself and took it out on you," she told him, struggling to her knees. Her feet tangled in the folds of her gown, and she sat down hard on her bottom. "But when I saw you'd passed out, I thought I'd help you upstairs." She babbled the excuse, feeling more foolish as she spoke the words aloud. Even to her ears they sounded inane now.

He looked around blearily and then focused on her face once more. His expression was distrustful and wary. Shoving to his haunches, he grabbed her hand and stood, dragging her to her feet. He swayed, but righted himself.

"Stupid chit," he growled, shoving both hands through his hair and causing it to stand on end. "Don't know who asked for your help . . . damned sure wasn't me."

Patience flushed again and anger replaced her fear. She turned away from him, fumbling for the candle. She gripped the brass holder and winced as pain cut into the blisters on the pads of her hands.

Collecting her wits, she turned to face him, only to be met with an empty room. Confused, she rushed to the door and saw him making his unsteady way up the stairs.

"I hope he falls and breaks his wretched neck," she whispered, swiping at the tears of humiliation streaming down her face. She waited until she heard the door to his bedchamber slam shut, then slowly made her own way back to bed. Sleep would be a long time coming. And she had no one to blame but herself. What a fool she'd been to try to help him.

Idiot, she called herself over and over again as she shed her dress and donned her nightgown. She had no experience with drunkards or their mercurial moods. During his very brief, very intermittent visits, her father had never shown her that side of himself. Why had she thought to approach Reese Ashburn when she knew he'd be well into his cups?

She told herself it was out of guilt for the terrible things she'd said to him. She had spent a good part of the day cursing her loose tongue. But in truth, there was more to it than that. Seeing the pain her words had caused him, she'd felt something move inside her. Seeing how much he had cared for her father caused her to cast him in a new and more flattering light.

Obviously she'd been mistaken. There was nothing in Reese Ashburn to either pity or admire. And certainly nothing which would attract a sensible woman like herself.

Her eyes flew wide. Had she been thinking she was attracted to him? What a horrid thought. He was reprehensible and stood for everything she abhorred. He was entirely the wrong kind of man for her.

Besides, who was Rita?

Patience went down to breakfast early the next morning so she'd run no risk of encountering Reese Ashburn. Their catastrophic encounter the night before was still too fresh on her mind, and she didn't think she could face him.

As she entered the dining room, she skidded to a halt. There, already seated at the table, was her nemesis. And judging by the looks of him, quite the worse for his journey into the bottle.

He looked up and scowled, then bent back over his cup of coffee. She could see the steam rising from the cup from where she stood, but he seemed not to notice as he gulped the drink gustily.

She thought to turn and scurry from his presence, remembering her mortification at his skilled hands. But no, he'd already seen her, and it would only add insult to injury for her to show him how his behavior had disconcerted her.

Better to act the wounded party and let him try to smooth over the matter.

With a haughty sniff, she went to the sidebar and fixed a cup of tea. She placed a triangle of toast on a saucer and dolloped a spoonful of sour cream and jam onto it.

Taking her seat, she noticed the copy of the Mobile Press Register beside his plate. "May I?" she asked, motioning toward the paper.

Reese didn't look up. He grunted once, which

she took for consent, and went back to the study of his cup.

She sipped her tea, blew into it to cool it, and took another sip. Then she lifted the paper and rummaged toward the middle section for a rundown of the week's events.

Another groan came from Reese, and she lowered the paper with a snap. His head sank further into his shoulders and he scowled.

"Something the matter?" she asked.

He shook his head, moaned in pain, and went back to his coffee.

She cracked the paper into position once more and went back to reading. As her eyes scanned the columns, she lifted her toast and took a bite, chewing through the cream and jam with relish.

"Must you do that?" a rough voice demanded from behind the paper.

Patience peered over the top of the page and fought a smile when she saw Reese's bleary eyes meet hers. "What did I do?" she asked sweetly.

"You're chewing loudly."

"Chewing loudly? But it's only a piece of toast," she told him. An impish streak caused her to lift the toast for his inspection. "And I've covered it in sour cream and jam," she added, delighting at the look of horror that crossed his face as he watched the streaks of red jam mingle with the thick white globs of cream.

He jumped to his feet and turned away from the table, the silver coffeepot rattling as he poured another cup of the hot brew. Not knowing what devil drove her, Patience nevertheless couldn't resist making him pay just a little more in retaliation for his actions.

"Tsk, tsk, tsk," she muttered, folding the paper with more precision than the task should have warranted. "Just think how much worse you'd feel if you'd slept on that sofa last night."

He whirled around, pinning her with a sharp glare. She cursed her foolishness, reminding him of the embarrassing event. She set aside her cup, prepared to flee from whatever humiliating comment he would throw back at her.

She wasn't prepared for his statement or the fierce anger in his eyes. "How did you know that?"

Patience stared back at him with astonishment. The confusion in his eyes couldn't be fake. He demanded an answer with his harsh gaze, refusing to let her look away until she'd met the demand.

She stood hastily, pushing away from the table. Stepping back, she pressed her hands against the front of the workshirt she wore once more.

His gaze roamed over her hair and clothing, and he shook his head in disgust before returning to look at her face. "What did you mean?"

"N-Nothing."

"You were in the study last night," he accused her. "What were you doing there?"

She studied his narrowed eyes and the harsh tilt of his chin, and suddenly she understood. He didn't remember. He had no idea what had gone on between them. He probably didn't know how he'd gotten to bed either, or when he'd left the study. And he wanted her to fill in the missing pieces.

What a joke! As if she would recount to him that repulsive scene. No, he'd live in ignorance the rest of his life before she'd reveal her humiliation and open herself to ridicule once more.

"Are you experiencing memory loss now?" she clucked sympathetically. "That is not a good sign. Perhaps you should really reconsider your habits."

With a growl of displeasure, he made a move toward her. Finding her senses had not completely deserted her, she turned on her heel and sped from the room. Even she recognized the danger of baiting a wild bear.

Still, she felt easier knowing she'd never have to face him and wonder if he remembered the disgraceful scene. She even felt some delight in being able to once again point out the error of his ways to him.

But, she admitted to herself, above all that, she felt an odd sense of rejection. He'd been the first man to ever touch her in such an intimate and familiar way. And even if she hadn't found it in any way pleasant, she knew the memory would trouble her for a long time to come.

And he didn't even remember!

Chapter Eight

Patience added the finishing touch to the infirmary and smiled warmly at her new friend. Mag, the midwife, had agreed to run the small clinic for the slaves just as soon as the additional supplies arrived. Patience had instructed her in procedure, explained in detail each item which would arrive, and managed to get Cooper Hutchins to relieve Mag of her other duties so she could concentrate fully on the clinic.

The only thing she hadn't been able to do was talk to Reese and find out when they could expect the supplies. With a frown, she looked toward the house. He'd been holed up in the study for four days, with little more than liquor to sustain him. No one knew what possessed him, and no one had yet dared to invade his sanctum.

Patting Mag encouragingly on the shoulder, she

left the infirmary. Mag had been a surprise to Patience. She'd expected the midwife to be old and set in her ways. But Mag was barely thirty and very open to new ideas and suggestions. She absorbed everything Patience could tell her about caring for the sick and injured, and she added some very thoughtful insight of her own. Patience left knowing the place was in good hands.

"Not that it'll do much good without adequate supplies," she sighed, clapping hands on her hips. It was time to face the lion in his den, she thought with a twinge of trepidation.

Striding toward the main house, she chided herself for acting foolishly. How bad could he be? After all, he'd agreed to the idea of an infirmary for the slaves. He'd told her it would be no trouble getting the supplies from Mobile. All she needed was to know *when* he intended to get them.

She passed Ma Jewel in the main hall, giving instructions to one of the upstairs maids. The women stared in openmouthed astonishment as she turned down the hall toward the study door. Both stopped speaking in mid-sentence and followed her with widened eyes.

A swarm of apprehension fluttered through her stomach, and she wished the women weren't watching. She couldn't back out now without losing face. She bolstered her courage and knocked soundly on the door.

"Mr. Ashburn," she called when no response came to her knock. "Mr. Ashburn, I need to speak with you right away."

She listened, but heard nothing. With frustrated

fists, she knocked again, harder this time. "Mr. Ashburn, I am not going away until you see me. I warn you, I will stand here and pound this door until it falls down."

She punctuated her threat with another round of sharp raps, but still he did not answer. Turning to Ma Jewel, she asked brusquely, "Do you have the key to this door?"

The woman stared at her with horror. "Yes'm, I do. But I can't let you in there. Misser Reese told me he didn't want no one botherin' him."

"Well, I intend to bother him whether he likes it or not. Come on, unlock the door. I'll take responsibility if he gets angry."

"Ain't no if about it," Ma said, shaking her head firmly. "If I let you in there, he'll be angry plenty."

The fuse on Patience's temper shortened dangerously, and she had to remind herself that the woman was only following orders given by her master. No doubt Ma saw Reese Ashburn in that light despite their earlier camaraderie. She also had to stop herself short of issuing her own order, as she'd vowed to treat the slaves with respect.

Swallowing her irritation, she tried to look concerned. "Ma, he's been in there for four days now. He's not eating, he's probably not sleeping. All he's doing is drinking. For that matter, he might be dead. At the very least, he's probably unconscious. Please, open the door and let me check on him. If he orders me to leave, I will." She placed a hand over her heart and smiled. "I promise."

Ma grinned a savvy grin and shooed the young maid away with a word and a quick wave of her hand. The girl scurried off, and Patience heard her ascending the stairs.

She stepped toward Ma and held out her hand for the key. But the old woman shook her head and widened her grin. "You're not foolin' ole Ma with all them syrupy words. You like to turn Misser Reese's screws and watch him spin," she said knowingly. "You want in that room so you can plague him some more. Nope, I ain't gonna let you do it. No siree."

"Ma, I won't anger him, I swear." She saw the woman narrow her eyes, and she held up her hand. "All right, I did want to ask him about something. But truly, now I'm beginning to get concerned. If you'll open the door and let me see that he's all right, I promise not to even mention my request unless he agrees."

"Misser Reese is a grown man. He don't need no checkin' on."

"Reese Ashburn is a troubled man, Ma. You know that's true. Now please, I really want to help this time."

Ma studied her closely for a long moment, then finally nodded once. Patience breathed a sigh of relief. She hadn't been worried about Reese at first, but the truth was she now had an uneasy feeling. Why hadn't they insisted he come out sooner? Why hadn't someone demanded that he stop acting so childishly? Why didn't he answer her knock?

Ma went forward, key extended. But it was Patience who pushed into the room first. It took a moment for her eyes to adjust to the dim interior.

When she could finally see, what she saw made her gasp.

"Oh, Ma!" she cried, rushing forward. Reese lay in a heap on the rug before the sofa.

Ma moved with surprising agility to kneel beside Reese. Patience hurried to the window and yanked open the drapes. She raised the window and pushed aside the shutters, letting daylight and fresh air stream into the tomblike room. A shiver shook her as she tried to dispell the disturbing thought and image.

"Is he—he isn't—"

"Dead? No," Ma told her. She pried open one eyelid and shook her head. "But he sure is pickled," she said, her chins shaking with disapproval.

"Oh, my," Patience breathed, kneeling to have a better look. She'd never seen anyone pickled before. "It's not a very attractive sight, is it?" she reflected, wondering why she still found herself drawn to her ignominious guardian.

His shirt lay open to the waist, exposing a very broad, dark chest. His trousers were crumpled, his feet bare. Long, thin toes peeked up at her and she felt something soften inside.

With a huff, she pushed to her feet. I'm the one who's senseless if the sight of a man's toes has me weak in the knees, she thought, fighting a vivid flush.

"Well, we can't leave him like this, Ma. But I must admit I have no experience in this area. What do we do?"

Ma Jewel heaved her bulk to a standing position with a great sigh and shook her head. "I'll get the coffee boilin'. You get him on his feet an' walkin'."

Mumbling to herself, she left Patience standing in the middle of the floor, her face a mask of startled panic.

"Get him up? How am I supposed to get him up?"

Realizing she was talking to herself, Patience clamped her mouth shut. She approached Reese from different angles, trying to formulate a plan. Finally, she grabbed his hand, tugging with all her might.

"Mr. Ashburn," she called. "You've got to get up."

She yanked again, but he remained motionless. Patience dropped his hand, and it flopped to the rug with a thud. She frowned and studied the situation for another moment.

With her tongue pressed between her teeth, she straddled his outstretched legs. Bending at the waist, she grasped both hands and pulled. Like a marionette on a string, he sat up limply.

"There we go," she coaxed, though he still had made no response to her efforts. Working like a swift contortionist, she sat next to him, wiggled her shoulder beneath his left arm, and pushed to her knees.

"Oh, my, you're a big fellow," she groaned, struggling to get her feet beneath her. "Come on, the least you can do is help a little."

He muttered something and she slipped, almost losing her grip on him in her surprise. "That's right," she said. "On your feet."

To her amazement, he seemed to understand

her command. Leaning heavily on her, he finally rose.

"Oh, thank goodness." Perspiring from exertion, she wiped a quick hand across her brow and then clasped her arms around his waist. "Stand up," she encouraged him, propping her weight against his heavier bulk.

His eyes slowly opened and he peered at her through a red haze. "Not again," he muttered, slumping against her.

"Oh, no, you don't," she cried, pressing her hands firmly against his chest. "I insist you remain standing," she ordered staunchly.

"Has anyone ever told you what a worrisome pest you are, Miss Bentley?"

"Yes, Mr. Ashburn. My father mentioned it."

Reese shook his head, moaned, and disentangled her arms from around his waist. He slumped to the sofa and rested his head in his hands. Once again he'd managed to remind Patience of her father's death—and, more important, his lack of presence in her life.

"You're supposed to be up and walking around."

He looked up at her and grimaced. "Why would I want to do that?"

"To sober up."

He quirked one heavy brow, winced at the pain that small action caused, and scowled at her. "And why would I want to do *that?*" he demanded.

One of the maids interrupted then, pushing a cart carrying coffee, cups, and sandwiches. She didn't look at either Patience or Reese as she set the wheels and poured two cups of the steaming brew. Patience thanked her, and she hurriedly left without a word.

"Here." She thrust a cup beneath Reese's nose. She heard him mumble something, then he took the cup and gulped the coffee.

After he'd finished, she refilled it and added a plate of sandwiches. He made a face at the food, but once again accepted the cup. Feeling she'd at least assured herself that he wouldn't collapse onto the floor again, she took a seat.

"May I ask," she began cautiously, "what brought on such an indulgence?"

Reese emptied his cup, poured another helping, and drank that down. He walked from the sofa to the serving tray, paused, then paced from the window to the fireplace in the far corner of the room. Several times he raked fingers through his hair, sometimes smoothing, sometimes ruffling the dark strands.

Patience began to think he wouldn't answer. It seemed he didn't intend even to acknowledge her. She fought her ire at the shabby treatment, telling herself that no man would like to be found in such a way and then questioned about his actions—especially by a woman he disliked and barely tolerated in the first place.

She'd almost decided to rise quietly from the sofa and leave when she heard him clear his throat.

"You may ask anything of me you wish," he said, without facing her. "If you would be so kind as to give me time to make myself presentable, I will meet you in the dining room for dinner and we can have our discussion then."

He sounded every inch the sauve Southern gentleman, despite his rumpled appearance and bare feet. Patience feared he might go back to the bottle if she left him alone. However, he seemed to need privacy to collect himself, and she couldn't very well deny him that. She pushed to her feet.

"I'll see you at dinner," she said with as much dignity as she could manage after the bizarre encounter. Leaving the room, she wondered at the demons that drove Reese Ashburn.

He was at times a charming and witty companion. Yet always, beneath the surface, was a man tormented. She suspected her father's death was part of his trouble, but not all. She found she wanted to know everything about him so she could ease his pain. Why, she didn't know. He supposedly meant nothing to her. But somehow she knew that wasn't true anymore. He had come to mean something to her in the past week. She just didn't know what.

When she entered the dining room a few hours later, he was waiting for her. Dressed in an ebony frock coat, dove-gray trousers, and snow-white shirt and cravat, he was the most handsome man she'd ever laid eyes on. His hair was slicked back, his jaw fresh-shaven. She could smell the scents of his cologne and pomade as he assisted her into her chair.

"You look lovely tonight," he told her as he took his seat at the head of the table.

Patience could barely associate this princely companion with the sad, vulnerable man she'd found lying on the floor less than two hours earlier. This Reese Ashburn could pass for a pillar of the community.

She shook her head to clear the confusion and glanced down at her seafoam-green dinner dress. All her clothes had seemed the height of fashion in Boston, but since coming South she thought they seemed frilly and somewhat juvenile. She wondered now if the clothes were wrong for the climate or if something in her had changed.

"Thank you. You look very nice yourself."

"A slight improvement over our last meeting, I'm sure."

She saw the flash of self-disgust in his dark eyes, and she smiled to ease his dismay. "A definite improvement," she said, trying to convey her understanding with her gaze. Their eyes met and held for a long moment, and a shaft of awareness pierced her stomach. Something vague and sensuous passed between them, causing her heart to flutter against her breasts. She tried to look away but found she could not.

It crossed her mind why Reese Ashburn had a reputation as a ladies' man. His eyes held her enthralled, and his mouth made her wonder what it would be like to kiss him. The shocking thought snapped her out of her ridiculous musings, and she lowered her head to hide her scarlet cheeks. What on earth had possessed her? She'd never acted so foolishly in her life!

Gay arrived to serve their soup, and for the moment Patience was spared having to make small talk. After the slave filled their bowls and water glasses, she left them alone once more.

"So, you said you'd tell me what was bothering you," she began, gently stirring the seafood bisque with her spoon.

"I don't recall saying anything was bothering me." He took a spoonful of his soup and eyed her across the table.

"So you're not going to tell me after all. That is a shame. I thought perhaps I could help."

"I don't see how you could."

She arched an eyebrow. "Then there is a problem?"

He studied her for a long moment, then seemed to make some kind of decision. He nodded. "Yes, there is a problem," he admitted.

Patience set aside her spoon, her interest in dinner forgotten. "Is it a problem with Bonne Chance? I managed father's estate in Boston, you know. If you would let me, I could help you."

"No one can help now, I'm afraid."

"How is that?"

He battled his thoughts for a moment, then faced her squarely. "Cooper Hutchins has very nearly bankrupted Bonne Chance."

Patience gasped. "You're not serious?" But she could see that he was very serious. "How? Why would he do that?"

"Oh, I don't believe it was intentional. He's gotten old, possibly senile. Our factor must have known, since he's been paying well below the going rate for our cotton for nearly three years. Meanwhile, all the expenses have continued to rise, some of which I have no one to blame for but myself. Together it was a recipe for disaster."

She could see the despair on his face, the guilt, the blame. She wished they weren't so far apart, or she'd reach out to him. Not that he'd appreciate the gesture. She wasn't even sure why she felt compelled to assist him. They certainly weren't friends, or even friendly most of the time. Still she said, "I'm sorry."

"So am I. Believe me, I had not anticipated this complication when I came home."

"You have had several shocks since your return. Not the least of which was me."

"Even that can't compare to the enormity of this disaster. If possible, I'm even less equipped to deal with this one."

"Nonsense," she said, surprised at her own vehemence. "You grew up here. This is your home. Who knows more about Bonne Chance than you?"

He laughed, but the sound held no humor. "Possibly anyone. I haven't exactly been a diligent owner."

"Then perhaps it's time you were."

He glanced up at her, and again they stared at each other for a long moment. Finally, he looked away. "I know nothing of the running of this place."

"You'd better learn, then. Because you're going to have to let Cooper Hutchins go."

His head snapped up, and he pinned her with a hard stare. "I can't fire Cooper. He's been here longer than I have. He's the reason Bonne Chance didn't go under after my father's death. He has more right to all this than I do."

"He's also the reason you may very well lose it now. He's an old man, Reese. He has a right to slow down and enjoy his old age, not work until he falls dead in the fields."

Slowly, he nodded. "You're right. But I couldn't just fire him. Pension him off, maybe. Although there's very little money for even that. If I pay Cooper a stipend, I can't afford to replace him with another overseer."

"Then I suppose you'll have to do the job yourself."

"What are you talking about? I'm not an overseer."

"You aren't a dimwit, either. I'm sure you can manage whatever needs to be done."

Again he studied her, a glimmer of hope now in his eyes. "Do you think so?"

"Of course. And I'll help, too. I know how to deal with merchants, take care of accounts. I know something of your slaves, too, since I've been spending time with them. Together I'm sure we can pull through this."

"Together?"

Reese grinned at the irony. All he'd wanted was a way to get rid of Patience Bentley and return to Mobile. Now, she was suggesting that he stay on at Bonne Chance indefinitely, with her as a constant companion.

And, what was even more surprising, he found the idea didn't appall him as he'd thought it would.

Chapter Nine

"You're still not pleased?"

Reese shook his head, his eyes never leaving the field of workers. He heard Patience's ruffled sigh.

"I know it'll be close for the next few months. And things are still bad. But you're are not going to lose Bonne Chance. That should make you happy."

After two weeks of steady work—Patience budgeting and alloting, Reese following first Cooper and now Ran through the fields—he failed to see what he had to be so damned pleased about.

"If we get the entire cotton crop to market, and if we bypass the factor and sell directly to the shipper, and if you don't start a rebellion before all that can come about, we might just break even." He tossed aside the weed he'd plucked from the edge of the field and stared down at her. Her usual sprightly expression was pinned expectantly in place, and he met it with a scowl.

"Yes, that's right," she said, her exuberance shining in her wedgewood-blue eyes.

"And you see that as a reason to celebrate?"

"Of course. Good grief, Reese, you've proven you can run this place under the most dire circumstances. What's wrong?"

Reese bent to pluck another weed, more for something to do than out of concern for the crop. He didn't want to look into those eyes, so wide and trusting. He couldn't bear to see the newfound belief in him that he sensed growing in his ward. It was undeserved and unwarranted.

So he'd stuck around for a while, helped get the crop in the ground, helped set the accounts straight. Randolf, their main driver, had done most of the actual work of directing the other workers, setting schedules and fulfilling them. He'd make a damn fine overseer. Better by far than Reese ever would.

"So put him in the position."

Startled, Reese swung around to stare dumbfounded at Patience. "What?"

"Ran. You said he'd make a fine overseer. So why don't you give him the job?"

Reese didn't know which disturbed him more. The fact that he'd spoken aloud without realizing it, or the fact that once again Patience was right. Only this time, there was nothing he could do about it.

"You still don't understand," he told her, looking back out over the fields. On this one point they were finally in agreement, he and his headstrong ward. But it was an impossible situation. Ran did the work of three men. He was a born leader, smart and capable. And unmistakably black.

"I've already explained to you, Patience. No one in these parts would stand for me putting a slave in a position of authority, no matter how well-deserving he might be. It simply isn't considered safe."

"Oh, pooh," she huffed, smoothing down the folds of her skirt. She'd done away with the fluffy, frilly dresses she'd brought with her, now choosing instead to wear simple skirts and blouses. But sometimes she reverted to the familiar motions that soothed her. "I told you that's a lot of rubbish. It's your estate, and you should have anyone you like as overseer without giving a fig what those other zealots think or say about it."

"Perhaps that's the way it should be. But it certainly isn't the way things are done here."

"So, change the ways," she said firmly. "Someone has to make the first move toward reform."

He snapped out of his troubled thoughts and turned on her with a fierce grimace. "You are assuming I want reform. I've told you before I do not. I don't make society's rules, Patience, but I will abide by them, as we all do, for the betterment of the whole."

The gleam of righteous anger flared to life in her eyes, and he saw the start of another round of debate—a battle he was not up to in his present state of mind. She opened her mouth to speak, and he whirled on his heel and strode away without a backward glance.

Why couldn't she understand and accept Southern ways? She was bright, beautiful, and dedicated. She'd stepped in and helped him out without a word of reproach. She'd carried a mammoth weight of responsibility, all the while seeming to enjoy the toil. So why did she continue to fight him on this one issue?

He passed the overseer's cottage, Cooper Hutchins's home for longer than Reese had been alive. He thought about going to the door and talking to the old man for a few minutes. But his guilt stopped him. Cooper hadn't been the same since Reese had relieved him of his duties.

Reese had offered him the use of the cottage indefinitely, out of contrition, and because he wouldn't be hiring another man any time soon so the place wasn't needed. But just the day before, Cooper had told him he would be going soon.

Where would the man go? Bonne Chance had been his home for most of his life. Reese would have to come up with a workable solution. He didn't want Cooper going off alone somewhere to spend his last years. At the same time, he could see the pain it caused the other man to look upon the fields each day and not be able to do the job he'd always done.

With a disgusted sigh, Reese headed for the main house. God, he needed a drink. If only he hadn't sworn off the stuff for the time being. Between the mess with Bonne Chance and his certainty that something had happened between him and Patience that he couldn't remember, he'd decided to curtail his drinking for a while. Unfortunately, he couldn't have chosen a worse time to embrace temperance.

In the study, he sank into the huge leather chair behind his desk. With a groan, he raked rough fingers through his hair. Why did everything have to be so complicated? He'd like nothing better than to walk away from the whole cursed situation.

But for the first time in his life, he was truly needed here. Patience needed him to keep her in line and out of trouble. Cooper had obviously needed him for years but had never let on. Even Ran, though skillful, needed him.

Why didn't he feel the choking, stifling burden of responsibility he'd been running from for more than a decade? Where was the weight of unwanted obligation he'd dodged like a curse? Where did this strange feeling of pride come from?

But mixed with the pride was guilt and remorse. He had to do something about Cooper. And he had to talk to Ran. Both men deserved better treatment than finances and society currently allowed.

On that issue Patience was right. While a slave owner, Reese had never been of the mind that slaves were merely property. He'd been taught by both his parents to respect folks, no matter their color. In return, you usually had more content workers. But to make a slave overseer—that would be asking for trouble Reese could ill afford at the moment.

He focused on the accounts spread across his desk. Patience had done a lot toward cleaning up the mess Cooper had made of the books. But money would be tight until the first crop was shipped. And that time was still six months away.

Good Lord, what would he do for that long to keep his sanity in this place with that hellcat ward of his?

He needed solutions. For the first time he would be called upon to make important decisions. He had to keep a clear head. But, dammit, he missed the blessed oblivion of alcohol.

"It's going to be a long six months," he said, shaking his head.

"I'm so pleased with the way you've handled everything, Mag," Patience told the woman with a genuine smile. "You only received the supplies a few days ago and already you've put everything in order. A few of the slaves have told me they've been to see you, and they're very pleased with your efforts, as am I."

The woman's *café au lait* cheeks creased in a wide grin and her black eyes danced with pride. "Thank you, miss. I've been real happy here. I always wanted to put my mama's teachin' to good use. I feel like I'm doin' that now."

"You just keep up the excellent work, Mag."

Patience left the infirmary, a smile still tipping her mouth. She really liked Mag, and the woman had become a good friend as well as a trusted employee. She'd talked to her about reform, and Mag had listened attentively.

Patience could tell the woman mostly did it out of courtesy, because she liked Patience and didn't want to hurt her feelings. She, like most of Reese's slaves, didn't see any point in touting something they could not imagine coming about in their lifetime. But it was a start, and Patience, though she claimed otherwise, could be patient at times.

"Howdy, Miss Patience," a deep, smooth voice said.

Startled, Patience gasped and clasped her hand to her chest as she whirled to face one of the younger workers. When she saw who it was, she relaxed and released a shaky breath.

"Oh, Monroe. You startled me. Were you heading for the infirmary? Is everything all right?"

"I'm fine," he said, rubbing his bare chest where his shirt parted in front. "But I was wanting to hear more of what you had to say 'bout this freedom movement."

Patience's spirits soared, and she couldn't keep the pleasure from her voice. "Oh, I'm so glad," she breathed. "I'd be happy to tell you everything I know about the movement in the North to pass bills in Congress and even enact laws for reform." She glanced around at the fields, dotted with the dark forms of the slaves at work. "But shouldn't you be working right now? I don't want you to get into trouble."

"I told Ran I had the headache real bad. He told me to go to the clinic for some powders."

Hearing the bitterness and self-satisfaction in Monroe's tone, Patience felt a moment of unease. "Well, you certainly should go and let Mag give you something, then."

He laughed and leaned close to her, and Patience couldn't help but draw back.

"I ain't got the headache a'tall," he told her, grinning wickedly. "I just told him that so I could talk to you. He don't like us listenin' to you, you know."

"He—he doesn't?" Patience cleared her throat nervously, wondering how her concern had gotten her into this uncomfortable situation.

"Nope. So maybe we ought to step behind the old shack there, so's he can't see me."

"I don't want you to get into trouble, Monroe. Maybe we should wait until later. After your work is finished."

"Then you'd have to come to my cabin," he said. "I couldn't get away to the big house without someone seeing me. I'd be caught for sure."

"Oh, I wouldn't want you to do that," she hurriedly assured him. The thought of going into Monroe's cabin alone gave her the chills for some reason. Was it his eyes or the subservient tone he used that didn't ring true? She couldn't put her finger on why she didn't like Monroe. His actions seemed genuine, but he unnerved her.

"Maybe we should wait until some of the others show an interest and then we could put together a meeting," she said.

A flare of intense and sudden anger lit the dark depths of his eyes, and Patience drew a deep, shaky breath. Then the look disappeared and he cocked a grin at her.

"Ain't no one but me gonna listen to you as long as Ran tells them not to."

"Randolf is ordering the slaves not to talk to me?" she gasped in outrage. "He can't do that."

And to think she'd encouraged Reese to make the man overseer. Why would he be so set against her talking to the workers? He was a slave—he should want to hear what she had to say as well. It made no sense.

"If you was to talk to me, then I could tell them all what was what. Ran wouldn't have to know nothin' about it. We could work together, you and me," he said, a note of insolence in his voice.

Was he acting so boldly because he didn't want her to think he answered to Ran? That must be the reason. Simple male pride. It was silly of her to feel threatened. The man came to hear her ideas. And, if what he said about Ran's dictate were true, he might be the only one she got the opportunity to talk to. Despite her unease, she couldn't pass up this chance.

"All right, Monroe. I'll meet you tonight after supper. But I can't go to your cabin. Someone could see me and you'd still be in trouble."

He looked annoyed for a second, then his expression cleared. "Good thinkin', Miss Patience. I knew you was a smart lady. We could meet at the edge of the orchard. You from the front of the house, me from the back of the quarters. That way no one'll see neither of us."

Swallowing a hard knot of apprehension, Patience slowly nodded. "At the orchard, after supper." She cleared her throat again. "I'll be there."

"That's real good, Miss Patience," he said. "Real good."

He sauntered around the side of the infirmary, whistling a tuneless melody. A grin split his ebony face. His hands were tucked into the hip pockets of his work pants, and his broad shoulders pushed forward as he strode away.

Turning her palms over, Patience saw that sweat had pooled there. She was acting foolishly. The man had done nothing to bring on such distress. He simply wanted to know about reform. And she intended to tell him everything she knew on the subject. Despite Reese's warnings, Patience had determined to fight the injustice of slavery on the battlefields of the Southern plantations. She refused to let a bout of nervous jitters keep her from her purpose.

As she walked quickly back toward the house, she tried to tell herself it wasn't Monroe's actions that had caused her anxiety. It was knowing how Reese would react if he found out about it.

And, she had to admit, a measure of guilt plagued her. She and Reese had been getting along well the last two weeks as they united in their efforts to pull Bonne Chance from the jaws of ruin. He wouldn't appreciate her meeting one of his slaves for a secret reform conclave.

All the more reason to take this opportunity, she thought. Her mind made up, she pushed aside the twinge of conscience. She'd told Reese Ashburn exactly what she intended to do during her stay in Alabama. If he didn't expect some sort of action from her, it was his own arrogance that blinded him. She had made no secret of her intentions.

Chapter Ten

Patience was still battling a case of nervous jitters when she went down to supper. She hoped Reese couldn't tell that the fluttering in her stomach had stolen her appetite.

As he swept into the room to join her, she knew she had nothing to worry about on that level. He was in an exceptionally good mood, smiling and complimenting both Gay and Ma Jewel on the meal. By the time dessert arrived, her curiosity was whetted and she couldn't stop herself from questioning him.

"You seem unusually happy tonight," she said, dipping into her berries and cream. He'd devoured his own with relish already.

"Yes, I am." He grinned, and Patience's heart jolted at the sight. She'd never been the direct recipient of one of Reese's blinding smiles and the effect left her dazed.

Quickly averting her gaze so he wouldn't notice her surprise, she toyed with the dessert. "Well, I must say it's a nice change."

She could have said a lot more. About tickles and tingles and feelings that shoot from your head to your toes. She almost sighed with delight just looking at him tonight in his formal clothes and with his familiar slicked-back hair. His eyes had begun to shine since he'd abstained from the bottle, and his cheeks had a fuller, less harsh look to them.

"Yes, I imagine it is," he said with a chuckle. "I haven't exactly been the ideal host since your arrival."

"I haven't exactly been the model guest, either," she admitted, thinking shamefully of the meeting she'd arranged for later that night.

"Nevertheless, I made some decisions today. They were difficult and complicated, but I'm pleased with the results and I think you'll agree they will be satisfactory to all concerned."

"Decisions? About what?" She glanced up and met his glowing gaze, nearly catching her breath. He was so incredibly attractive when he smiled. His whole face changed, welcoming her attention rather than spurning it as he had for so long.

"You know how troubled I was about letting Cooper go."

Yes, she'd seen the depth of his concern for the old overseer. It had aroused in her the first glimmers of doubt about his feckless nature. No one could care so much for an employee and be totally self-absorbed. She nodded.

"Well, I found the perfect solution. There's a five-acre plot on the far northern border of Bonne Chance. My father purchased the property from a settler when he planned to enlarge the fields. The enlargement never took place, and the land is still there, small cabin intact. As part of his settlement, I've given Cooper the land and the cabin. He can stay on Bonne Chance, and it doesn't cost me a dime."

Patience felt an answering smile tip her lips. He was so pleased with his solution, and she couldn't blame him. It was truly a wonderful idea and she told him so.

Reese grinned and nodded. "It felt good to take some positive action. Really good," he admitted somewhat shyly.

This need for reassurance was also a new facet to Reese's character that Patience hadn't expected. He didn't like her—why should he care what she thought of his decisions?

"I also talked with Ran about the overseer's position," he stated, leaning closer to the table and holding her gaze all the while he dropped his bomb.

Patience remembered Monroe's words about Ran discouraging the other slaves from listening to her. If Reese made him overseer, he would have the power to forbid them.

"You—you said you couldn't offer him the position. You said it would cause trouble."

"Yes, it would," he said with enthusiasm. "But I've found a way around all that—a solution I think you especially will appreciate."

"Me? Why me?"

"Let me tell you what I have in mind, then you'll understand. I couldn't pay to hire an overseer, as you know. And Ran was the best man on the place to fill the job. So I offered him credit toward buying his papers in exchange for his taking over most of Cooper's duties. Officially, I'm the owner and manager of Bonne Chance. But in reality, Ran is buying his freedom with his efforts."

Mouth gaping like a beached bass, Patience stared speechlessly at Reese. She couldn't believe what she was hearing! It was too incredible.

"You're serious?" she finally managed to ask.

Reese laughed out loud at her expression, thrilling to her reaction, which was just what he'd expected.

"I'm very serious. And I won't have stepped on anyone's toes in the process. Slaves are allowed to buy their freedom. Only none ever have the means to do it. This way I'll be paying Ran, but it won't cost me any real cash. Of course, when his price is paid I'll lose his value as a slave, but by then we should be on firmer ground financially and it won't be such a hardship."

"Well," she muttered, somewhat breathlessly. "You certainly have figured everything out, haven't you?"

She glanced up then and caught a brief flash of chagrin cross his face. She narrowed her gaze for a better examination, but he'd covered the look—

if it had been there at all. Seeing his friendly expression, she thought perhaps she'd imagined it.

Clearing his throat, Reese lifted his water glass and took a long sip. "Yes, I think I have," he said, enigmatically.

Meeting her questioning gaze over the rim of the goblet, he tried to hide his thoughts. He'd decided early on, after first reading her father's will, that there was only one way to solve the problem of his rebellious ward. But it wasn't a solution he suspected she'd find as satisfactory as the others they'd discussed.

The will made it perfectly clear that she would remain on Bonne Chance until she reached the age of twenty-five, unless he could find her a suitable husband. Only then could he rid himself of the problem of Patience Bentley without feeling he'd once more let James down.

He'd been distracted from his plan for a little while, but last night he'd come to the conclusion it was time to see the chit well wed and rid of as soon as possible. Not an easy task, but one he now felt competent to handle.

With her skirt gathered close to her legs, Patience made her way out the kitchen door and around the side of the house toward the orchard. Guilt ate at her as she crept surreptitiously toward her meeting with Monroe.

Reese had been a different person at supper. He'd been charming and cordial and had treated her with deference and respect. She hated deceiving him this way when they'd been getting along so well. She knew without a doubt that he'd be furious if he found out.

But she'd made up her mind to fight slavery. She couldn't let her guardian's overwhelming charm and good looks keep her from what she felt was right. The slaves at Bonne Chance, as well as all over the country, were depending on her. Whether they knew it or not.

And no matter how nice Reese had been of late, or how attractive, she couldn't forget that he was a slaveholder. A trader in human bondage. She'd been encouraged by his plans for Ran, but arranging for one slave to be freed wasn't nearly enough.

Still, she felt like a Judas, accepting his hospitality while sneaking around behind his back to enlighten his workers. At least before this, their battles were forthright.

But it couldn't be helped, she told her bothersome conscience. This need for secrecy had been forced upon her; she hadn't chosen to be deceitful.

She approached the orchard cautiously, searching the shadows for a sign of Monroe. Her uneasiness hadn't lessened in the interim. If anything, she was more nervous now that she was here. What was it about the young man that troubled her? If she could only put her finger on what caused this feeling . . .

"Miss Patience."

Again she spun in surprise to find the man behind her. How had he crept up without her hearing him? Was that what had her so jumpy? That he seemed always to sneak up on her from behind? It certainly didn't help her nerves any.

"Monroe, please don't do that to me. You nearly gave me a nervous shock."

"Didn't know I was here, did you?" he asked, his tone boastful.

He actually seemed pleased to have scared her. Why? She was there to help him.

"Just don't startle me any more, all right?"

"Whatevers you says, miss," he drawled, his speech overly idiomatic.

Patience knew he spoke proper English well enough. Why was he mocking her with the slang? Her disquiet grew.

"Maybe this wasn't such a good idea, Monroe."

"You always have a lot to say about equality and freedom. You're always preachin' about reform." Again he moved toward her. "I want to know if you really believe all that stuff you been spoutin'."

"Of—of course I mean it. I feel very strongly that all men are created equal, no matter their color."

"So I'm as good as any white man?"

"Yes, certainly." She cleared her throat, trying to calm her unsteady nerves. All the man wanted was a chance to hear her ideas—why was she behaving like such a ninny?

"Well, that's where you're wrong, Miss Patience," he said harshly, emphasizing her name. "I ain't as good as white men. I'm a damn sight better."

Backing away, Patience knew in that instant why she'd felt so uneasy. Monroe wasn't there to hear her ideas on reform. And the apprehension she'd always experienced in his presence was an instinctive reaction to the bitter hostility he harbored just below the surface of his affable demeanor.

"Monroe, I think I should go. We can continue this discussion another time."

"What's the matter, Miss Patience? I thought you said I was equal to any white man. Now you're actin' like you don't want me near your precious self."

"It isn't that, Monroe. The way you're behaving frightens me."

"How is that?" He took another step toward her and she backed up, right into the trunk of a big apple tree. He'd been purposely trying to pin her in, to trap her out of sight of anyone else. Terror blossomed in her chest, and she could taste the acrid fear creeping up her throat.

"Let me go, Monroe."

"I want to see you put your fancy words into action," he said, reaching forward to slam a hand against the trunk over her head.

Patience cried out, and she could see his teeth gleam as he grinned widely. "Show me you think of me as your equal, Miss Patience. Show me I'm good enough for the likes of you and your kind."

"Monroe," she pleaded, hating the frightened tremor she heard in her voice. "Please stop. There'll be trouble."

"Only if you tell, Miss Patience. And who's gonna believe you? They all know you been leadin' us a merry chase, tellin' us how we got to stand up for our rights. I'll say you asked me out here. I'll say you wanted it, said as how no white man had ever satisfied you."

"No, that's not true. They'll believe me," she cried, tears of shame and humiliation filling her eyes. "Don't do this, Monroe. Please, I was only trying to help."

"You was tryin' to show us what a good person you was, standin' up for the poor black man. Well, we can take care of ourselves. We don't need to be the charity of some fancy rich bitch."

No amount of talk was going to help, Patience decided. Monroe's hatred festered too deeply. She would have to save herself from this mess she'd gotten into. The blame, and the responsibility, were hers.

Gathering her strength, she crossed her arms and barreled past him, knocking him to the side. Stunned by her unexpected action, he stumbled backward. She darted from beneath the apple tree, hampered by her whipping skirts.

Monroe recovered quickly and overtook her. He whirled her around, wrenching her arm. She cried out and struck out at him, scraping her nails across his cheek.

With a scream of rage, he slapped her hard on the face, making stars dance crazily behind her eyes. She slumped, and he yanked her up by the shoulders. Grasping her hair in one hand, he used the other to rip her blouse from neck to waist.

She fought him, but he was muscled and strong and he subdued her. She tried to call out, but he clasped a hand over her mouth. With a mighty shove, he toppled her to the ground and fell on her.

With the breath knocked out of her, Patience

couldn't even scream. Gasping and choking, she bucked hard, trying to dislodge him. He chuckled and settled himself between her spread thighs.

Shoving her hand into his face, she pushed hard with all her strength. "No!" she screamed.

His weight shifted, and she was stunned when she felt the pressure of his body lift from hers. Rolling to the side, she gasped and drew her breath in sharply. Turning, she saw Monroe being lifted by the neck like a rag doll.

It was too dark for her to see much, but she heard the unmistakable crack of fists meeting flesh and bone. Then Monroe's unconscious form fell beside her.

Patience shrieked and climbed hurriedly to her feet. She turned to run, and strong arms encircled her.

"Miss Patience, you all right?"

Opening her eyes, she peered up at Ran. His lean face was pinched in rage. She shrank back, and he instantly released her.

"Yes. Yes, Ran, I'm fine now. Th-thank you. Thank you so very much. I—I don't know what I'd have done if you hadn't come along," she stammered, holding her blouse together with one trembling hand.

The sound of footsteps rustling through dry leaves met their ears, and they both turned to see Reese running toward them. He slid to a halt, staring from the crumpled form on the ground to Patience's tattered blouse. Quickly, he removed his frock coat and slipped it around her shoulders.

"Patience, are you hurt? What happened?" He

turned to Ran, his gaze shooting sparks of fury. "What the hell happened here?"

"I don't know, Mista Reese. I heard what sounded like a scream and I came runnin' to see. I found Monroe there attackin' Miss Patience."

"Attacking her?" He gathered Patience's trembling body against his side. "Why would he do that, Patience? What happened here tonight?"

"I—I don't know. He said he wanted to talk to me about my ideas for reform," she stammered, struggling through the tremors of shock washing over her. "But when I arrived he was so angry, so bitter. And then he—he—"

To her horror, she broke down then, sobbing against Reese's shoulder. He gathered her against his chest and softly smoothed the hair at the back of her head.

It felt so good to be in safe arms, to be held and comforted. No one had ever comforted her this way. Not even when she was a child. Her tears subsided, but she couldn't make herself move out of the haven of Reese's embrace.

Ran walked over to Monroe and lifted him by the shirt collar. Shaking him like a dog, he set the dazed man on unsteady feet.

"What you want to do with him, Mista Reese?"

Patience lifted her head, watching the emotions cross Reese's face. She felt his rage, saw the barely restrained violence he fought to control.

"You're in charge, Ran. He's your man."

"He ain't no man, you don't mind me sayin' so," the older slave bit out savagely. "And there ain't but one thing to do with scum like him. Anyone does what he done deserves to be hung."

"No!" Patience cried, grabbing the front of Reese's shirt.

Monroe came alive at the pronouncement and began to struggle. Ran subdued him by catching his hands behind his back and lifting until his elbows met. The younger man bellowed, then wilted in submission.

"Reese, please," she begged. "You can't let him do that. You know how I feel. Maybe I brought the situation on myself. I didn't mean for anything like this to happen, though."

He took her gently by the arms and shook his head. "Ran is in charge, Patience. I gave him the authority. I can't take it away the first time he's called upon to make a difficult decision."

She whirled to face Ran and saw Monroe's terrified expression in the glow of moonlight. A shiver rocked her, but she forced herself to step closer. "Ran, please," she entreated. "Don't do this. As a favor to me, please find some other way to handle the situation."

He looked past her to Reese. "I reckon we could whip him, Mista Reese. But I don't think that'd do no good. 'Sides, the other overseers find out what he done, they'll come after him for sure." He shrugged. "Only one other thing we can do."

Patience glanced over her shoulder and saw Reese nod his head. "I'll take care of it, Ran," he said.

"I'll make sure he's locked in 'til you do," Ran said, shoving Monroe ahead of him as he led him toward the quarters.

"What?" Patience asked, her gaze darting from the slaves to Reese's hard-set features. "What are you going to do?"

"You didn't want him killed. We'll try to see that doesn't happen. But we can't keep someone like that on the place. It isn't safe. Besides, Ran's position with the slaves will be seriously undermined if word gets out that he didn't punish Monroe. He'll have to be sold."

Clutching her hand over her heart, she gasped. "Just like that? You're going to sell the man like a barrel of apples?"

"I don't have a choice, Patience. He's proven he's dangerous, and it'll only get worse now that you've interfered with Ran's control. If Ran doesn't make an example of Monroe, the other workers will never listen to him again. Despite what you think, most of them would have understood and agreed with Ran's punishment."

She shivered again, this time with shame. She'd made such a mess of things. How had her good intentions turned so bad?

"I'm sorry," she muttered. "I'm really sorry."

Tears filled her eyes, and Reese flinched from the look of despair on her lovely face. He wanted to rail at her for her stupidity. He wanted to shake her until her teeth rattled for putting herself in such danger. But he couldn't bear the look of hopelessness she wore.

He'd seen her fighting mad and spitting with anger. He'd seen her fired with righteous indignation—none of which he thought he'd liked, until now. But he realized he'd much rather see her bristling with fury than shrinking in fear.

"Come on," he said, putting his arm across her shoulders. "Everything'll be fine. I promise."

Chapter Eleven

Patience watched from the balcony outside her bedroom as Reese rode his horse along the fields. Ran directed the workers as they weeded the sprouting cotton plants. She could see Mag sweeping the porch of the infirmary.

Her gaze swept the emerald and brass of the new fields, the blue of the bay in the distance. The line of trees bordering Bonne Chance were full and richly colored kelly and moss greens. Even the slave quarters, with their red roofs and royal-blue shutters, looked picturesque.

It was another hot day, the humidity already climbing. But on the upper gallery, a breeze from the bay could be felt. Patience leaned against the French doors and sipped her morning tea.

For the first time, she felt comfortable in her surroundings. Even in Boston, on her father's estate, she'd sometimes felt like a stranger, an interloper. But she knew she belonged at Bonne Chance now. These people thought of her as part of their big, strangely connected family. Even with her many faults, which she knew troubled them deeply, they'd accepted her.

Monroe had disappeared the morning after the incident in the orchard and had not been mentioned since. But Reese, Ran, even Ma Jewel, now treated Patience with a protective tenderness.

She'd made it clear to Reese that she didn't intend to stop preaching reform, telling him Monroe was the exception, not the rule, when it came to the slaves on Bonne Chance. Instead of arguing with her, he'd actually smiled at her!

Such an odd man. Reese Ashburn was an enigma Patience couldn't quite figure out. She knew her beliefs riled him, yet he'd seemed glad she wasn't giving them up after the terrible incident with Monroe. He'd been pleasant and attentive to her for the past two weeks.

Which was the only explanation Patience could find for the bizarre feelings, thoughts, and dreams she'd been having about her guardian.

Her breasts tightened and her stomach knotted at the memory of last night's dream. She'd imagined Reese holding her—with desire this time, not comfort. Her lips tingled as she closed her eyes and relived the imaginary kiss he'd bestowed on her. She could almost feel the strength of his arms encircling her, drawing her against his broad, hard chest.

Unexpectedly, she felt a warmth of moisture

pool at her most private spot. Stunned, her eyes flew open and she drew a deep, shaky breath. Heartbeats pounded against her chest, and her fingers felt almost numb with the need to touch Reese.

What was happening to her? She'd never felt this way about a man before. In Boston, she'd had her share of kisses. She'd even been courted once, by a young man from an adjoining estate. But nothing she'd experienced with Carl Garrard had prepared her for the feelings Reese aroused in her.

Foolish, foolish thoughts, she chastised herself. Setting aside her cup, she went to the armoire and started to dress for the day.

"You're looking very pretty today," Reese greeted her as he entered the parlor before dinner. The afternoon meal was always a casual affair.

"Thank you," she replied, feeling herself blush. She'd donned a soft lavender blouse and a skirt of deep lapis. A fitted tapestry vest completed the ensemble, and she'd swept her hair into a loose bun.

She preferred the style since the days had grown hotter and she'd continued her work around the plantation. But she knew it also gave her a more mature look than the carefully coiffed ringlets she'd worn on her arrival.

"Would you like a glass of sherry before we go in?"

Reese always offered her refreshment, but until now she'd refused. This time, instead, she smiled and nodded. "That would be lovely."

She thought she saw a brief glimmer of surprise

cross his face, but he hid it well as he went to the sideboard. She'd also noticed of late that he didn't indulge in any of the fine spirits laid out. The level in the decanters had remained unchanged for several weeks.

Feeling she'd somehow brought about that change, she felt a small measure of pride. Without liquor for a crutch, Reese stood very tall in her eyes.

She thanked him for the sherry and slowly sipped the garnet-colored beverage. It wasn't half bad, she thought, feeling the warmth of it slide smoothly down her throat.

"Shall we?" he asked, motioning toward the dining room.

Feeling as though she'd stepped into a young girl's fantasy, she took his proffered arm and smiled up at him. He returned the smile, and the sherry hit her stomach with a jolt.

Again she was struck with the magnitude of his good looks. His easy charm could knock her off her feet when it was directed toward her.

Forcing herself to look away, she cleared her throat and tried to slow her racing heart. The sound of a carriage rolling over the oyster-shell drive stopped them both.

"Are you expecting company?"

Reese released her arm and Patience immediately mourned the loss of contact. "No, I'm not."

The front bell rang and they turned toward the main hall as Ma Jewel bustled by on her way to answer it.

Patience could hear mumbled voices and then

Ma appeared in the doorway of the parlor, a sour look on her face.

"Misser Symmons and his daughter to see you," she announced.

Patience felt Reese stiffen beside her, and she glanced up to see the look of irritation in his eyes. She couldn't imagine why these guests would cause his sudden mood shift. She'd never heard their names mentioned before.

"Show them in, Ma. And set two more places for dinner."

She hustled off, and Patience turned to Reese. "How do you know they'll want to stay for dinner?"

He frowned, meeting her eyes. His were full of disdain. "No one arrives at this time of day unless they're planning to be invited for dinner."

She was about to tell him she thought that a rude custom when an older man and an attractive brunette entered the parlor.

Extending his hand, Reese walked forward. "Samuel," he greeted the man, clasping his outstretched hand. "How are you?"

"Fine, fine," the portly man replied.

"And you, Virginia. You look as beautiful as ever."

"Thank you, Reese," she drawled, her accent thick and slow.

"Come in. I'd like you to meet my ward. Patience Bentley, this is my nearest neighbor, Samuel Symmons, and his daughter Virginia."

Pleasantries were exchanged all around, and Reese made the invitation to dinner.

"Oh, no," Samuel blustered. "We wouldn't think of intruding."

Patience blinked in confusion as she looked from Reese to their guests. Could he have been wrong?

"Nonsense. You're not intruding at all. I've already told Ma to set two more places at the table."

"Well, if you're sure it's not an imposition." The man nudged Reese with his elbow. "You know Ma Jewel is the best cook in the country."

"Yes, indeed," Reese said, satisfied that the tactful two-step had been completed. "I couldn't agree more."

As they went into the dining room, Samuel took Patience's arm, leaving Reese to escort Virginia. Patience frowned at the arrangement, but didn't have time to fret about it as Samuel began to question her.

"So, how is it you've come to be Reese's ward?"

"Patience is James's daughter," Reese said as he pulled a chair out for Virginia.

Immediately both father and daughter donned sympathetic expressions.

"I was so sorry about James," Samuel said to both of them. Reese nodded, and Patience whispered a polite thank-you.

"I think it's just dreadful the way the docks have deteriorated," Virginia put in. "It simply isn't safe to go there at all anymore."

Patience could see that Virginia had directed her comments to Reese, and the woman's eyes filled with concern and compassion. Patience didn't see any hint of attraction on either Virginia's or Reese's part, but she noticed they seemed uncomfortable together. And Samuel continued to eye them both closely as though expecting, hoping, for some spark.

"Such ugly business. I know it must be especially disturbing to you, Reese," Samuel added.

Reese's mouth tightened and thinned with ire. Patience glanced at Samuel, but saw only sympathy.

"Of course," Reese said, not meeting the man's eyes. He took an inordinate amount of time smoothing his napkin on his lap, and when he looked up, his expression had cleared.

"So, what brings you to Bonne Chance, Samuel?"

Something in his tone made Patience think he already knew the answer to his question. She watched the byplay between the men with interest.

"Business. But we can discuss that after dinner. And Virginia wanted to meet your guest."

"Then you knew Patience was here? And how did you learn about that?" Reese asked Virginia.

The woman looked slightly embarrassed, then smiled and gave a light laugh. "You know how servants talk, Reese. Nothing is a secret for long around here."

"I see. Should I talk to my people about gossiping?"

"Don't you dare," Virginia teased with a flirtatious grin. "I depend on those little tidbits of information when father leaves me alone for days at a time."

Samuel smiled at his daughter endearingly. Reese's mouth turned down, then he too smiled. Patience couldn't help but be charmed by the other woman's open demeanor.

Dinner was served and they exchanged light discourse about the weather, other neighbors, and even politics. Reese shot Patience a warning glance when Samuel mentioned the effects the coming election would have on the growing move toward emancipation in the North. Before she could interject her opinion, Ma announced coffee and dessert in the parlor.

"I thought we could skip coffee and maybe go to your study for whiskey and a smoke," Samuel suggested, as the men pulled out the chairs so the ladies could rise.

Again Patience saw Reese's easy mood being swallowed up by irritation. But he quickly hid the look and nodded.

"If the ladies will excuse us?"

Virginia and Patience offered their approval and were escorted to the parlor and left with a tray of coffee and a plate of small, spongy white cakes.

"Tell me how you like living at Bonne Chance," Reese heard Virginia say as the men left the parlor.

He led the way to the study and poured a single glass of whiskey for Samuel. Handing it to his neighbor, his rancor increased. He suspected he knew the reason for Samuel's visit, and he had no intention of answering the man any differently than he had in the past.

"I'll get right to the point, Reese," Samuel said.

Reese opened a humidor on the desk and offered Samuel a cigar. After accepting the smoke, he waited while Reese lit both cigars.

Puffing so the fire would catch, Samuel looked up through a ring of smoke. "I heard about Cooper Hutchins."

"What did you hear?" Reese drew on the cigar, masking his resentment that Samuel felt justified in probing into Reese's private business.

"You put him out to pasture. And before you say anything, I know you haven't been looking for a replacement."

"So?"

"So, who is going to oversee Bonne Chance?"

Blowing smoke toward the ceiling, Reese shrugged one shoulder. "I am."

Samuel coughed loudly and lowered his cigar. "You?"

"Yes, me."

"But you don't know anything about running a plantation. And it's no secret you've never exactly hankered to learn."

"I've changed my mind."

"Have you? Or have you had it changed for you?"

Lowering his own cigar, Reese narrowed his eyes. "Meaning?"

"I also heard you put one of your strongest bucks on the block and didn't purchase another to replace him."

"I really will have to have that talk with the slaves. It seems their idle talk has gotten out of hand."

Samuel waved his hand, clearing smoke and cutting Reese off. "No, really. I would have heard sooner or later from someone at the auction. You know how word gets around. I didn't come here to get your dander up."

"Why did you come?" Reese asked bluntly.

"To offer you a way out of your present situation."

"Don't bother. You know my answer."

"I know you've been stubborn about selling in the past, but you must admit it's the only practical thing to do now."

His jaw clenched, Reese asked simply, "Why would I admit that?"

"Obviously you are having financial difficulties; otherwise you'd have hired another qualified overseer. And that would also explain why you sold that slave when you need every hand you've got this time of year."

"You're speculating, Samuel. Besides, we've been through this time after time and my answer is always the same. I will not sell you Bonne Chance."

Seemingly not at all perturbed, Samuel only smiled. "You'll never stay on here for any length of time. You love the city life, the freedom to do as you please. You won't tie yourself down here for long."

"I've changed," Reese said, wondering if he had. He hadn't been longing for the nightlife so much the past few weeks. He hadn't missed Mobile as much as he thought he would. In fact, he'd found the days spent in the fields very rewarding. And the evenings with Patience were cozy and restful.

She never seemed to run out of ways to both entertain and exacerbate him. She had a quick mind and a rapier wit that he rather enjoyed. Even though he disagreed with most of her ideas, he found it stimulating to discuss them with someone who embraced them whole-heartedly. Patience's rare passion and fervor for what she believed in made him seriously consider her comments.

And her beauty was easy on his eyes after a long day of toil.

He remembered with a twinge of regret his decision to marry her off and realized he would miss her when that task had been completed.

"You'll never change," Samuel said, the harshness in his tone breaking through Reese's musings. "I've known you too long. You'll soon be chomping at the bit to return to Mobile—and Rita Mallory. A chit like your ward can't hold your attention very long."

A red haze of anger swept over Reese, and he deposited the cigar in the ashtray on his desk. "What the hell is that comment supposed to mean?" he demanded.

Seeing the fighting look in Reese's eyes, Samuel held up both hands and chuckled. "Nothing. Nothing at all."

"Patience Bentley is my ward, and my best friend's daughter. If you ever imply, to me or anyone else, she's anything other than that, I'll break your face, Samuel."

Samuel only laughed. Poking the stub of his cigar into the crystal ashtray, he turned and offered Reese a wry grin. "You see, you haven't changed after all. All that pent-up energy is just bursting to be let loose."

"Remember that."

Again Samuel only chuckled. "You remember my offer. I think you'll come to see it in a different light very soon."

"Don't count on it," Reese warned.

Samuel went to the door and opened it, glancing back over his shoulder. "Oh, but I am, Reese. I am counting on it. Very much."

Chapter Twelve

"They seem very nice," Patience said as the door closed behind Samuel and Virginia.

"Virginia is a sweet lady," Reese admitted, his brow still furrowed with anger at Samuel's comments. He'd never liked the man. He'd heard rumors from his own servants about Samuel's cruelty to his slaves, and it was no secret that the man was ruthless in business, almost to the point of suspicion. But the only thing he'd ever done to Reese personally was pressure him to sell Bonne Chance.

And he couldn't find fault with the man's offer, or even his remarks about Reese not wanting the burden of the place on his shoulders. Reese had never let on by word or deed that he wanted to take over where his father left off. So Samuel's proposition couldn't be taken as any kind of personal slight.

Still, Reese didn't like him. And he liked him even less for pointing out a fact which he himself should have realized before now.

Patience's presence in his house was bound to cause talk, talk his reputation would only enhance. He'd worked hard at building a name for himself as a rogue and a rakehell. In sixteen years the title had never bothered him even a little. But now he knew he couldn't let the taint of his past tarnish Patience's reputation.

"Reese?"

He shook off the troublesome thoughts. "Yes, what did you say?"

"I said, you seemed angry at Mr. Symmons. Did he do something to upset you?"

Reese could hear concern in Patience's voice. The softness was a sound unfamiliar to his ears. How long had it been since someone had worried about him? And why now? Why her?

They'd spent most of the time since she'd arrived at each other's throats over one thing or another. She hated the South, the plantation, and him in particular.

"No, I'm not angry," he hedged. "Samuel's been trying to get me to sell Bonne Chance since my father died. I've told him before that I won't sell, but he refuses to give up."

"Why would he want another plantation? Isn't his own home as large as Bonne Chance? I understood as much from what Virginia said."

They strolled back into the parlor and each took a seat. Patience arranged her skirts while Reese leaned back and propped one booted foot on the other.

"Oh, Emerald Acres is the largest plantation in the entire Alabama Black Belt right now. But Samuel would like to make it the largest in the country. The only thing stopping him is me. If he had Bonne Chance, he'd have what he wants. So he keeps after me to sell."

"I'm glad you refused."

He met Patience's gaze and saw the soft glow of approval in her blue eyes. They'd become accustomed to sitting like this, having discussions after a meal, particularly in the evenings. Sometimes they'd put aside their animosity and share a game of chess. He'd been surprised to find she played expertly. But when had she begun to look at him with such receptiveness? As though she supported him, if not his convictions?

She arched a golden-brown eyebrow in his direction and he realized she was awaiting a response. What had she said? And why had he been so absorbed in looking at her that he'd missed her words altogether?

"You don't, do you? Plan to change your mind?"

"About selling?" he asked, still not quite sure what her question had been. "No, I won't. But why do you care? I thought you hated Bonne Chance and all it stood for."

"I deplore slavery—you know I will never relent on that issue." He nodded. "But I have come to appreciate the beauty of Bonne Chance and its eclectic composition. I've also come to realize that while I cannot abide the right of one human being to own another, these people could be a lot worse off somewhere else."

"My," he said, with a broad smile, "that's quite an admission from you. Dare I hope things will be peaceful around here for a while now?"

She laughed openly at his wide-eyed enthusiasm and pursed her lips as she shook her head. "No, you may not," she told him frankly.

As Reese lay in bed that night, thoughts of Patience continued to haunt him. A lightness touched his heart when he remembered the satiny softness of her laughter. An unfamiliar smile crossed his lips.

Was it possible for them to find peace together in one house, while still battling their differences of opinion? He thought of the other men he'd known in his life, and especially the ones with wives. None of the women of his acquaintance had ever shown one tenth the spirit and mettle Patience demonstrated daily. But then, he'd never been attracted to any of those women either.

Attracted? To Patience Bentley? Was he truly drawn to the girl in such a basic way? Was it possible the feelings he'd been experiencing for her were more than those considered appropriate toward his best friend's daughter?

He'd noticed her beauty immediately, of course, but her loveliness had been overshadowed by her troublesome actions. However, he'd begun to understand and accept her attitudes and, surprisingly, had found he couldn't fault her for them. In fact, if he were going to be painfully honest, he'd admit he admired her for standing for what she believed in against such fierce opponents.

He also had to concede she'd been a great help since he'd retired Cooper. Her intelligence and knowledge of running a household had certainly pulled his bacon from the fire. And she hadn't uttered so much as a word of complaint, though she'd worked as hard as anyone.

Oh, Lord, was he completely insane? He couldn't be thinking about Patience as a woman. Thoughts like that could only lead to trouble for them both. He had to remind himself that she was his ward, his responsibility. It was time he started acting like a guardian.

Therein lay the problem. Unfortunately, he had no idea how to begin.

"Oh, I'm glad I caught you," Reese said as he strode into the dining room the next morning. He'd risen early and dressed hurriedly so he'd have time to speak with Patience before she went about her duties.

Patience sat, sipping the last of her tea. "You almost didn't. I was just finishing up. Mag needs my help in the infirmary today. Several of the children have come down with a skin rash. We're going to make a poultice and apply it to them all, then we're going to see if we can find out what is causing the outbreak."

"Can't Mag get one of the other women to help? I have something for you to do."

"I'm sorry, I told Mag I'd help her. What's come up that's so important?"

"A party."

She blinked in surprise and pursed her lips. "A party? You must be joking."

Reese watched the familiar moue she made with her full, pink lips and his gut knotted. He could imagine her using that sweet mouth to kiss a man with all the passion and intensity with which she did everything else. The small pout was an invitation he wouldn't have passed up in the past. Now he choked down the unexpected need. His voice was rough as he spoke. "I'm serious."

She set aside her cup and stood. "You want to give a party? Somehow I don't see you as the typical country host."

"It's true, I haven't entertained in the past. But things are different now, and Samuel and Virginia reminded me of my duties."

Her spine stiffened, and he saw a gleam of suspicion in her eyes. "What duties?"

"My duty as your guardian, of course," he said, going to the sideboard and pouring a cup of strong black coffee. He swallowed a mouthful and let it burn its way down his throat.

"And what do you see as your duty?"

He shrugged as though it were a minor matter. "I should have introduced you to some of our neighbors. I should have invited people in to meet you so you could make some friends and meet some suitable young men."

"Suitable for what?"

He flushed and stammered. "For—for you to—see."

"You must be joking. Why would I want to spend time with a bunch of Southern slave owners? I have to spend time with you, and believe me, one is enough."

"Nonsense. You're a young woman. All young women want to go to parties and socialize. Don't they?"

He'd thought about this long and hard last night. And he'd tried to determine what exactly a guardian did. He felt certain he should encourage her to get out and associate with other young people.

That would also benefit the other plan he'd come up with as he lay in bed pondering the problem of Patience's presence in his home, and his strange reaction to her lately. If he ever hoped to find her a husband, he'd better do something about getting her into contact with acceptable young men.

"Not me. Besides, you really can't afford it," she said, waving her hand dismissively as she turned to leave the room.

"Wait," he ordered, seeing the years of shared confinement with her stretching out before him. He had to find her a beau. And soon.

She turned and quirked a golden brow, as if to ask what more he had to discuss.

"I said we're having a party, and that's final."

She frowned. "You're forcing me to have a party I don't want? Isn't that a bit autocratic, not to mention extravagant?"

"We're having a party, and that's final," he told her. "Now stop being such a churl. You're going to help Ma Jewel plan this party, and you're going to have fun. Send word to the seamstress, too. Money or no money, I want you to have a new dress. Do I make myself clear?"

Patience could only nod in stunned disbelief as Reese slammed his cup down on the table and charged past her.

He left her wondering what had gotten into him. They'd been getting along better recently, and now he was back to his old ornery self.

Imagine, forcing someone to have a party. Besides, she had work to do. Important work. She was needed in the infirmary. Mag was counting on her. The children required immediate attention.

Patience ignored the small voice that nagged her, telling her Mag could manage without her. She brushed aside the whisper of her conscience, accusing her of thwarting Reese purposely to get his ire up.

It wasn't such a big request, anyway. She could have agreed to help him, as soon as she'd seen about the children. After all, maybe he missed the excitement of city life and wanted a little diversion. Didn't he deserve it after the weeks of hard work he'd put in?

But something about his rigid declaration continued to bother her as she went out the door and toward the clinic. Why had he decided she needed to socialize now? And what was all that nonsense about meeting suitable men? Was he up to some sort of mischief?

If he truly missed Mobile, wouldn't he just go there for a few days? If he wanted her to make friends in the upper echelon of society, he could take her there with him.

But no. He wanted to host a party in her honor. To show her off to his friends and neighbors? Not likely, since he thought her a troublesome piece of unwanted baggage and feared that a discussion about her politics would be disastrous. Then why would he arrange a social engagement? Why risk her infuriating the other plantation owners? Why subject his associates to such a vexatious hoyden?

She paused midstep, her foot poised above the walkway. Yes, he thought of her that way. He'd warned her about declaring her unpopular beliefs while in the South. More than once he'd indicated his desire to actually be rid of her.

Was that the answer? Could that be his ultimate plan? Had he devised this party as a method to foist her off on some Southern bumpkin?

Fury boiled in her chest as she stomped toward the infirmary. Well, if Reese Ashburn thought he could unload her on some backward-thinking Southern aristocrat, he had another think coming.

She didn't question the pain her heart felt knowing he didn't want her around. She didn't even question her overreaction to what was at present only a guess. All she knew was, he didn't want her. And that thought wounded her more than it should have.

* * *

"What do you mean she's not here?"

Reese scanned the interior of the main hall as though searching for some sign of his missing ward. Ma Jewel stood, damp hands twisting the apron at her generous waist.

"I ain't seen the missy today," she told Reese again.

"But I told her hours ago that I wanted her to get together with you about the arrangements for the party. Didn't she find you?"

"There wasn't no finding to be done. I've been in the pantry all morning stockin' the bins. 'Sides, since when does that girl listen to you or anybody else?"

"Stubborn little chit," he mumbled, grabbing his hat off the hall tree and stomping toward the door. He'd about had enough of his willful ward. It was time Patience Bentley realized who was in charge now.

Maybe in the past she'd been left to her own devices—a deficiency her wayward parent should have corrected. Obviously she didn't understand that things were different here. She was his responsibility, and he fully intended to discharge that duty until such time as he could palm her off on a husband.

"Which can't be soon enough to suit me," he said, striding across the yard to the infirmary. He didn't need these complications right now. How much was a man expected to put up with? His life, as well as his plan to further the search for James's killer, had been postponed indefinitely because of the little minx.

Slapping his hat angrily against his thigh, he charged up to the door of the clinic, peered inside, and skidded to a startled halt.

The room was full of little black children, all lined up and wearing a thick pink concoction on their faces and arms. Mag stirred something in a huge clay bowl, her strong arms straining and her sleeves rolled to the elbow.

But it was his impetuous charge who caught—and held—his eye.

His frown dissipated like fog under the hot summer sun. A softness touched his mouth, and his eyes narrowed slightly as he watched her.

A stream of morning sunshine sliced through the doorway and caught her in its shimmering beam. With her golden hair in a long braid over one shoulder and a pink gingham apron covering her clothes, she looked like an angel from heaven. She held a small child in her arms, its chubby hands touching her cheeks lovingly. She was smiling, and the affection he read in her sparkling blue eyes sent a twist of longing through his gut. A flame of desire ripped across his loins, sending his body into a whirlwind of sensations.

Arousal, need, passion, swamped him. But it was the other feelings—the aching tenderness, the unfamiliar yearning—that grabbed him and refused to let go.

She laughed lightly, pressing her full, pink lips to the child's ear to whisper something.

A shaft of primitive hunger engulfed Reese. He wanted to feel those lips pressed against *his* ear.

He longed to hear her whisper secrets for *him* alone.

With a rough, dry sigh, he rolled away from the doorway. Leaning against the wall of the clinic, he painfully dragged air into his lungs.

What was happening? How could he feel such an intensity of emotion for a woman he claimed not to even like?

His hat suffered as his fists clenched and unclenched around the wide brim. This was Patience Bentley, James's daughter! He couldn't think of her the way he did other, more experienced women. He couldn't think of her with less than pure thoughts. And he could never entertain an idea of conquest where she was concerned.

Dear God, he'd been trusted to care for her. And now he found himself lusting after her.

He'd been away from Mobile far too long. That had to be the answer. It was the only reason he could or would accept. A night with lovely Rita, and he'd be seeing Patience as the irritating, insufferable brat he knew her to be.

But his heart denied the unfavorable thought even as it raced through his dazed mind. She might be headstrong, even obstinate, but only about things she truly believed in. Only when it came to the convictions she embraced with her very being. And those principles were not selfish or self-serving. They exhibited her strength of character, her love of humanity, her sense of fairness and justice.

Lord, he wanted to despise her for making his life a living hell. He wanted to, but he couldn't.

With each day that passed, each new facet of her personality he uncovered, it got harder for him to think of her as nothing more than an encumbrance.

God help him, he didn't know what was happening to him. But Reese knew in his soul that it meant trouble.

Chapter Thirteen

Sipping the bright pink punch she held in her gloved hand, Patience scanned the multitude of guests. Everyone in Alabama must have been invited tonight. And judging by the crunch of people milling through the house, they must have all shown up.

Her gaze lit on the familiar sight of her guardian almost immediately, and she felt the jab of awareness hit her full in the stomach.

He looked so fine in his formal attire—somber black coat and trousers, snowy white shirt and cravat. On him, the outfit looked almost scandalous, for it made him so handsome, she couldn't stop staring at him.

She had found herself looking at him a great deal lately. For the past two weeks, she'd tried to define the attraction she felt growing between her and Reese, to no avail. She didn't agree with his ideals. He loathed her persistence. His way of life contrasted with everything she stood for. Her beliefs taxed his forbearance.

Still, she felt the desire growing inside her every time they were together. And she suspected Reese felt it, too. He'd been avoiding her lately, but she'd caught him watching her closely when he thought she couldn't see him. He'd argued with her at every turn, but she could see the pride shine in his eyes when she verbally bested him.

Why had he insisted on this farce tonight? If she were right, and he'd devised the plan to find her a suitable husband, then he must know he was wasting his time. She'd never have any of the men she'd been introduced to tonight.

Young boys barely out of short pants. Old men with young ideas toward an attractive female. Rough-mannered merchants Reese occasionally did business with. None held any fascination for Patience. None, she had to admit, except her guardian. He held her eye and, she feared, her heart.

When had she come to know the good in Reese? When had she recognized the honorable man hiding beneath the rogue? Why did he pretend to be so feckless and dissolute, when she'd seen the way the slaves loved him and respected him? And why did he claim to be a cold, inhuman flesh-peddler when she'd seen many times the true affection he felt for the people of Bonne Chance?

It made no sense, yet she didn't mind anymore. She'd determined to find out the truth about

Reese, and she thought she had. If only he could see the reality himself.

He was no more a rakehell than she was. He didn't think of his slaves as mere property, the way most Southerners did. He simply didn't understand what was required of him in this place. He'd never felt at home here. He behaved the way he thought people expected him to behave.

But she'd seen in the past few weeks how happy he could be here. She saw how hard he would work when he was needed. She understood the pride he took in a job well done. She'd experienced the same feeling with Mag in the infirmary, with Ma Jewel in the kitchen, but especially with Reese. When they worked together on the accounts. When they planned and executed a new idea. When they sat in the parlor in the evenings and shared a game of chess or a conversation.

She felt as though she belonged here. With him.

He glanced across the room and caught her eye. After a brief flash of surprise, he smiled. She returned the smile, feeling her heart melt with emotion. She couldn't single out the exact moment when she'd fallen in love with him. It had slowly crept up on her minute by minute, touch by touch. But the details didn't matter. All that mattered were her feelings. And Patience knew her heart.

She'd never been a witless miss. She'd always known her mind, in all things. And she knew, without a doubt, that she loved Reese Ashburn.

Reese watched as the young son of a local plantation owner claimed Patience's hand for a dance.

She set aside her cup with the grace of a princess and curtsied to the youth as they reached the dance floor.

A sharp stab of jealousy ripped through him. He covered it by sipping from his glass of punch. He frowned, making a face as the sweet concoction filled his mouth.

Damn, he'd give anything for a shot of smooth whiskey. But he'd chosen not to cloud his mind with drink when he was forced to deal with Patience. She was clever and cunning, and he needed all his senses alert to handle her.

Even tonight, she'd nearly triumphed over him. She'd refused to plan the party, forcing him to arrange everything himself with the help of Ma Jewel and Virginia. He now knew more than he'd ever wanted to know about hosting a gala.

Reese couldn't help the quirk of a grin that tipped one corner of his mouth. By God, that girl could be stubborn. She'd even refused his suggestion that she have a new gown made, telling him she'd prefer to wear something she'd brought with her. He'd expected one of the frilly fashions she'd seemed so fond of when she arrived. Nothing could have prepared him for the simple, yet elegant gown she'd chosen.

Not at all the latest style, it was basic in design—a smooth, flowing creation that resembled a silky chemise, it slid down her body to the toes of her low-heeled biscuit-colored slippers. A smoky, sensuous pearl gray, it made her blue eyes stand out like a slice of bright sky in an overcast day. Her creamy ivory skin seemed to glow with health; her cheeks were rosy and her lips a full pink.

He'd never seen anyone so beautiful. All the other women in the room paled in comparison, despite their fashionable gowns. The men danced attendance on his ward, vying for a dance or the privilege of sitting with her at supper.

His plan was working out better than he'd ever dreamed. So why was he so miserable?

Across the room he saw Virginia making her way toward him. Wanting to avoid a long discussion and an awkward session of flirting and countering, he ducked behind a large potted plant set at the side of the dance floor.

Virginia glanced around as she approached the spot where he'd stood; then her eyes lit on another male guest, and she veered toward that gentleman.

"How are you enjoying yourself?" Reese heard her say in a sugary tone.

The man smiled with delight at the attention and stepped closer to Virginia.

"The evening has suddenly taken a turn for the better," he drawled, claiming her arm as he led her toward the French doors onto the balcony.

Reese was about to breathe a sigh of relief when two men stepped close to the dance floor, their attentions focused on Patience.

"She's a pretty little thing," the first man said.

Reese drew farther behind the plant, feeling foolish for the subterfuge in his own home. But he took advantage of the opportunity to learn what his neighbors thought of his ward.

"Yeah," the second, younger man said. "But if

you ask me, that's the ugliest dress I've ever seen."

Reese glanced across at Patience and saw the outline of her ripe, lush figure beneath the smooth satin. Was the callow youth blind? Couldn't he see that the dress was intended to highlight a woman's best features with its simplicity?

"Clothes can be changed. It's her personality I found unattractive."

The other man nodded and sniffed distastefully. Reese studied Patience, searching for anything that a man might find unpleasant about her tonight.

"How Ashburn thought he'd ever palm her off as a gently bred lady of refinement is beyond me. When I danced with her, she never shut her mouth. Going on about the North and their advanced thinking."

"And how slavery would soon be nothing more than a dark blot on America's history. The girl is a trial. Did Ashburn truly think no one would notice?"

"Well, I noticed. And so did the rest of the men invited here to compete for her affections."

"She does come with a sizable dowry," the first man admitted, a note of disappointment in his voice.

"Bah. If you ask me, there isn't enough money in the world to compel a fellow to saddle himself with such a harridan. I for one am going to run in the other direction if Ashburn starts to eye me. As fast as I can."

The other man grunted in agreement, and the two turned to stroll out onto the balcony. Reese stood beside the potted plant, seething with rage.

The stupid bastards, he fumed, eyeing Patience with a look of long-suffering understanding. They couldn't see past the obvious. Blinded by their prejudice, they saw only a troublesome piece of baggage. Much as he had when she first arrived.

But he'd changed his mind. It had probably begun when she stood up for the slaves against an army of opponents. Or maybe it was when she'd pitched in to help him, despite her hatred for slavery and plantation life. Or was it when he'd watched her hold the black child so lovingly in her generous embrace?

Regardless of the moment when he'd opened his eyes to her true character, he thought he now understood her better. And with understanding came acceptance and favor. And if these stupid country yokels were too ignorant to see a diamond amidst a mass of coal, that was their loss.

He stepped from behind the plant and set aside his cup. Striding onto the polished floor, he boldly claimed Patience for a waltz.

"Are you enjoying yourself?"

His arms held her, his body's heat teasing her with its nearness. Patience could barely draw breath, much less respond. She settled for a nod and a small smile.

"Good. I've noticed you haven't been long without a partner. I had to cut in just to dance with you."

She could hear the teasing quality in his voice, and her heart settled into place. He knew how to put her at ease, even if he had no idea why she seemed flustered.

"Your friends are very kind and attentive," she confessed, a hint of remorse in her tone.

Reese's mouth hardened, and his eyes narrowed in remembered anger. It set his teeth on edge to hear Patience defending the very people who ridiculed her behind her back. He longed to tell her that none of the persons here tonight were his friends. Few of them even qualified as acquaintances. In fact, Virginia had been the one to draw up the guest list, since Reese wasn't familiar with most of the prominent members of society.

Instead, he felt himself draw her closer into the protective circle of his arms as they continued across the floor. She settled against him with ease, fitting the curve of his body like a glove. His eyes drifted shut for a second as he savored the soft, womanly feel of her curves. His hands clenched, as he fought the desire to touch her more intimately.

Had the whole world gone mad, or had he? Couldn't these men see what a prize Patience was? A woman who not only had a mind of her own, but wasn't afraid to speak it. A woman with courage and conviction. So what if she didn't conform to their standards? She had her own ideals of what was right and wrong, what should be and what shouldn't.

She would never surrender her beliefs for any man, nor should she. They were what made her unique and exceptional.

And they were what made him love her.

Reese stumbled and trod heavily on Patience's toe. He cursed beneath his breath as she winced in pain.

"I'm sorry," he mumbled, regaining his footing and counting off the missed steps in his mind. He started again, only to go the wrong way and, again, step on her foot.

"Damn it all," he muttered, stopping in place. It was hopeless. He couldn't keep his scattered thoughts on something as mundane as a waltz when he'd just made a momentous discovery. He took her arm and forced a smile.

"Would you like a glass of punch? I could use some fresh air." He motioned to the balcony, and she nodded.

As they started toward the heavily laden refreshment table, Patience could think of nothing she'd like less than another glass of the sugary beverage. But she could think of nothing she'd like more than a stroll with Reese. All the men she'd danced and spoken with tonight had paled sharply in comparison with the man at her side. And she'd spent the better part of the evening doing just that. Comparing.

She'd come to the conclusion that the abundance of single gentlemen present could not be coincidence—which only served to reinforce her deduction that Reese wanted to marry her off.

A month ago, the thought of being married held no appeal. However, only recently Patience's views toward marriage had changed. Ever since she'd begun spending time with Reese, sharing meals and engaging in lively discussions about everything from politics to poultry, she'd started thinking of what it would be like to share more of her life with a man. But not just any man. Only her irritating, infuriating, primitive guardian would suit her.

As they strolled together in the light of a hundred Chinese lanterns, she could almost imagine them doing this each night before they went off to bed and did whatever else it was married people did.

She had her suspicions about that mystery, and she'd shared whispered speculations with the other girls at school. But she couldn't be certain of her facts since she'd grown up motherless.

Still, many times in the past weeks she'd envisioned her and Reese together this way. And the visions had grown, almost taking on a life of their own, expanding and developing into daydreams and nightly fantasies.

"So, how do you find our neighbors?"

She snapped out of her musings and looked up into his moonlit face. His eyes shone with starlight and glistened as they seemed to study every detail of her.

"I—actually I find them quite boring. Not one can hold a thread of conversation for more than a minute. And the ones who can converse think I'm suppose to talk incessantly about nothing at all for hours."

Reese laughed, delighted that she hadn't been captivated by one of the witless wonders he'd encountered at the edge of the dance floor. He should have known Patience wouldn't be taken in by the likes of those weaklings. None of them was man enough for a woman like Patience.

Did he consider himself man enough? He stopped alongside a blooming hedge of azaleas, and Patience drew her breath in as she inhaled the flowery scent. He thought of her scent, more musky and womanly, and wished he could hold her close and breathe it in at that moment. It was a fragrance he would forever think of as hers alone.

"I remember now why I spent so little time with these people. They're decidedly dull."

She giggled and he felt himself smile as they meandered around the garden. "I thought you'd enjoy a bit of tedium after the weeks of excitement I've lent you," she said.

Reese took her arm as they stepped carefully along a flagstone path. Patience absorbed the feel of his strength and the warmth of his touch.

"It hasn't been so bad," he told her.

Again she laughed, and Reese found he enjoyed the sound much more than he should. He longed to hear it more, and often. Directed at him alone.

They'd walked quite a distance from the house, and Reese pulled to a stop as he realized that they were quite alone now.

"We've wandered away from the guests," he observed with dismay.

"Yes, it seems so," she said in a breathy voice.

Reese's loins tightened, and he slowly turned his gaze toward her. Could she know what her whispery tones did to his nerve endings? he wondered.

Did she suspect how her hushed murmurs enflamed his desire?

Of course not. She was an innocent, unaware of such things. He was a man of experience and knew better than to spirit a young woman off alone into the night. If anyone should see them, it would be disastrous. For her future and his plans.

"Come on, we need to get back."

"Reese," she whispered, halting him with a hand on his arm.

His gaze fell to the creamy expanse of her neck, highlighted in the glow of moonlight. The silvery gown billowed in the breeze, flattening against her breasts, her stomach, the outline of her long, shapely legs. He swallowed hard, certain she wore a chemise and petticoat beneath the finery but wondering why it hid none of her attributes.

"Reese, do you want to kiss me?"

He very nearly choked on his shock. His eyes widened and his mouth fell open. Then he realized that it was just like Patience to cut to the heart of a matter. He fought a grin.

"Yes, I do." In the spirit of their relationship, he saw no reason to lie to her.

"Would you?" she asked.

He fought the urge to grab her and crush her against him. He never remembered wanting a woman this way in his life. No woman, not even Rita. But Patience was no ordinary woman. She was James's daughter.

"No, I won't," he said, hoping the pain he felt wasn't apparent in his voice.

"Why?" She stepped closer. "I wouldn't mind,"

she admitted, ducking her head shyly.

The timorous movement surprised him. He'd never seen Patience any way but forceful and commanding. Her sudden reticence also aroused in him deep feelings of protectiveness and a surge of defensiveness. She was an innocent. And she was his responsibility.

"I don't know what is happening between us, Patience. But it can't continue. I'm—jaded. Hell, I'm more than that. I have a reputation as a rogue, and it's a name I've well earned. You're naive about such things."

"I wouldn't be so naive if you kissed me."

"I'd be a bigger scoundrel than even I confess to be if I succumbed to that temptation."

"I don't believe you're as big a blackguard as you claim. This past month you've shown the depths of your caring and thoughtfulness. I've seen examples of your regard for Cooper and the slaves, and the love you feel but try to hide for Bonne Chance. I suspect, Reese Ashburn," she said with an impish grin as she poked a finger lightly against his chest, "that your renown as a miscreant is a lot of bluster."

Reese took her hand from his chest and engulfed it in his big palms. Holding it close to his heart, he closed his eyes and slowly stilled his racing heart. Opening his eyes, he forced himself to look down into her upturned face.

"I'm not the man you've seen here on Bonne Chance the past month. That is only a character I've been forced to play temporarily. Soon the plantation will be back on solid footing and Ran will have everything under control. When that time comes," he told her, pushing her hand toward her own chest, "I will go back to my previous life, and soon enough you will see the real Reese Ashburn. I've no doubt that person will shock and disgust you, and you will be horrified by what you've proposed here tonight. And you will count yourself lucky I refused your foolish offer."

As she gaped at the hard visage he turned on her, he released her hand and stepped away.

Chapter Fourteen

Patience awakened with a long, sensuous stretch. Her flesh tingled as the hint of a morning breeze tickled her body. The faint image of a mischievous smile teased her lips, her dreams still fresh in her mind as she slowly rose to the surface of consciousness.

All the guests were gone, all signs of the previous night's festivities removed. The furniture was neatly back in place as though it had never been disturbed. But Patience knew it would all look different to her.

"Because I am different," she whispered, her hands inching up over her sensitized skin. She lightly brushed her thighs, her belly, her breasts. Reese might have refused to kiss her, but he'd wanted it as much as she had.

Tossing aside the covers, Patience went to the

chiffonier to carefully choose what she would wear. For the first time in her life, she hesitated over the perfect ensemble. Everything seemed too frilly or too plain, too juvenile or too prissy.

She couldn't see herself in any of the garments hanging in the cherry-wood cabinet. Who was the girl who'd worn such clothing? Surely not the woman she faced in the mirror this morning. She'd changed, grown, matured.

She was different all right, she thought with a satisfied smile. She was a woman. A woman in love.

"What do you mean he's gone? Gone where?"

Ma Jewel clucked her tongue as Patience fretted with the fine chiffon lace marching down the front of her robin's-egg-blue blouse.

"To the city," Ma told her directly, brushing past a startled Patience on her way to the parlor. A host of servants were still working to put the house to rights after the gala, but for once Patience barely noticed their presence.

"Why would he leave now?"

Ma turned to face her, her small black eyes narrowed. "What's so different 'bout now? That boy's been runnin' to the docks to find his fun ever since he could mount a horse. And he's been chompin' at the bit to get back to the nightlife for a while, less I miss my guess."

Patience felt her dreams shrivel and die within her. Pain iced through her stomach, binding it in knots. She'd been so certain Reese cared for her. Hadn't she seen desire in his eyes as they'd stood in the magical beams of moonlight last night? Hadn't she heard the rough whisper of need in his voice as he spoke? Even when his words were harsh, she'd heard it.

He'd accused her of being naive, innocent. Was she so inexperienced that she'd mistaken disgust or disappointment for passion?

She was loath to admit it, yet Reese had always been an enigma she couldn't quite figure out. But she was certain of her own feelings; she loved Reese Ashburn, and she always would.

"Well, well," Rita Mallory said as she opened the door wider. "You look a damn sight better than the last time I saw you."

Stepping aside, she made room for Reese to enter. He walked into the house, bussing her cheek as he passed. "You look beautiful as always, Rita."

"Thanks," she said, smoothing a strand of rich auburn hair into place. She wore a low-cut gown of raw red silk. The dove-white mounds of her breasts showed like rising half-moons above her neckline. The dress tapered down to her incredibly small waist, then fanned out over full, generous hips.

Reese looked his fill, hoping the familiar flame of need would seize him. It didn't. As he studied Rita, all he could see were blue eyes staring up at him as he clutched a petite figure close in his embrace.

"How have you been?"

"I'm fine," she said, arching a brow at the inane conversation. She'd seen him eyeing her body, and it had sent her into immediate arousal. So why didn't he move to take her in his arms? Why didn't he claim her lips and carry her to the bed as he usually did? They'd had a very satisfying relationship for years, but small talk had never been a part of it.

Could he be waiting for her to make the first move? He never had before, but then they'd parted under less than amiable conditions the last time he'd been at her house.

She decided she'd ease the way for him. Reaching for his coat, she spread her hands wide and raked the garment off his shoulders and down his back. He swallowed hard, and his eyelids drooped as he inhaled sharply. Satisfied, she reached for the buttons of his shirt.

"No, Rita," he said sharply. "We have to talk."

"Talk?" She fingered the placket of his shirt, wriggling her fingers between the fasteners until she could feel the warmth of his chest. He jerked away, pressing his hand where hers had been.

"Yes, talk. Please," he said, motioning toward her little sitting room. "Can we sit?"

"You really want to talk?" she asked incredulously. He nodded, and she swallowed her disappointment. "All right, Reese."

Conversation might not have been a part of their relationship until this moment, but Rita had been in the business of pleasuring men for a long time, and she knew when to improvise. If he wanted to talk, they'd talk. First.

"Would you like a drink? I have whiskey."

She could have sworn he made a face at her suggestion. Confused, she watched him quickly shake his head.

"No, thank you."

They'd always been forthright, even blunt with each other. Rita decided to cut through the niceties.

"No sex, no liquor," she said, eyeing him up and down. "If I didn't know better, I'd think you weren't Reese Ashburn at all. In fact," she told him with a puzzled frown, "you don't look much like the man I left here a little over a month ago. Care to tell me what's been happening while you were away?"

"A lot," he murmured, raking a hand roughly over his face. He tried to arrange events in a particular order in his mind, from when he first laid eyes on Patience until the moment last night when he'd known beyond a doubt the depth of love he'd developed for his ward. But in the end, he couldn't form an intelligent sequence.

"I'm broke, Rita," he blurted out.

She nodded sagely and touched his hand. "I know—I've heard the talk."

He met her eyes and a hint of distrust crossed his expression. "You knew?"

"Well, I must admit I was hoping the gossip was exaggerated, but I'm not surprised to find it was based in fact. Most rumors are."

He sighed deeply. "The house is yours, you know that. But the monthly income . . ."

Her hand closed around his fingers and she smiled. "I suspected as much. Don't worry so. You've taken good care of me over the years, and

I was very careful with my money. I'll be fine. In fact, if you need a loan . . ."

"No," he snapped, removing his hand from beneath hers. "Hell, no. You'll need that money. Besides, I haven't sunk that low—not yet."

His tone held a large measure of self-disgust, as though he suspected he'd come close. "I'll work it out."

Rita instantly missed the feel of his hand in hers. She felt bereft. Reese had never been overly demonstrative, but he seemed to have distanced himself from her even more than usual. Was that the difference she'd noticed?

She stood and paced to the empty fireplace, poking at leftover ashes for something to do. Busy movements kept her from reaching for Reese. In her heart, she knew he wouldn't respond. Not this time, maybe not ever again.

Could it be the girl, his ward? She'd heard the reports of James's will and his daughter's appearance in Reese's life. Rita had to know.

"I understand James left you a pretty package in his will."

She didn't turn to look at him. She didn't have to. She could hear the truth in his voice as he spoke.

"Yes, Patience is definitely beautiful."

Rita winced and bit hard on her lip to stifle the dismay bubbling in her chest. She'd never considered herself in love with Reese Ashburn. She was too smart for that. But they'd had something special, and for a moment she grieved at the loss of it.

"She's certainly a handful, too," he said, his voice full of something that sounded suspiciously like pride.

"So I understand. She must have come as quite a surprise."

Reese's laughter caught her off guard and she whirled, watching him through widened eyes as he chuckled with appreciation.

"It was a shock, no doubt about it. But I think we've come to an understanding. For the time being, anyway."

"An understanding?" She quirked an eyebrow at his choice of phrase.

Reese looked up and noticed Rita's pained expression for the first time. He stood and walked to her, lowering his head to gaze into her brown eyes. "What is it?" he asked.

"Oh, nothing," she said, brushing aside her foolish emotions. "But I think you should know. There's been talk."

"Talk? What about? Patience? Her ideals? So she's a freethinker. At least she has a brain to think with."

"It isn't Patience's notions fueling most of the rumors, Reese. It's you."

"Me?"

He clutched her shoulders hard and forced her to face him. He saw something in her eyes—not physical pain, but a certain sadness and discomfort at having to be the one to tell him the hurtful truth.

"You're a reputed philanderer. Hell, you've made no secret of your conquests. Why do you think the same mothers who parade their daughters before you in hopes of a marriage proposal wouldn't think of leaving one alone in your presence? You were considered a great catch, between your fortune and Bonne Chance. But you were also considered notoriously self-indulgent."

"I'm well aware of my reputation, Rita. What is your point?"

"You know my point," she said, pinning him with a hardened stare. "You just don't want to admit the truth. Everyone believes you're bedding that girl, Reese."

"That's a damn lie!" he bellowed, slamming a fist against the wooden mantel.

"They don't see it that way," she told him. "And, I understand, with good reason. I've already heard about last evening's festivities. At the market this morning, the details were buzzing through the stands. I heard about the dances you shared. The way she gazed up at you. The way you held her closer than propriety allows. Then, if there had been any doubt in anyone's mind, you took her into the garden where you disappeared for nearly a half hour."

"Good God, I never intended for any of that to happen. That party was specifically designed to find Patience a husband." He looked up and saw the wry grin on Rita's face. "Not me, dammit. A proper husband. Someone respected and suitable. Someone—someone James would approve of."

"And you're certain James wouldn't approve of you?"

Reese opened his mouth in stunned disbelief.

"You just said yourself that no one considers me reputable. Oh, they might put up with me because I have—had—money. No doubt many of them covet Bonne Chance. But not even James would mistake me for a prize when it comes to husband material."

"Maybe not before," she said, slowly walking around him. She narrowed her eyes and pretended to study him closely. Reese spun on his heel to watch her movements, a scowl furrowing his brow.

"What the devil are you doing?"

"Noting the changes."

"What the hell—oh, stand still, for God's sake."

"You've changed in the past month, Reese," she told him, covering the ache in her heart with a knowing grin. "Whether that girl did it or not, I don't know. But you're different. I couldn't put my finger on it at first, but now I see."

"See what? Dammit, Rita, I said be still!"

She stopped, and a small smile tipped one corner of her lush, generous mouth. Her eyes softened. "I believe you've matured, Reese. You carry yourself like a man who knows his own mind, not a boy who's searching for himself in the bottom of a bottle. How long has it been?"

"How long has *what* been?"

"Since you've gotten drunk. How long since you've been falling down, stumbling, horny drunk?"

Reese gaped silently, staring stupidly at this woman he thought he knew.

"You always were, you know. Horny when you

were drunk." She pushed her tongue against her cheek to keep from bursting into laughter. He looked so funny with the startled realization on his face.

"That must have made for some interesting encounters with Miss Bentley."

A scene flashed across Reese's brain. Himself on the hearth rug in his study, Patience clasped in his arms lying beneath him. Her face held fear and something else, something oddly foreign to the delicate features. He slammed his eyes shut and blocked out the disturbing image.

"It was a mistake to come here," he said guiltily, searching for his coat. He found it lying on the floor by the door and swept it up hurriedly and pulled it on.

Rita followed him across the room, her expression suddenly solemn. "I'm sorry, Reese. I didn't mean to tease you." She clutched his arm, and he turned to face her.

The hopelessness in his eyes made her forget her own sadness, and she placed her palm gently against his cheek.

"Dammit, Rita," he breathed, momentarily taking the comfort she offered. "I wanted to do this right. I needed to be everything James hoped for when he drew up that damned will. But I'm not any good at this."

"Shhh," she whispered. "Don't talk like that. James knew exactly what he was doing. He knew no one would work harder to take care of his daughter than you would. He knew you loved him, and he knew you'd love his daughter—if only because of who she was."

He glanced away, and she saw the harsh reality he couldn't hide. "Oh, my God. You do love her, don't you? Not because she's James's daughter, either. You really are in love with her."

"Rita, girl, I've made some messes in my life, but none like this."

"I don't know what to say. I guess I thought you were immune to genuine feelings. You always seemed so detached, so removed from real emotion. I'm shocked. I'm sad, because I feel like this is the end for us. And, dammit, I'm jealous. You never fell in love with me all the time we were together."

"It would have been a hell of a lot easier if I had," he said roughly. Suddenly he tossed his jacket aside and grabbed her, crushing her in his arms. "Make me love you, Rita," he said, clutching her desperately to his chest. His hands roamed her curves, searching for some response in himself. She opened her mouth beneath his, and he kissed her hard and hungrily.

"Make me want you the way—"

She pulled back and he let her go, realizing what he'd almost said. The hurt in her eyes tore at him, and he lifted a hand to touch her.

She took another hurried step back and forced a resigned smile. "Go home, Reese. Go back to Bonne Chance. Go back to her."

Already he was shaking his head. "I can't, Rita. Don't you understand? All the gossip, the rumors. I'm ruining any chance she might have had to find a decent husband. I'm destroying her hopes of making a life for herself here. As you said, everyone's going to think she's my latest paramour, if they don't already. Dammit, why did James send her here? That fool. That stupid fool. Couldn't he see that everything I touch turns bad?"

Rita reached for him again, but he opened the door and, without bothering to collect his coat this time, slammed it shut behind him.

Chapter Fifteen

Reese drew back on the reins, slowing his mount to a stop on the long, tree-lined drive leading to Bonne Chance.

The overhanging branches of the moss-draped cedars formed a canopy of cool shade above him. He felt the familiar knot of longing grip him as the house came into view. Was it any wonder he'd stayed away from Bonne Chance for nearly a week? Patience's presence was permanently etched into every inch of the place now, from the balcony outside her bedroom to the infirmary bustling with activity.

He could almost see her standing at the railing, waiting for him to return at the end of the day—no doubt to present him with yet another problem.

As he approached, a young boy ran to take his horse.

"Hello, Aaron," Reese greeted the youth. The boy grinned, pleased the master had remembered his name, and led the horse back around the side of the house.

Striding onto the veranda, Reese was surprised—and a little disappointed—that no one had come to the door to welcome him.

Who was he fooling? he thought with a snort of disgust. He didn't want just anyone. He wanted Patience to greet him. He ached to see her after seven long, lonely days away.

In the hall he removed his hat, tipping his head toward the sound of raised voices drifting from the parlor. He tossed his hat onto the parson's bench, a silly grin pasted on his face, and followed the noise.

At the parlor door he stopped, propping himself against the frame for a moment to soak up the blessedly familiar scene.

Cooper was yelling and waving his hands frantically at Patience, who was shaking a pointed finger in the man's face. Ma Jewel, in a pose he recognized well, was acting as referee between the two volatile opponents.

"Not again," he said with a smile.

The three turned to him, shock registering on each face. Cooper and Ma met his gaze, and their faces fell. Reese felt his own smile fade slightly.

"Oh, Reese," Patience cried, rushing to him. "I'm so glad you're here." She flung herself into his arms, and he didn't have time to think about his reaction. He clutched her to his chest.

Eyes closed, he absorbed the feel of her in his arms. Love, so long suppressed, surged through him. She felt so good, so right in his embrace, that he actually trembled.

"Hey, hey, what is this all about?" With a mammoth effort, he gently pushed her away. He could see the startled looks on both Ma's and Cooper's faces. Clearing his throat, he lifted Patience's chin with his finger and smiled at her. "Tell me why you're so worked up."

"I didn't know what else to do, Reese," she said, naked despair clouding her sky-blue eyes. "You'd been gone so long, and I knew something had to be done soon. So I sent for Cooper."

Reese barely had time to ponder the fact that she'd turned to Cooper for help. His eyes darted quickly to the old man, and he saw the wretched hopelessness in the vague eyes. "What the hell's happened?"

"Misser Symmons was jus' here," Ma said, her hands wringing the apron at her waist. She shook her graying head with sorrow and dabbed at her eyes.

"Would someone please tell me what is going on?" Reese demanded. Remembering that first encounter with Patience, he turned to Cooper. "Thank you for coming, Cooper, but I'll take care of things now."

This time the old man made no move to argue. He hastened out of the parlor, and Reese heard the sound of the front door slamming.

"Ma, will you leave us alone for a moment?"

The slave patted Patience's hand as she left the room. Reese felt a shiver of alarm rip through him. Ma hadn't said one word to him before taking her leave.

"Patience?"

"Reese, it's really bad," she said, motioning him toward the matching chairs flanking the fireplace.

Reese wanted to stay where he was, with Patience's hands clasped in his. He wasn't ready to let go of her just yet. For days he'd suffered, trying to stay away from her. But it was no use. He hadn't been able to stay away, despite knowing it was his only option.

"What did Samuel want, Patience?"

A flash of anger crossed her otherwise perfect features, and Reese drew back, startled. He'd never seen her look so bitterly angry, not even when Monroe attacked her.

"He wanted what he's wanted all along, Reese. Bonne Chance."

So the little spitfire was now defensive when it came to the plantation. He couldn't help wondering if she felt equally protective of him. The thought brought him more pleasure than it should have.

"I told you I would never sell, Patience. You don't have to worry about Samuel."

"But *you* do, Reese," she told him. "He's been busy this past month."

"Doing what?" he asked, his tone still soothing.

"Buying your markers."

The room shifted. Or maybe it was the world, Reese thought dizzily. His world. "What are you talking about?" He jumped from his seat and strode toward the window, his guts shaking with dread.

Patience followed him, her hands clasped at her waist. "Apparently you gambled heavily in Mobile those three months. Samuel has been buying up your markers all over town. He came here this morning to see you, but you weren't here. So he gave me a message to deliver. He said"—her voice broke and she swallowed hard—"he said you have one month to come up with the money to pay him."

Reese reeled from the shock of Patience's words. One month! How could Samuel pull off something like this? But Reese knew the answer. Samuel had money. Lots of money. And with money went power. Hell, Reese knew that better than anyone. Hadn't he used his own money and influence to open doors in the past?

But he no longer had the money. And the influence he still possessed, if indeed he had any, wouldn't compare to Samuel's.

"He won't get it," he murmured heatedly.

"What?"

Reese turned to face Patience. Fear and anguish haunted her features. He took her shoulders and forced a bright smile for her benefit, although his insides were being torn apart with guilt and self-loathing. "I said, he isn't going to get his hands on Bonne Chance, Patience. So don't worry. I'm going to take care of this. It isn't anything you need to be concerned about. Do you understand?"

She nodded and Reese longed to kiss her sweet, trusting mouth. No one had ever put faith in his abilities. No one had ever run to him when something went wrong.

Before he could reconsider and talk himself out of the impulse, he pressed a quick, hard kiss against her parted lips. It felt so good to allow himself that small liberty.

Patience blinked in surprise, her mouth turning up slowly in a wary smile.

"I'm going to fix everything," he said, releasing her. "Everything."

As he rushed from the room, collecting his hat as he went, Patience brushed her fingertips across her lips. She didn't understand Reese's words—or his actions. But she knew that when he said he would fix everything, he was talking about more than the debts Samuel held over him.

As he rode toward Samuel's plantation, Reese slogged through the quagmire of emotions in which he suddenly found himself bogged down. He'd never felt so ashamed in his life. How had he let his behavior deteriorate to the point of nearly losing Bonne Chance? Why had he never realized how much the place meant to him before now? First with Cooper and now with Samuel, his disregard had nearly led to disaster.

He felt shame and remorse. Never before had he cared what people thought about him. But he found he cared very much about Patience's opinion of him. Why hadn't she turned from him in disgust this morning? She knew only too well what kind of man he'd been. And yet, she'd touched him with concern, looked at him with understanding and deference. She'd come to him looking for a solution, and her eyes told him she believed in his capacity to succeed.

Reese now knew what it felt like to be in love—and to be loved. For surely that had been love he read in Patience's eyes when she first saw him standing in the doorway. It had been love he felt in her embrace as she went eagerly into his arms.

Love, undeserved, but more precious because of its unpredictability.

Reese was damned if he would let Samuel and his greed steal the one good thing he had ever found.

The long, winding drive to Samuel's house gave Reese time to gather his thoughts and devise a plan. He would not give in to Samuel, and when he realized Reese had no intention of giving in, they could sit down and work out a reasonable solution to deal with the debts Samuel held.

He reined in and tied the leather straps to the post in front of the stately mansion. Four Ionic columns supported a semi-circular roof over the Paladian-style porch. The balcony jutting from the front of the upper story was braced by ten smaller columns. Samuel Symmons had everything a man could want. Why wasn't it enough?

Reese took the eight steps to the porch two at a time. He knocked heavily on the massive carved-oak front door.

A servant answered his call and showed him into a lavish sitting room off the main hall. He waited for nearly twenty minutes for Samuel to appear.

Temper high from cooling his heels, Reese considered ignoring the man's extended hand. Then he remembered his pledge to resolve the situation amiably.

"Samuel, I heard of your visit upon my return to Bonne Chance this morning. I only wish you had waited to speak with me in person. You've thrown my household into an uproar."

"Yes, I daresay," the man gloated. "But you can't be all that surprised."

"Oh, but I am," Reese admitted, a hint of his anger echoing in his harsh words. With Herculean effort, he reined in his choler. "How could I know you'd bought up my markers? You've certainly gone out of your way to hide the fact."

Samuel smiled and lifted his hands out to his sides. "I confess, I acted furtively. Didn't want to jinx the deal."

Reese bit back an embittered retort and shrugged casually. "Well, it's obvious that matter is settled now."

Samuel arched a thick black eyebrow and nodded sagely. "Oh, indeed, it's a fact. And it's all here for you in black and white."

He reached into his inner coat pocket and retrieved a sheaf of papers. He unfolded them, handing them to Reese with a cluck of his tongue. "Nasty business, gambling. Especially when you're too drunk to know whether you've won or lost."

Fury boiled freely through Reese, and he longed to knock the man on his sanctimonious ass. Samuel had been known to gamble himself on occasion. But Reese ignored the jibe, feeling certain it was well deserved, as he perused the documents.

The sum at the bottom of the last page nearly knocked him off his own feet. The wind sailed out of his lungs so fast, he felt the room spin around him. Dear God, what had he done?

He quickly composed himself and faced Samuel.

"So what are your terms?"

"I want Bonne Chance."

Reese forced a small smile, pasting an amused expression on his face. "I would never have guessed," he said sarcastically. The smile died, and he fixed his mouth into a hard, firm line. "It'll never happen."

"Actually, there's a good chance it will. These," he said, waving to the documents Reese held, "are considered legitimate debts in this country, and property can be seized to cover arrears."

He rocked back on his heels and tucked his thumbs into the small side pockets of his pinstriped vest. "Of course, if you'd rather sell now, I'm still willing to offer you fair market value for Bonne Chance and everything on it."

"You bastard," Reese seethed, forgetting his promise to himself to handle the situation peaceably. He shoved the papers into Samuel's chest. The man fumbled to catch the floating pages, and Reese grasped his collar and lifted him to his toes. "I'll pay you every cent of the money I owe, but you will never so much as set foot on Bonne Chance. Do you understand me, Symmons? I'll see you in hell before I'll let you have one inch of what is mine."

He shoved the portly man back, watching as he pitched and swayed, trying to regain his balance. The papers fell haphazardly to the floor around Symmons's feet.

"You're making a mistake, Ashburn," the old man yelled as Reese strode toward the sitting room door. "You'll be sorry you didn't accept my offer when the month is up and you don't have enough to pay your debts. I won't offer again. Do you hear me?" he screamed. "I'll have Bonne Chance. And you'll have nothing. Nothing!"

Reese walked straight to the front door and out into the bright sunshine of the day. He slammed the door behind him and felt a small measure of satisfaction when he heard the etched glass panel crack.

That was nothing compared to what he'd do to Symmons if he saw the man again. He longed to throttle the blackguard. He wanted to crush his fist into the fat jowls dangling like saddlebags on the man's jaws.

But as he mounted his horse and turned it in the direction of Bonne Chance and Patience, Reese knew he wouldn't do either of those things. Not that Samuel didn't deserve them after his deceit. The man had sat down to dine with Reese, all the while planning to stab him in the back.

Reese knew Samuel wasn't to blame for the mess he now found himself in. This time he had no one to blame but himself. He'd made this muddle while grieving over James's death. It was up to him, and him alone, to correct it.

Samuel bent to retrieve the papers, a grin on his face. Ashburn had reacted just the way he'd expected him to. And it brought Samuel a great deal of pleasure. When you did business the way he did, it was imperative to know your opponent. Reese Ashburn was the type of weak, self-indulgent man Samuel most enjoyed besting.

And he would beat him this time. Samuel had planned his acquisition carefully. No possibility had been ignored. No possible pitfall had been overlooked. He knew everything he needed to know about Reese Ashburn and his wealthy ward.

He chuckled. He'd bet he knew more about them than even they did.

Going to his desk, he took paper and pen and began to scribble the telegraph message he'd composed earlier. He had an ace in the hole Ashburn would never expect. And it would ensure his success.

Just a little longer, and all his plans would come to fruition. He'd waited so long that he almost rubbed his hands in gleeful anticipation.

Chapter Sixteen

The brush slid through her hair rhythmically, soothing her with every stroke. Dressed in a night-gown and matching robe of delicate sea-green silk, Patience watched her reflection in the dressing table mirror.

How could she look the same, when she felt so very different? Setting aside the engraved silver hairbrush, she leaned closer to the wavy likeness staring back at her. Her hand touched her cheek, her forehead, her lips. All the same. Yet not.

Love. Until now, it was only a word she'd heard but never paid any mind to. A convenient term used by men who sought to woo or entice. In poems, a pledge with a nice sound. But it was so much more.

She was now a player in the sonnet. A heroine in a Brontë novel. A verse in a song.

Laughing at her ridiculous musings, she nevertheless felt transformed. Reese had kissed her. More than that, he'd held her, comforted her, embraced her to ease his own troubles as much as hers. They had shared a moment, and she knew without a doubt that it had changed them both.

She couldn't wait until she saw him again. She alternately feared and anticipated their next encounter.

Would he be distant, regretful of showing her his feelings? Would he try to kiss her again? She knew that if he did she wouldn't stop him.

A knock sounded on her door, startling her. Her heart crashed against her ribs and she forgot to breathe for a long moment. Then she jumped to her feet and walked to the door, telling herself she was behaving like a foolish schoolgirl. It could be anyone, Ma Jewel, Gay . . .

"Reese," she breathed, pulling the door open wide.

"I didn't mean to disturb you," he said, his eyes dropping to her neckline and lower. She saw his throat work as he raised his eyes to gaze at her.

"I wasn't sleeping," she told him. She stepped back. "Come in."

"No, I shouldn't." He frowned, then took one step into the room. "Well, I do need to talk to you."

"What is it? Is anything the matter?"

"Only the mess you already know about. I was wondering. . . ." He paused, shaking his head. "I would have thought you'd be repulsed by what I'd done. But you seemed so supportive." He took another step, and she let the door slowly swing shut behind him. He heard the latch click into place, but he was too intent on what he was trying to say to hear it.

"You didn't need me to berate you. I could tell you were doing a very good job of that yourself. We all make mistakes, sometimes foolish mistakes. But you immediately took responsibility for your lapse and began to figure a way out of it. That's very commendable."

He shook his head, gazing at her with wonder. "How do you do that?"

"What?"

"Find the good in a rotten situation? Find something noble in the ignoble?"

"Don't paint me as an idealist. If I gave you credit, it was deserved."

He looked as though he wanted to touch her, and she longed for him to do it. She leaned closer, and he stuffed his hands in his trouser pockets and stepped farther into the room, his head lowered.

"I'm going to Mobile tomorrow."

"Again?" she cried, without thinking. He glanced quickly up at her and she clasped her hands in front of her. "I mean, you only just returned."

"I need to go and see about a loan. Samuel refused to negotiate. He wants Bonne Chance, and he sees this as his only way to get his hands on the plantation. He won't grant me so much as one day past the deadline."

"I see." Her lips formed a hard, white line and her eyes narrowed in anger. "I suspected as much when he delivered his message. He seemed to be gloating."

A bitter sound escaped Reese's throat. "Oh, yes, he's very proud of his resourcefulness. He could never sway me, no matter what argument he used, so he found a way around my opposition. And I played right into his hands."

"He hasn't won yet," Patience said firmly, going to stand directly in front of him.

"No," he agreed, a quick flash of admiration in his dark eyes as he gazed at her. "He hasn't won yet. And if I have anything to say about it, he won't. That's why I have to go to Mobile."

"No you don't."

Reese met her eyes as a smile tipped that luscious mouth he craved. It took all his strength to resist the temptation, but now was not the time to press that issue. However, it was a matter he intended to examine very soon.

"What do you mean?"

"There isn't any need for you to go to Mobile. You have all the money you need to stop Samuel. I can't believe I didn't think of it sooner, but I suppose I was too upset to think clearly."

"Patience, you know Bonne Chance is nearly bankrupt. We barely have the funds to see us through until we sell the first crop."

"I have all the money you need, Reese," she told him with a wide smile. "And you have the control over it."

He studied her for a moment as the truth dawned. His eyes flashed angrily and he set his jaw. "No! Absolutely not."

"But, Reese—"

"My God. What do you take me for? I admit I've done some base, despicable things in my life, but I would never take money from you."

"Why?" she cried, clasping his arm. "I'm offering it to you. I think Bonne Chance is worth saving. I think you're—"

"I said no." He shrugged her hand away and turned his back to her. "I don't know why James sent you here, why he entrusted me to be his executor. But I'm not about to take advantage of his trust. There is no way I'd touch a cent of your money."

"All right," she said soothingly, realizing too late that she'd obviously said something wrong. "All right, whatever you say. But I want you to know, if you need the money—"

"No!" He whirled and clasped her arms. She gasped, startled. Then, meeting his eyes, she relaxed. She knew he would never hurt her.

"No, but I appreciate the offer," he choked out.

She doubted if her suggestion were truly valued, but he was trying to be generous and she didn't want to say anything to upset him further.

Suddenly his hands gentled on her arms. Patience met his glance and saw that the anger had been replaced with a very different emotion. Smoldering in his eyes was the same attraction, the same need she'd been feeling for days.

His gaze seemed to caress her, tingling along her flesh, although he continued to stare into her eyes. His fingers moved, and sparks of fire shot through her, tightening the muscles in her stomach. A moist heat pooled in her core, sending flames licking out in every direction.

He would kiss her now, she thought longingly, and wet her lips in anticipation. His eyes followed the movement, and a grin tipped his mouth as though he could read her thoughts.

"Yes," he murmured, leaning closer. "Yes, I'm going to kiss you this time. If you still want me to."

Want? Need, desire, crave. The feelings she was experiencing went beyond anything she'd ever felt before. Her body ached for his touch; her lips begged for the feel of his mouth. Plunging ahead as she always did, she pressed herself against his chest and wrapped eager arms around his neck.

She heard his hungry groan as his mouth claimed hers and his arms tightened around her. His lips explored the tender, sensitized flesh of her mouth.

Patience gave herself freely to their passion, standing on tiptoe to deepen the kiss. He responded by letting his hands roam over her back, to her sides, around her waist. He lifted her gently, tilting her body closer into the curve of his.

The kiss was surprisingly gentle, though thorough. He pressed her lips and she opened to him. Somewhere inside her chaste mind she was shocked by her ardent response, but her heart cried out for more, and she answered the call by letting her own hands touch and caress as his were doing.

Reese lost all control as Patience's hands stroked and surveyed the muscles of his back and neck. Her soft fingers found the sensitive spot at the base of his neck and sent shivers of desire coursing through him. He ached to sweep her into his arms and carry her to the bed on the other side of the room.

The thought barely crossed his mind before it was replaced with another. This was no dockside harlot, this was Patience Bentley! He might entertain thoughts of love and desire, but simple lust had no place between them. She would not be just another conquest.

He forced himself to release her, though it took all his strength to pull away. She clung to him for a moment, still lost in the depths of her passion, and he fought the urge to clasp her in his embrace and finish what he'd started, what she seemed to want also.

He reminded himself that she was an innocent. She didn't know what she was asking for, what he longed to give at that moment.

"Patience," he softly called her name.

She opened her eyes, the dazzling blue depths captivating him and pulling him into the whirlpool of emotions he saw there. He had to swallow hard before he could continue.

"Patience, I have to go. We'll have a lot to talk about when I return. Starting with this," he said, indicating their clasped arms.

She nodded mutely, and a deep sigh escaped her slightly parted lips. He couldn't resist. He leaned in and pressed another long, drugging kiss on her mouth.

Then he released her, leaving the room hurriedly before either of them could speak the words that would ignite the inferno again.

Pale light filtered through the drapes as another frantic knock sounded on Patience's bedroom door. She drifted up from a deep, dream-filled sleep, the feel of Reese's touch still on her lips and skin.

Realizing the knock was real and not part of the memory of Reese's visit, she shoved aside the light covers and rushed to the door.

Swinging it open, her heart sank. Had she thought he would return? Had she been hoping he'd change his mind about the money and stay at Bonne Chance with her?

"Ma, what's wrong?"

"It's Nancy, miss. She's laborin' and Mag asked if you'd mind helpin'. Nancy's askin' for you."

"She is? Oh, yes, of course. Tell her I'll be right there, as soon as I change."

The old slave nodded, her chins quivering in anticipation as she hurried off again.

Patience yanked off her nightgown and hastily donned a clean white shirtwaist and dark skirt. She collected a fresh apron from the tallboy in the hall and slipped her feet into flat kid slippers, then rushed toward the side door of the main house.

Dawn was just peering over the horizon as Patience scurried toward the infirmary. She tied her hair back at her nape as she sailed through the door. Nancy lay on one of the new cots, gripping the straps of leather Mag had had fastened to the iron footrail. The woman had insisted on placing them there, and now Patience understood why.

She'd been present at a few births in Boston, for good friends who'd married before her. But she'd never heard of using leather straps to assist a birth.

She watched in amazement as Nancy used the straps to pull herself up as she pushed. Hurrying behind the woman, she placed her hands behind Nancy's back and helped her lean forward. A long, low wail rose from the woman's throat as she bore down, moving the baby into position.

As the contraction passed, Nancy slumped back against the pillows. A basin of water was on the table next to the cot and Patience wet a cloth and dabbed the sweat from the dark, furrowed brow.

"How is it going?" she asked Mag.

"Fine, fine. Nancy's strong—she won't have no trouble. Just a little longer, right, Nancy?"

"That's what you keep tellin' me." She clutched Patience's arm. "I wanted you here, miss. You was so concerned 'bout my young'un before, I knew you wouldn't let nothin' happen now."

Patience stared, stunned at the woman's words of confidence. She didn't know what she could do. Then her doubts fled as another contraction moved over Nancy's abdomen, and she screamed as she gripped the straps and pulled.

Patience put her arm around Nancy's shoulders and helped her into position once more.

Sweat dotted her own forehead as another quarter hour passed. Nancy's contractions seemed to come one on top of the other without cease. The woman's strength was being taxed as Mag finally announced the crowning.

Patience laughed and patted Nancy's shoulder. "Just a few more," she said encouragingly. "You're doing really well."

The woman clenched her teeth and pulled, releasing a wail as she pushed with all her might.

Mag's cry of triumph followed, and the sound of a wet, raspy cry filled the room. Nancy slumped back onto the pillows, gasping, and Patience sponged her face with the cool cloth once more.

"It's a girl," Mag announced, holding up the squirming infant. She handed the baby to Patience, who held it for Nancy's inspection. Nancy glanced up, and the two women shared a happy smile.

Nancy touched the toes and fingers, the soft, wiry hair on the tiny head. She sighed and closed her eyes, and Patience went to the table set up in the corner. She cleaned and wrapped the baby while Mag finished up with Nancy.

After the woman had been bathed and the sheets changed, Patience laid the baby in her arms and watched as mother and daughter fell into an exhausted sleep.

"Thank you, Miss Patience," Mag said, washing up. "I'll keep an eye on 'em for a while. Tomorrow we can move her back to her own cabin."

"Is there anything else you need?"

"No, ma'am. We'll be fine," she said.

Patience went to the door, then turned to look back at the cot.

"You done real good, too, Miss Patience," Mag told her with a smile.

"Nancy did all the work," she said. "But I'm glad I was here."

Mag nodded, and Patience opened the door. Ran was standing outside, an expression of concern on his dark face.

"Oh, Ran, how are you?" She relayed the news of the birth to him, then stepped outside. She saw his gaze move around the infirmary until it settled on Mag.

The woman turned at the sound of voices and met Ran's gaze. Patience watched as the overseer's eyes softened and filled with emotion. She arched a brow and stepped lightly away as Mag started toward him.

So there was something going on between Mag and Ran. Funny, she'd never noticed it before. She pondered the situation as she made her way toward the kitchen, where she found Ma Jewel.

She imparted the news about Nancy and the baby and accepted a freshly brewed cup of coffee as she sank down on a chair, exhausted.

"Ma," she said, sipping slowly. "I noticed something just now. I know it isn't any of my business, but is something going on between Ran and Mag?"

"Going on? Not if you thinkin' they're up to mischief."

"No, no, I know it isn't anything like that. But—well, I never noticed Ran's paying so much attention before."

"Ran's a different man now," she said cryptically.

"Different? How do you mean?"

"He'd never take a wife, start a family a'fore."

"Why?"

"Slaves are allowed to marry, but it ain't recognized as legal by white folks. We got no rights over our young'uns. Any child born to a slave mother is born a slave. The property of the master."

"Oh, Ma, that's horrible," Patience cried, her heart constricting in her chest as she thought of Nancy's new little baby girl.

"Ran would never marry, since he thought he'd always belong to someone else. Didn't want to see his family sold off and sent away where he'd never see 'em again. So he jus' never let on he needed that kind of companionship a'fore."

"Oh, I see," she said, brightening. "And now that he knows he'll be free one day, he's willing to show Mag how much he really cares about her. But what about Mag? She'll still be a slave, and so will their children. You just said so."

Ma nodded. "Yep, but Ran figures if Misser Reese lets him buy his own papers, he'll let him buy Mag's too. After he's free, he'll jest keep workin' 'til he works off her price."

"Oh, Ma, that's wonderful." Her enthusiam dimmed, and she bit the side of her lip. "I only hope she returns his feelings."

"Oh, Ran's had her heart since she was a girl. But nothin' she did would sway his determination. So she kept her feelings to herself. But she never looked at no other man."

"Now they're finally going to be together." Patience's romantic heart swelled with emotion. She felt she'd had a hand in bringing about the circumstances which allowed Ran and Mag to declare their love at long last. She and Reese together.

It made one believe all things were possible with love. Maybe she could convince Reese to give the couple Mag's freedom as a wedding gift.

Or better yet, maybe she would one day convince Reese that *all* the slaves deserved the chance Ran was being given. Perhaps this was the beginning of the end of Reese's slave holdings.

And if she could change his mind about an issue so paramount in his life, she knew her happiness would be complete, because then she would have no doubts about her own feelings for Reese. She loved him. She'd been proud of the way he stood up to Samuel and rose to the challenge of saving Bonne Chance. If she could change his mind about slavery, the last obstacle between them would disappear. Then she could give her heart completely and without reservation.

"Dammit, Woolsey, you've known me all my life. I've never borrowed a cent from this bank, but I've damn sure put a sizable sum into it over the years."

"Reese, you know if there was any way I could help you, I would. But you won't consider using Bonne Chance for collateral, and I can't just give you that kind of cash on your signature."

Reese leaned forward in his chair, his hands flat on the edge of the man's desk. He'd known Darius Woolsey all his life. They'd gone to school together. He'd come to him first thing that morning, only to hear the same words he sat listening to now.

He'd left in a huff earlier, angry that their friendship hadn't carried any weight with the banker. But after visiting every other bank in town, he was back. Without his pride and indignation.

The answer had been the same at every bank. No one was willing to give him a loan without Bonne Chance, or something of equal value, for collateral.

He suspected Samuel's influence had something to do with his suddenly being an outcast among the businessmen who used to cater to him. But deep down, Reese knew his own reputation was as much to blame. No one knew how he'd react to being broke. They knew him as a wastrel; they couldn't know he'd changed. Or tried to. They couldn't know how important it was now for him to prove that he was more than a reprobate and a ne'er-do-well.

All the way to Mobile, he'd thought about his encounter with Patience. It still stung that she had offered him the money to save Bonne Chance. As though he'd accept such a degrading proposal.

No, he wouldn't use her money. Not now, not ever. But he needed to save Bonne Chance just the same—mainly because it had been his father's dream and he couldn't allow it to fall victim to his debauchery. More important, he needed to prove to himself, and to Patience, that he really had changed.

He would never ask her to marry him if he didn't feel he was the best choice for her. He owed James that much, and no matter how much he longed to tell her how he felt, he wouldn't relent on that point.

"Woolsey, I told you I'd sign over the profits from the first crop as collateral. I've been talking to shippers, and if I bypass the factor and do the negotiating and shipping myself, I'll make a much larger profit."

"Reese, crops fail. We have storms, insects. Hell, you never know when a hurricane's going to hit and wipe out the whole field. It's too risky." He twirled the pen he held in his hand. "Reese," he said, meeting his friend's gaze. "The truth is, man, *you're* too risky. If I gave you an unprotected loan, I'd lose my job. You've made a spectacle of yourself for months, shocking even your staunchest defenders. Me included. I'm sorry, but there's nothing I can do."

Reese wanted to grab the man and shake him. He longed to tell him how important it was that he succeed this time. But he knew it wouldn't do any good. If his reputation as a rounder were well known, it was nothing compared to his reputation as a womanizer. He could just imagine Woolsey's reaction if he told him he was doing this for the sake of a woman he wanted to think he was worthy.

The man would laugh him out of the office. He choked down his defeat and offered his hand.

"Thanks for your time, Woolsey."

The man stood quickly, his hand extended. "Reese, if there were any way . . ."

"I know. It's all right. Hell, I've got no one to blame but myself."

The banker looked chagrined, and Reese knew he'd been thinking the same thought. He grinned to ease the man's discomfort.

As he turned toward the door, Woolsey called his name and Reese looked back.

"The girl—James's daughter?"

Reese nodded, a frown sliding over his forehead.

"I hear she's a pretty thing."

Again Reese nodded, the frown creeping into his soul as he watched the light of an idea form in the banker's eyes.

"I hear she came with a nice little settlement. Why don't you put those charms you're famous for to good use? A wealthy wife can solve a lot of problems for a man."

Fists clenched at his sides, Reese stepped toward the man he used to call friend. His jaw set rigidly, he barely found the forbearance to keep from burying his fists in Woolsey's unsuspecting face.

"I'm going to forget you said that, Woolsey, because I know you're only trying to find a way to help me. And because, just maybe, I deserve it after the way I've acted in the past. But hear this, and don't forget it. If you ever say anything like that about Patience Bentley again, I'll kill you."

The man's face turned a sickly gray, and Reese slammed out of the office before he changed his mind and hit the banker. One good thing about a bad reputation, he thought with revulsion, people were never sure just how low you'd sink. Woolsey would never mention Patience's name again, because he couldn't be sure Reese wouldn't carry out his threat.

Although he'd never been violent in the past, Reese had to admit he wasn't sure himself. Woolsey's comment about Patience had gone through him like a knife—because he realized at that moment that if he asked her to marry him now, that was exactly what everyone who knew him would think.

Chapter Seventeen

Patience paced the parlor, worried and despondant. Reese had returned from Mobile two days before, but he refused to see her or talk to her. He'd locked himself in his study again.

Her periwinkle robe and nightgown floated out from her feet as she walked to and fro in front of the empty fireplace.

Why wouldn't he let her in? What had happened in Mobile? He'd said they would talk when he returned, but all that had obviously changed.

She heard the door of the study closing and rushed to the parlor door and peered out, jubilant to see Reese ascending the stairs.

Should she go after him now? What would she say? How would he react if she told him what she'd been thinking?

He disappeared around the landing, heading toward his bedroom, and she tiptoed into the main hall. Her flat-heeled slippers made no sound as she eased toward the stairs.

All her life she'd been bold and headstrong. Why had shyness claimed her now? Always before, she'd gone after what she wanted. She told herself she could—should—do that with Reese now.

Before she had a chance to change her mind, she followed him up the stairs. At the door to his bedroom, she paused for a moment, then knocked soundly.

"Go away," he called out.

"Reese, can I speak to you a moment?" To her dismay, her voice broke. She caught herself looking over her shoulder nervously.

For a long minute she didn't hear a sound from the other side of the door. She feared he would just ignore her. Then she heard the shuffle of feet and the click of the latch.

Taking a stumbling step back, she met Reese's eyes as he opened the door.

"I don't really feel like talking now, Patience. I'm tired."

Her hand reached for the edge of the door, afraid he'd close it in her face before she built her courage enough to speak to him.

"I was worried," she finally said, not sure where to start or what she could say to make him listen to her. "When you didn't come out of the study for so long, I thought . . ."

"That I was drunk again?" he asked derisively. He shrugged. "Sober as a judge, as you can see. I haven't had a drink in weeks. Not that I couldn't use one right now."

"No, I didn't think that." She realized it was the truth. She'd worried that he needed her but wouldn't come to her, that he regretted the kiss they'd shared. But she hadn't believed he was drinking again. "I gather things didn't go well for you in Mobile."

He laughed dryly. "No, things did not go well in Mobile. And I'm exhausted right now. So if you don't mind . . ."

She clutched the door anxiously. "Please, could we just talk a minute?"

He studied her face closely, and she took the opportunity to return the scrutiny. She read hurt, resolve, and something more in his eyes. How had no one noticed the vulnerability he'd hidden behind his carefree facade? She'd recognized it almost immediately. It was one of the things that drew her to him. He felt pain and loneliness—the same feelings she'd lived with all her life.

Why couldn't he see that they had so much in common with each other? Perhaps he didn't recognize the changes she'd undergone since her arrival. He still saw her as the cheeky little pest who'd disrupted his life.

But she wasn't the same any more. She'd grown accustomed to the slow-moving South. The oppressive heat made her appreciate the breeze off the bay even more. She'd made friends with most of the slaves, and, although she still wanted to see them freed, she understood more about this way of life.

Should she just tell him how she felt? Could she blurt it out in her usual outspoken fashion?

He was still watching her, waiting for her to make some kind of move. She took a tentative step into the room. His eyebrow climbed toward his hairline, but he didn't show any other reaction.

Apprehensive, she nevertheless refused to show him how frightened she truly felt. Boldly, she pushed the door behind her and heard it click into place.

"Patience." His voice sounded harsh, weathered. "This isn't a good idea."

"Why?"

He shook his head. "The fact that you don't already know the answer to that question only proves my point."

Frowning, she cocked her head and stepped closer.

"You're too innocent, Patience, to understand what just being alone in the same room with a man like me could do to you."

"But we've been alone a great deal of the time I've been here."

"Yes, yes, that's my point. I'm ruining any chance you might have had of finding a suitable beau here."

Shocked, she froze in place. "A beau?" she asked disdainfully.

"Yes, someone who would suit you. Someone your father would have approved of."

She shook her head, dizzy with confusion. "How did we get on this subject? I didn't come in here to talk about my finding a husband."

"Then why did you come?"

Tears burned the backs of her eyes. Why was he being so cold? How could he pretend that the precious moments they'd spent together before he left had never happened? Couldn't he see he was hurting her?

Suddenly the tears backed away and she stiffened her spine. It made sense to her now. He hadn't found help in Mobile, and he feared he would lose Bonne Chance. Shame or guilt made him lash out. He'd purposely brought up other men to remind her how unsuitable he considered himself.

She was having none of that.

"I want to know what happened in Mobile."

"I told you, nothing."

She strolled past him, farther into the room. "You weren't able to get a loan?"

He growled low in his throat and lowered his head before facing her squarely. "No, I wasn't able to get the money I needed. Not from the bank, not from any of the individuals I went to see."

She could see the anger, the humiliation he sought to hide.

"It seems that since I've lived the life of a miscreant and a prodigal for sixteen years, no one has faith in my ability to actually work for a living." He quirked one dark brow sarcastically. "Can you imagine that?"

Patience went to stand before him, her gaze never leaving his eyes. Placing her hand on his arm, she shook her head. "No, I can't imagine it. I can't believe no one noticed the change in you."

She felt him stiffen, his eyes widening in surprise. "What are you talking about?"

"Reese, did you think no one cared? Did you think I wouldn't see the way you've worked to save this plantation? Or the fact that you haven't had a drink in weeks? You didn't go to Mobile to visit the taverns, you went to visit the banks. You've changed, Reese. And so have I."

He shrugged away from her touch, but Patience refused to back down now. "Why can't you see that I have faith in you? I believe you can save Bonne Chance, that you'll work longer and harder than anyone to see it succeed."

"Well, I appreciate your confidence, but it's misplaced this time."

"No, it isn't." She met his gaze, a look of tender assurance on her face. "You have to save Bonne Chance, no matter what it takes. Admit it."

His dark eyes showed the dullness of defeat. "It's no use. I've tried. Samuel seems to have won this time."

"You can't let that happen, Reese. I've talked to the servants. They've told me horrible things about Samuel Symmons and the way he treats his slaves. We have to stop him."

"Dammit, Patience, you haven't been listening to me. I couldn't come up with the money. I've spent two days trying to figure out how much I could raise if I sold everything except the house and land, and it just isn't enough."

"I have a solution," she told him quietly.

He stopped, staring down at her. Then his mouth hardened, and his jaw clamped tight. "I've already told you I won't take your money. It isn't—"

"Marry me."

"—an option. What did you say?"

"I said, marry me. Then the money won't be mine any more. It'll be yours, and it's more than enough to pay Samuel."

Reese stared in stunned disbelief. His heart wanted to cry out to her that he'd like nothing more than to make her his wife. But his head knew he never could. Not now. Not as long as Bonne Chance was in financial difficulty. People would assume he'd married her only to get his hands on her money, and she'd be the laughing stock of the county.

Besides, he would never take advantage of James's trust in him by using Patience's money to bail himself out of a mess of his own foolish creation. James had intended that money for his daughter's future.

"Patience, you don't understand. I can't marry you."

She swallowed hard, and he saw a flush creep over her cheeks. But she hid her embarrassment and brazenly took a step toward him.

"Why? Don't you think we'd suit? I've enjoyed our evenings together, our discussions. I told you I've become accustomed to this place. I don't miss Boston any more. I'm very well trained to run a household—you've seen me do it."

Already he was shaking his head. "It isn't any of that, Patience. You've been a pleasant companion and a great help to me. But there's more to a marriage than that."

Again her hand found its way to his arm and he covered it with his own. Her touch soothed him, and despite his resolve to avoid another encounter with her, he needed to feel the warmth of her fingers on his skin.

"I'm aware of that, Reese. Don't you think we would suit . . . that way?"

He gulped down a lump of desire as she moved closer. Her scent reached him, and he drew a deep breath. The air around them seemed to crackle with energy, like the wind before a summer storm. Her nearness nearly stole his senses.

"No," he said, stepping away quickly. "It isn't that simple. I wouldn't be any good for you, Patience. Hell, I'm not good for much right now. Maybe I have changed over the past weeks, but it isn't enough. I've got a long way to go before I'd be the kind of man your father would have wanted you to marry."

"My father sent me to you, Reese. Why do you think he'd object to our marrying?"

"Because of what I am, what I've always been. Dammit, Patience, why can't you see what I'm really like?"

"I know what you are. I see you clearly. More clearly than you see yourself. And I think my father saw it, too. That's why he sent me here. And that's why he'd agree with me now."

Raking rough fingers through his hair, Reese paced the rug in front of the huge sleigh bed. "You don't understand," he whispered. "You don't know."

"Know what?"

He slid one large hand over his face, trying to clear his muddled thoughts. He didn't know why James had done what he had, but Reese felt certain it wasn't for the reasons Patience mentioned. James knew him better than anyone, knew the scrapes he'd been in.

He faced her, a burning, faraway look in his eyes. She saw the painful memories reflected there.

"I killed him."

"No, Reese . . ."

"I was responsible. It was my idea to go to the tavern that night. The place was deplorable—and dangerous. I knew that, but it only added to the excitement."

"Reese," she called, drawing him back from his recollection. "Reese, don't. None of that matters now. We have to remember Samuel's threat. That has to be our prime concern now."

"*My* concern," he told her firmly, shuttering his expression. "I appreciate your interest, and I'm glad you've come to like it here, but this is my problem and I'll solve it, somehow, on my own."

"But that's what I've been trying to tell you, Reese," she said, pushing forward. "You don't have to do this alone."

"Patience, I . . ."

She moved forward again, closer this time. Watching his eyes carefully, she put her heart out on her sleeve where he couldn't miss seeing it.

Hoping he wouldn't tell her the feelings were one-sided, she glanced up at him and smiled.

"I enjoyed our kiss the other night, Reese. Didn't you?"

He tried to look away, but his eyes were locked on hers. He nodded. "Yes, but . . ."

"I wondered why you didn't come see me when you returned. I waited for you."

"I'm sorry. It's just . . ."

"You said we'd talk. About us. About what happened."

"That was a mistake. I can't offer . . ."

"It didn't feel like a mistake. It felt good."

"Dammit, Patience. Would you be quiet for once and let me get a word in edgewise?"

"Go ahead, Reese. What is it you want to say?"

"Before I left, I thought there was a chance we could make things work between us."

"I'd like that, Reese."

"But my plans didn't pan out, Patience. That's what I've been trying to tell you."

"Things could still work out. I've been drawn to you since the day I met you. Even when I thought I hated you, I felt something deep inside for you."

"Yes, I felt it, too. But that's desire, Patience."

"Yes, desire." Her hands came up to rest on his chest. He closed his eyes and groaned deeply.

"But you need more than that," he forced himself to say. It was getting difficult to talk. More difficult to remember why this couldn't happen between them.

"It's a good start," she said, her fingers roaming up to his neck. They trailed around to his nape, where she found his sensitive spot.

Reese sucked his breath through clenched teeth to keep from grabbing her and crushing her to him. She whispered his name softly, like a refrain. Her nails raked down his back, and he lost all control.

His head came down in a flash, and his lips claimed her mouth hungrily. The kiss sent spirals of ecstasy through him. He'd tried to tell himself it hadn't been this good between them. He'd nearly convinced himself that he'd blown the whole encounter out of proportion in his mind. But now he knew he hadn't. If anything, they were more explosive together than he'd thought. One touch, one caress, and they ignited with fiery passion like nothing he'd felt before.

How could she, an innocent, enflame him so? What magical element did she possess that the other, more worldly women of his acquaintance lacked? For none had ever so completely robbed him of his senses.

His arms went around her, and he folded her into his embrace. Her body curved into the line of his, her head tucked just under his chin.

He rained kisses along the line of her jaw, her throat. He pushed aside the soft fabric of her robe and nightgown and let his lips follow the ridge of her collarbone.

Standing on tiptoe, she strained to get closer. His hand drifted down the curve of her waist to her hip and lower. He touched her thigh and eased her leg up, gripping the bend of her knee. With his other arm around her back, he lifted her, setting her down on his outstretched thigh.

She gasped and threw back her head, sighing with need. The sound went through him like a torch. Suddenly the blood in his veins turned to hot molasses, heating him with molten desire.

Patience dropped her chin to Reese's massive chest. Her trembling arms clung to him as her weakened knees gave out. His touch brought her untried senses to life. She couldn't get close enough. He couldn't touch all the places yearning for the feel of his hands.

She'd never felt anything like the sensations he roused in her. His warm, moist breath brushed her face, sending shivers through her body. His thigh sparked an ache in her very core. Straining against him, she sought to satisfy the longing, but the closer she got, the higher the need rose until she felt she would fly apart with the pleasure and pain of it.

"Oh, yes, Reese, I want this," she whispered, arching her back until her breasts flattened against his chest. The thin fabric of her nightgown brushed the peaks of her hardened nipples, and she trembled with rising passion. "I want you."

She felt his body go rigid beneath her hands. His lips stilled their tantalizing exploration. Slowly, slowly, he raised his eyes and stared into her flushed face.

"Oh God, Patience," he moaned, pushing her slightly away. His arms still held her tightly, as though he tried but couldn't quite release her. "This is wrong. It shouldn't be this way. Not with you."

"Why not with me?" she cried, struggling to find her way out of the passion-induced haze still surrounding her. "What's the matter with me?"

"No, I didn't mean that. You deserve more, much more." This time he set her gently away, straightening her clothing and brushing a stray lock of hair behind her ear. "More than someone like me can offer you."

"But you're what I want," she told him.

He shook his head. "No." Breathing deeply, he went to the door and pulled it open. "It isn't that simple."

She took one step toward him, and he put out his hand. "Go back to your room, Patience. Now, before it's too late."

"Reese?" The word was a plea, and he closed his eyes and his heart against the sound.

"Just go, Patience. This is one time you can't have what you want."

Chapter Eighteen

"Come on, Phillip," Reese said, stepping around the desk in his study. He leaned against the corner and crossed one booted foot over the other. "You've been after me to sell you my stud for two years."

"I'd love to have that horse—he's a fine animal. I just don't have the money right now."

He wouldn't meet Reese's eyes as he shifted nervously in his chair. Reese studied the man, trying to fight the irritation boiling within him.

"What's he got on you?"

Phillip Bell glanced up, chagrin lining his thin features. "Hell, Reese, he's got something on all of us," he said, not even pretending he didn't know what Reese meant. "We've all done business with him. I've still got a few irons in that fire, and he could make things difficult if he wanted to."

"And if you helped me, he would?"

Bell nodded, lowering his head. "He hasn't made any outright threats, but he's been throwing his weight around. God, just knowing the spot you're in makes the rest of us shudder. Who'd have thought he could get this far?"

Reese laid his hand on the other man's shoulder. "I understand, Phillip. Dammit, the bastard's got to be stopped. Somehow . . ."

Suddenly Phillip stood, a white line of determination circling his mouth. He tugged on the tails of his coat and adjusted his trousers over his thin frame. "You're right, Reese. As long as we bow down to him, he's only going to get stronger and more unscrupulous. Something has to be done. If we band together, he can't ruin us all, can he?"

The fight slowly drained out of his clear blue eyes, and his pale face turned gray. Reese clapped him lightly on the back.

"I just don't know, Phillip. But you don't have to take the chance. I'll figure something out."

"Well, there might not be much I can do about Symmons, but one thing's for damn sure. I want that stud, and he can't stop me from buying him from you. It won't help much, I realize, but maybe if I stand up to him others will follow."

"Are you sure, Phillip? I may just go down on this one. I'd hate like hell to take my friends with me."

"And I'd hate like hell to see Samuel with that stud. No, I've made up my mind. I'll take the horse."

"I'll draw up a bill of sale," Reese said, going back around the desk and snatching up paper and pen before the little man's brief flash of courage deserted him once more. "You won't be sorry—he's a champion."

"Oh, I know that," Phillip said, taking the paper Reese handed him and tucking it into his pocket. "I'll have a bank draft drawn up today, and I'll be back to pick up the horse in the morning."

"Would you like to walk out to the stables and see him again before you go?"

Patience left the kitchen and crossed the yard, a basket of fresh fruit and pastries over her arm. Ma had prepared the basket for one of the older slaves who'd been suffering from a bout of severe bursitis and Patience had offered to deliver it to the woman.

She stopped beside a large oak and watched Reese and another man walk toward the stables and go inside. She paused for a moment as a host of feelings swept over her.

For three weeks, she and Reese had managed to pretend nothing had happened between them. They'd kept to their routine of dining together and spending evenings in the parlor. But conversation was stilted now. Always the carefully banked embers of their passion simmered just beneath the surface of cordiality.

Reese refused to discuss the emotions that had nearly carried them both away. He preferred to act as though he'd never kissed her mindless, or touched her until her body screamed out in need.

But Patience would never forget the moments she'd spent in his arms. Each time she saw him, her heart raced out of control. When he spoke, she couldn't take her eyes off the lips that had promised so much pleasure.

Stepping slowly toward the quarters, she shook her head, then sighed deeply. Would he ever realize they were meant to be together? Couldn't he see that nothing mattered except the love they shared?

Oh, he'd never actually said he loved her, but she knew he did. He was just too stubborn and honorable to admit it when he thought he had nothing to offer her.

Samuel's deadline loomed before them, and Patience knew he'd had no luck raising the money Symmons demanded. Soon Reese would have to face the truth and, she hoped, accept her offer.

She had a few qualms about marrying him under such peculiar circumstances, but she felt sure he would come to see it was the best solution in the long run.

After delivering the basket and visiting for a minute with the old woman she'd come to know and like, she made her way back to the house. Reese was just waving good-bye to the thin blond man he'd been shut up in the study with all morning.

Patience ambled over to him, watching a trail of dust follow the visitor down the long drive.

"How did your business go?"

"Better than I expected," he said, not realizing that he'd gotten so comfortable with her that he didn't even pause before answering.

Patience noticed, though, and she felt a lightness ease her doubts. Reese shared everything with her—everything, except his passion. In every other way, they were almost like a married couple already. Why couldn't he see he was only denying both of them the fulfillment of a true union?

"Well, you seem pleased. What did you two have your heads together about?"

"He bought my horse."

Whirling to face him, Patience gasped and clapped a hand to her chest. "Your horse?"

He nodded, still staring down the tree-lined drive.

"But you love that horse." Just how she knew that, she couldn't have said. She'd seen him ride the animal and tend him in the evenings. But it was more than that. The man and the horse seemed to have a special bond, a oneness she'd noticed and envied when Reese rode.

He looked down at her and grinned crookedly. "What makes you say that? He's just a horse. There are several other horses in the stables I can use."

"But—but that was *your* horse. He was special."

"Yeah, and tomorrow I'll have a bank draft showing just how special."

He nodded at her and turned, taking the porch steps two at a time. Without a backward glance, he went into the house and closed the door.

Had she been mistaken about the attachment between Reese and the animal? She would never have thought he'd sell the purebred. Could she be wrong about other things as well? Like the way

Reese felt about her? After their encounter, she'd felt certain he loved her as much as she loved him. It was the only thing that allowed her to go ahead with her plan to marry him. But if she were wrong, and all he felt for her was desire, as he'd said, could she continue to hope he would change his mind and accept her offer?

She went quietly into the house, still lost in her troublesome thoughts. As she passed the dining room, she stopped. Standing before the long windows facing the east side of the property, Reese stared out at the stables in the distance. A pensive look filled his eyes.

Patience ached to go to him, to tell him not to sell the animal if it brought him such pain. But she knew he didn't want her to know how losing the horse affected him. She tiptoed silently away.

The sun had recently set—the days were getting shorter already—when they sat down to supper. Patience had changed into the lavender blouse, lapis skirt, and tapestry vest. Her hair was once again in a loose topknot. Reese looked deliciously handsome in black frock coat and trousers, with the traditional white shirt and cravat.

But the shadow had not left his eyes. Patience wished there was something she could do to ease his burden, but this was one time he didn't want her help. He needed to beat Symmons on his own. She didn't understand his feelings, but she'd decided to respect them nonetheless.

Each of them picked at one course after another until Ma Jewel herself came into the dining room.

"Somethin' wrong with the food tonight?" she

demanded, slapping meaty fists on her hips.

Patience sat straight, spooning a bite of cobbler into her mouth. She shook her head and swallowed. Everything tasted like old paper. She couldn't even tell what filling had been used in the dessert, but she forced a smile for Ma's benefit.

Reese just shook his head and pushed the dish aside.

Ma clucked her tongue and went off mumbling beneath her breath. Patience set her spoon aside and dabbed her mouth with her napkin.

"Why don't we play a game of chess, Reese? You beat me the last time, and I'd like a chance to get even."

At first he didn't respond, and she thought he hadn't heard her. Then he stood, pushing his chair back. "Not tonight, Patience. I've got work to finish."

She rose to her feet. "We could just talk for a while if you'd like."

He glanced at her across the table and smiled briefly. "Another time," he said, but she noticed that the smile didn't reach his eyes.

Reese didn't want Patience to know the true depth of his concern. Only a week remained until the deadline Samuel had given him. And he hadn't come up with a fraction of the money he owed. He'd spent days, weeks, selling everything he could find a buyer for. But it would never be enough. He'd known that from the beginning, but he'd had to do something, anything to keep from feeling totally helpless.

He touched Patience's shoulder and offered her

a reassuring smile as he passed her. He should accept her invitation to a chess match. Maybe it would take his mind off the decision he'd made earlier that day.

After putting off the inevitable as long as he could, he'd come to the conclusion that he would have to mortgage Bonne Chance.

It wasn't an idea he relished, and not just because he knew how disappointed his father would have been at the prospect of a bank holding the title to his beloved home. Reese feared that Samuel would somehow get his hands on the note and then he would have no way of stopping the bastard.

As he reached the main hall, a knock sounded at the front door. He called out to Ma that he'd see who it was, then went to the door and pulled it open.

"Rita?"

"Hello, Reese. May I come in?"

Stepping aside, he held the door open for her, then took her hat and gloves as she removed them and placed them on the parson's bench.

"What are you doing out here at this time of night?"

She grinned crookedly up at him and rose on tiptoe to place a kiss on his cheek. "Don't you mean, what am I doing here at all?"

She glanced past him, and the smile faded from her face. Her eyes widened in surprise, and a flash of green fire lit her gaze.

"Well, this must be James's daughter. Reese,

you didn't tell me she was so damned young—and flawless."

He could see the hint of envy she tried to hide behind the light reprimand. Her gaze slid slowly down Patience's form, as though memorizing every detail. A strained look crossed her attractive face before she forced a bright smile and took a step forward.

"How do you do, Miss Bentley. I'm sorry to disturb you at this time of night."

"Patience," Reese cut in, remembering his manners. "This is Rita Mallory. She—um, knew your father."

Patience stared from Reese's uncomfortable countenance to the twinge of sadness in the woman's bright green eyes. Dressed in a traveling suit of forest-green serge, the auburn beauty was stunning, Patience had to admit. Not even the slight hardness around the full red lips or the tiny lines at the corners of her eyes could detract from her loveliness.

It took her a moment to realize that Rita Mallory was extending her hand. Clearing her throat nervously, Patience accepted the greeting.

"I need to speak with you right away, Reese," Rita said, turning back to him in her urgency.

He glanced around and motioned to the parlor. "Come in, please."

Patience made to follow and he stepped in front of her. "Patience, if you'll excuse us for a moment."

She opened her mouth to protest, then closed it and nodded. "Of course."

He followed Rita into the parlor and closed the

large double doors behind them. Patience stood still for a minute, battling her own bout with jealousy. Who was the woman? And why had she come to see Reese so late in the evening? And why did Patience get the feeling they were more than friends?

She took one step toward the doors. Leaning close, she could hear muffled voices coming from inside. Ashamed at her devious behavior, she whirled on her heel and went to find Ma Jewel.

"Rita, what are you doing—"

"She's fabulous, Reese. Beautiful and gracious."

"What? Who? Patience?" He glanced guiltily toward the doors. Blinking away his shock, he strode to the sidebar. "Would you like a drink?" he asked, ignoring her comment.

"Yes—a good, strong one."

He nodded. "Well, you didn't come all this way to get a glimpse of my ward, did you?"

He poured her a drink and handed it to her. She glanced at his empty hands, and her eyes widened in astonishment. Quirking a brow at his brusque manner, she lifted her glass toward him. "Still not drinking?"

"You didn't come all this way to discuss my thirst, either, Rita. What is it?"

"Trouble," she snapped. "Maybe more than you can handle this time."

"I've got all I can handle right here. What the devil has happened now?"

"Did you know James had a brother?"

He nodded. "In England, yes. James said he was

a duke or an earl or something."

"A titled Englishman, yes," she said, facing him squarely, "but not in England. He's right here in Mobile."

"The hell you say. James hadn't seen his brother since he left England over twenty-five years ago. Why would he come here now?"

"Apparently he sailed to Boston when he received word of James's death. Somehow he learned Patience was here. He just showed up two days ago."

"How is it you know all this?"

"I have a new friend who's a barrister—or rather a lawyer, as they call them here."

Reese glanced sideways and noticed that Rita's eyes were fixed on the amber liquid in her glass. He understood the implications of her admission and realized that after the years of association they'd shared, he should feel angry or jealous.

He didn't. In fact, he felt slightly relieved and that added to the ever-increasing guilt he carried.

Pressing his thumb and forefinger against his closed eyes, he slowly shook his head. "And just what did your friend tell you?" he asked.

Rita set her drink aside and met Reese's questioning gaze. "James's brother has come to Mobile to challenge James's will." Her expression held sympathy and a hint of protectiveness. "He's petitioning Judge Carson to overturn the directive naming you executor of the estate and guardian of his niece."

"He can't do that. James's attorney told me the will was ironclad. If I had refused guardianship,

Patience would have become a ward of the state. James never made any mention of his English relations at all."

Reese strode briskly to the sidebar and hungrily eyed the liquor in the cut-glass whiskey decanter. "James made his wishes clear. How can this man—this stranger—hope to overturn that?"

Again Rita's gaze dropped. Reese's confidence spiraled downward with it, and a feather of foreboding skimmed along his spine.

"He's using your reputation and the unorthodox relationship you shared with James to claim you're an unfit custodian for a young girl. Especially a beautiful young girl, with a rather large inheritance."

"Dammit, that son of a bitch," Reese bellowed, causing Rita to start. "Who does he think he is? He can't just sail in here after all these years and start saying what is right for Patience. He doesn't know anything about her. Besides, whatever his reasons, James chose me to look after his daughter. And I'll be damned if I'll let him down again."

"What do you intend to do, Reese? The man is Patience's uncle."

"I don't care who he is. James sent her here, to me. And this is where she's going to stay. I'll fight him in court if I have to."

Rita arched her brows and nodded slowly. The sad smile said she'd known all along he would.

"I hired a carriage," she told him. "You can ride back with me."

"Tonight?"

She went to the parlor doors and pulled them

open as he continued to stand in place in the middle of the room.

"Tonight," she said, collecting her gloves and hat from the parson's bench. "He has an audience with the judge in the morning."

Chapter Nineteen

Three people climbed from the carriage in front of the Mobile County courthouse. A cream-colored stone building three stories high, it had a triangular set of steps stretching across the entire front and two massive carved lions standing guard at either end.

Patience bit the corner of her lip and stared up at the imposing beasts. Inside that building lay her fate.

Reese had called her into the parlor the night before and related the news of her uncle's appearance. He explained that he would honor her wishes if she decided to go with the Englishman.

Of course she'd been horrified at the prospect. As much as she'd despised moving South to Bonne Chance, she couldn't imagine anything worse than leaving now.

Especially to go to a strange country with a man who'd never been anything more to her than a name inside the cover of a Bible.

"Patience, are you ready?"

She blinked and met his tense gaze. He hadn't argued with her when she'd insisted on accompanying him to Mobile. He'd understood her need to have a say in what became of her this time. His only hesitation had come when they'd returned to the main hall, where the auburn-haired woman waited.

Patience decided right then that it didn't matter who, or what, Rita Mallory had been. She'd come to warn Reese and to help Patience. She instantly became a friend.

"I'm as ready as I'll ever be," she finally answered.

They walked up the steps and into the dim hall of the building. Doors opened off either side of the hall. They hurried along, their heels tapping loudly on the marble floor, until they came to the door they sought. Painted in neat block letters on the frosted glass panel was Judge Carson's name.

Patience heard Reese draw a deep breath before raising his hand to knock. A rotund man in a snug vest and tiny round spectacles answered the summons.

"We're here to see Judge Carson," Reese said.

The man smiled amiably. "I'm afraid the judge is engaged at present, but if you'd like to make an appointment . . ."

"We don't need an appointment," Reese told him, pushing into the anteroom.

"But—but the Judge has another appointment with him right now," the man stammered as Patience followed Reese toward the double doors on the other side of the room. Rita hung back slightly, reluctant to interfere.

"You can't go in there."

"Watch me," Reese warned.

"You haven't been announced," the man sputtered.

"We don't need announcing, either," he said, taking Patience's hand as he burst through the inner doors.

Three heads snapped up at their entrance, and Patience quickly scanned the occupants of the room. The judge sat behind his desk in a dark suit, his balding pate beaded with sweat. A young man in a drab, slightly threadbare suit sat poised over a pad of paper, pen in hand.

Patience's gaze went to the third person present, and her breath caught in her throat. Pain sliced through her heart and she gasped.

"Oh, Reese," she whispered throatily.

Glancing up, she saw that his face had gone white. His hands clenched at his sides and a look of anguished regret flooded his face.

Without thinking, she reached out and took his hand. Her uncle's eyes caught the motion, and the corners of his mouth turned down sharply, diminishing, albeit slightly, the uncanny resemblance he bore to her father.

"You were twins," she heard Reese mutter.

"Born eight minutes apart," her uncle acknowledged with a satisfied nod.

Dear God, this was going to be harder than she'd ever imagined. Despite her love for Reese, she wanted to go to the man who'd come across an ocean to claim her. She wanted to feel his arms close around her the way her father's used to. She wanted to hear him say her name and imagine, for a moment, that it was her father's loving voice she heard.

She realized in that instant that even if her father had never been very conscientious, he had loved her. Very much. Enough that she now sought a stranger's touch for one last chance to hold on to her father.

She heard Reese breathe a curse beside her, and she whipped around to face him. His expression echoed her thoughts. This meeting was going to be more difficult than either of them expected.

"What is the meaning of this?" the judge demanded, darting confused looks between her, Reese, and her uncle. Patience realized that the whole encounter had lasted only seconds. It had seemed eternal.

Reese looked at her, a question in his stare. After only a minute pause, she nodded.

"We have business here, your honor," Reese said.

"I'm busy right now. You'll have to come back later." He waved a hand, and Patience turned to see the flustered assistant standing in the doorway behind them.

"I tried to stop them, Judge Carson," the little man told him defensively.

"We have business with *this* hearing, your

honor," Reese reiterated, planting his feet as though to indicate that he wouldn't be moved without force.

Judge Carson looked at the man seated in front of his desk. "Do you know these people?"

"I believe the woman is my niece, Patience Bentley."

Patience nodded slightly.

"Then that would make this man Reese Ashburn, your honor. The man my brother imprudently named executor of his will and guardian of my niece."

The judge rubbed a hand over his chin and made a sucking sound through his teeth as he studied the new arrivals. "I see," was all he said.

"Your honor, since this hearing is to determine Miss Bentley's fate, she would like the opportunity to address the court. And since I understand my character is in question, I feel I have a right to answer the charges against me."

"This isn't a trial, son," the judge told him. "You don't have any rights here except the ones I see fit to give you."

"Wait just a damn minute . . ." Reese said, stepping forward.

The judge held up his hand. "I didn't say you wouldn't be allowed to have your say. I'm just telling you the way it is. This is a hearing to determine if there's just cause for Mr. Bentley's case to be put before the courts. Don't wreck your chances before you even get started," he warned, a slight twinkle in his eye.

Patience gripped his elbow and Reese backed

off a fraction. But his spine remained rigid and his jaw set harshly.

"Bentley's presented quite a case already," the judge said, shuffling pages. "Letters from respected citizens, businessmen you owe money to, even the chief of police. Seems you had yourself quite a bacchanalia these past few months."

Reese stiffened and his arm snapped from her grasp. Her fingernails scraped his coat sleeve as she struggled to regain her hold, but he didn't notice.

"Mr. Ashburn was very upset about my father's death, your honor," Patience spoke up quickly.

"Yes," the judge said, glancing at the pages before him. "A murder you claimed—according to the chief—that you were responsible for?"

Patience couldn't hold back the gasp that escaped her suddenly dry lips. Reese shot her a wounded look, and she instantly regretted her reaction.

"I felt responsible because it had been my idea to go to the King's Inn tavern that night," Reese explained. He hated defending himself, but that was, after all, what he'd come here to do. And he'd swallow what was left of his pride if it meant Patience would stay with him.

He'd gotten quite a shock when he'd seen Albert Bentley. For a second, he'd been terrified that Patience would forget her desire to stay in Mobile. The man looked so much like James that Reese had feared she'd instinctively go to him.

When she hadn't, clutching his hand and offering him comfort instead, he'd been certain they were doing the right thing. He'd stand emotionally naked before the judge and meet whatever accusations Albert Bentley made against him.

"Yes," the judge said, eyeing the paper he held. "He did say that was your reasoning."

Reese knew then that the man had pushed him to see how he would react. At least the judge hadn't made his decision yet. There was still a chance he would be fair and impartial—if Reese could hold his temper and present himself as a suitable guardian with Patience's best interest at heart.

It wouldn't be easy. The thought of losing her, possibly never seeing her again, made him tremble with fear. And that made him realize how much he truly loved her—enough to want the very best for her, even if that meant not staying with him. He had a split second of doubt. Then he met her eyes. She smiled softly, and his uncertainty melted like a snowball in summer.

"Judge Carson," Reese began calmly, "James Bentley was my best friend. He was more than that. He was my mentor, a father figure, the one person in the world I looked up to and trusted. He knew me better than anyone. And he named me executor of his will and guardian of his daughter. Now since Mr. Bentley hasn't claimed that his brother was coerced or mentally unstable, I say James's decision should stand unopposed. It was, after all, his choice. And he chose me."

"I am this girl's flesh-and-blood relation," Albert spoke up. "No one could be a better custodian for Patience than her own family."

"A family she hasn't seen or heard from in her entire life," Reese pointed out. "She didn't know anything about you, except to know of your existence."

"That doesn't change the fact that I'm her only living relative. She should be with me."

"Why now? You never visited James while he was alive. He certainly never spoke of you with any fondness. Why don't you tell us why your own brother didn't name you executor? Perhaps that is the key point of all this."

"We had a falling-out years ago. I can only assume James thought I wouldn't agree to take over his responsibilities—a misconception, I assure you, your honor. I loved my brother, and I longed for a reconciliation. I was devastated by the news of his death."

"But the fact remains, you didn't come to America at any time in the past to seek this reconciliation you claim you wanted. You only came after you knew he was dead."

Reese turned to the judge, who'd remained silent throughout the exchange. "Your honor, how do we know Mr. Bentley isn't here now to claim his niece's inheritance for his own selfish or devious reasons? Shouldn't you check into his finances and character as well, if those are to be important issues in this case?"

"Now, see here—" Albert Bentley stormed, jumping from his seat.

"Settle down, gentlemen," the judge warned. "We don't have the time or the resources for that kind of investigation, Mr. Ashburn. That will have to be addressed in a formal court hearing. *If* I determine one is necessary."

"Your honor," Albert said, his tone wheedling and patronizing. "I've got a document here from a local banker who says Reese Ashburn is in danger of losing his plantation." He waited while the judge sifted through the stack of papers. "I honestly believe Ashburn's only interest is in my niece's fortune, not her well-being."

"That's not true," Patience cut in vehemently. "I offered to give him the money he needed to save Bonne Chance, and he turned me down."

Her gaze swept the room, and her heart sank. The judge's eyebrows were up where his hairline should have been, if he'd had one. Her uncle was smiling gleefully, and Reese looked as if he'd been spoon-fed glass.

"Oh, no," she stammered. "You don't understand. That isn't what I meant."

"I think we all understand perfectly," Albert said. "Your honor, this proves my point."

"Rubbish," Patience snapped. "How does that prove anything? I told you, he refused. If he was after the money, why didn't he take it?"

"The oldest trick known to man," her uncle told her, as though speaking to a backward child. "So you'd have to convince him. To make you think it had all been your idea."

"It *was* my idea," she spat angrily.

Bentley sat back in his chair and clasped his fingers together over his protruding middle, a self-satisfied smirk on his face.

Patience realized quickly that she was out of her

element. If she'd thought herself articulate, she'd discovered from which side of her family the talent originated. Her uncle made her look like a naive, unsophisticated innocent taken in by the charms of her worldly guardian.

Reese stepped in, once more stating that James's will had made his wishes clear. Patience saw the judge's gaze wander to the documents on his desk, and her uncle continued to look pleased. Desperate to correct the blunder she'd made, she backed out the door and into the anteroom.

Rita was seated on a tufted sofa, thumbing through a periodical. She sat up as she took in the look on Patience's face.

"You've got to do something," Patience said urgently. "I've really made a mess of things in there."

Rita blinked in surprise. "Me? What can I do? I don't know anything about the law or the legal system. Patience, my God, I'm Reese's—"

"I don't care," Patience cut her off shortly. "You're the only one who doesn't have a vested interest in this case. Maybe the judge will see you as an impartial witness. I know it's a gamble, but we've got to try."

Rita chewed her lip for a long moment, then shrugged. "Sure, if you insist."

She followed Patience back into the judge's chambers, and Patience closed the door behind them. As she turned around, she froze. All eyes in the room were focused on her, wide and disbelieving.

"This is Miss Mallory," Patience murmured,

wondering too late if she'd just made things worse for Reese. "I asked her to join us."

"Why?" Reese asked through his teeth.

"Because I know you so well, darling," Rita interjected, her accent heavy as thick syrup. She sashayed into the room, and Patience's jaw dropped. The men's eyes lowered to Rita's hips as they swayed suggestively. The clerk taking notes dropped his pen.

"You—you're a friend of Mister Ashburn's?" the judge stuttered.

"The best kind of friend," Rita told him, her tongue teasing the corners of her rosy lips.

Patience swallowed a hard knot of despair and noticed Albert's and the judge's throats working simultaneously.

"I think," Rita said, leaning low over the judge's desk, "that you might want to ask Miss Bentley to wait outside for a moment."

Albert snapped out of the trance Rita's entrance had held him in. He cleared his throat. "Your honor, Mr. Ashburn said my niece had every right to be here to hear the testimony. I say she should stay and listen to whatever this woman has to say."

Reese cut a scathing glance at Albert.

"If you have something to add to these proceedings, Miss Mallory," Carson said, "let's hear it. I haven't got all day, and this is beginning to look like it's going to get complicated."

"I've known Mr. Ashburn for several years," Rita said, boldly meeting the judge's gaze. "He came to visit me just a few weeks ago," she added, glancing at Reese.

"That's fascinating," Judge Carson said, a light of interest in his eyes. "But what does that have to do with this?" He indicated the tableau around him.

"Reese was very upset. We talked a while. He told me that Patience Bentley was a spoiled brat who tried his patience at every turn. She bedeviled him unbelievably."

Reese rubbed his hand over his eyes and mouth, shaking his head.

Patience took a deep breath to cover the pang of distress seeping through her stomach. Despair almost overcame her reason, but she stood calmly, even though Rita's words sliced through her soul.

Had Reese said such things about her to Rita? Or was Rita just trying to help their case in her own odd way?

"So why would he fight to keep her with him now?" Albert asked, his tone indicating that he knew the answer.

"That's what I asked him," Rita said. "And do you know what he told me?"

Her question had been directed to the judge, and he leaned in close, the beads of sweat on his crown increasing. "No," he said. "What?"

"He said James was counting on him to take care of Patience. Reese loved James like a father. James knew Reese would care for his daughter with everything that was in him. And Reese said he wouldn't let James down. He intended to do right by the girl, no matter how much of a trial she was."

The judge nodded, his eyes fastened to Rita's supplicating expression.

"By the by," she added, shooting a desperate look at Reese's and Patience's hopeful expressions. "You don't have to worry about his reputation as a lady's man. She isn't exactly his type."

Patience couldn't contain her gasp of surprise at the insult. Despite knowing what Rita was trying to do, she colored fiercely.

The judge suddenly directed his gaze at her, and she struggled to cover her reaction. Again, his bushy eyebrows climbed high on his forehead.

"Thank you, Miss Mallory," he said dismissively. "If that's all . . . ?"

"Yeah, I guess that's about it," Rita admitted ruefully. She turned and faced Patience, her back to the judge and Albert. She shrugged helplessly, as if to say she'd done her best, and walked out.

As the door clicked shut behind her, Patience jumped. The small noise sounded like a gunshot in the silence of the room.

"Miss Bentley."

Clearing her throat, Patience answered the judge. "Yes, your honor?"

"Before Miss Mallory's—interesting testimony, you said you offered Mister Ashburn the money he needed to save his plantation?"

She glanced toward Reese and nodded. "Yes, I did."

"And you went out there and collected that woman to speak on Mister Ashburn's behalf just now, didn't you?"

She nodded again.

"Why did you do those things, Miss Bentley?"

Patience couldn't look at Reese this time. She didn't know if she could stand to see his face when she answered the judge's question. For one brief second she considered lying.

But something told her the judge would recognize dishonesty. She swallowed the last shreds of her pride.

"Because," she said, lifting her chin defiantly, "I love him."

Chapter Twenty

"Thank you, Miss Bentley. That will be all. Please wait outside," Carson said.

"But your honor . . ."

"Outside, Miss Bentley. You, too, Jonas," he told the clerk taking notes. The secretary laid his pen aside and hastily departed the judge's inner sanctum.

Patience stood rooted to the floor for a full minute, her expression incredulous. Judge Carson arched a thick brow and tipped his head toward the door. Finally, she turned and left the room, closing the door behind her.

"It's obvious that Mr. Ashburn has used his charm to seduce my niece," Bentley chimed in, "in the hopes she would do exactly what she did—become infatuated with him and offer him her fortune."

"I'm warning you, Bentley, if you say that one more time, I'll put my fist through your face."

"Mr. Ashburn, please remain calm," Carson warned.

"If you don't mind, your honor," Reese continued, not daunted by the admonition, "I have a few things I'd like to say."

"Go right ahead."

"First of all, I never seduced Patience. Not for money or any other reason. I didn't even know how she felt until a minute ago." He forced himself to keep the joy and love he felt from showing on his face. But Patience's admission secretly thrilled him.

He cleared the emotion from his throat and continued. "Bentley is her only living relative, as he's been quick to point out. But he didn't even speak to her when she came into the room. There was no long, tender embrace. No comforting words on the loss of her father."

"I'm not the one under scrutiny here, Ashburn."

"Maybe you should be, Bentley. If you thought I had truly seduced your niece, you should be demanding I do the honorable thing and marry her. But you're not, are you? You're still trying to get her away from here. Well, I say you can't have it both ways."

He turned to Carson. "Judge, if you believe that Patience has been compromised, then it should be your responsibility to make sure I do right by her. However, if you believe me when I say I have never done anything to harm Patience, or endanger her in any way, then you have to agree I've been a satisfactory guardian. Again, it comes down to James's wishes regarding his daughter."

"That's ludicrous, your honor," Bentley objected strenuously. "If you allowed this man to marry my niece, you'd be falling right in with his nefarious plans to get his hands on her fortune."

"Bentley, we haven't established that Mr. Ashburn has any nefarious plans. Certainly the girl doesn't seem any the worse for her stay with him."

"She's a child, Judge Carson. She can't be expected to comprehend the intentions of someone with Ashburn's infamous experience."

The judge rifled the pages on his desk and hurrumphed loudly. "She's nearly twenty, not so much a child as a young woman. My own daughter is nearly that age, and she has a very intelligent head on her shoulders. Paula certainly would know a charlatan if she met one, even if he wore the disguise of a paragon."

He twisted his mouth, perusing the documents for another moment. Then he looked up and pierced Bentley with a firm stare. "You may step outside also, Mr. Bentley."

"Now see here, Carson," the man sputtered, "I am a baron with considerable influence in England . . ."

"Well, we're not in England, *Mister* Bentley, and I don't give a fig about your fancy titles. This is my domain, and I have all the power here. Now step outside."

Bentley had no choice but to do as the judge commanded. He cut Reese a fierce glare as he passed, but Reese ignored him. His attention was focused on the judge who held his and Patience's future in his hands.

The door slammed once more, and Judge Carson shoved aside the papers he'd been scrutinizing. "Now then, that just leaves us, Ashburn. Tell me, how do you feel about your ward?"

Reese opened his mouth to answer, then closed it again. He felt foolish, standing speechless when he'd been making speeches only moments ago. But what could he say? How could he explain to this man what Patience had come to mean to him? What she had meant to him before he'd ever met her?

"I'm very concerned with Patience's welfare," he said properly.

"Cut the crap, boy. That pompous continental windbag has been blowing hot air all over my chambers since I came in this morning. I haven't even had a chance to read my newspaper today. So don't squander any more of my time or patience. She said she loved you. What have you got to say for yourself?"

"I care very deeply for Miss Bentley," Reese hesitantly admitted. "Of course, I realize I'm not the sort—"

"Stop hemming and hawing. Has anything untoward happened between you two? And don't lie to me—I'll know if you do."

Reese resented the old man's attitude, but knew better than to rile him. Like it or not, Judge Carson held all the cards, and Reese had been a gambler too long not to know when to bluff and when to call.

"We've shared a few kisses," he said.

"Uh, huh," the judge muttered. "That all?"

"Dammit, she hasn't been compromised. I've already told you that. Despite my past escapades, I respect Patience Bentley, as I respected her father."

"I can see that," the judge told him, waving his answer away like an annoying fly. "What I'm asking is if you love her."

Reese wasn't ready to announce his feelings aloud. They were too new, too confusing. He wanted to hide his emotions away where he couldn't be hurt by them—or hurt anyone else until he sorted them out.

But the voice of reason spoke, telling him he would have to declare his feelings or renounce them. And his decision would determine what happened to Patience.

He raked both hands through his hair, plastering it against the sides of his head. He went to the chair Albert had vacated and slumped into it.

"Yes, I love her."

"You don't seem too pleased with the fact," the judge observed.

"Bentley was right, you know," Reese told him. "I haven't done much in my life that would make me a prime choice for a young woman's guardian." His head came up and a fire of determination lit in his eye. "But I've made an effort since Patience came to live with me, your honor. I've quit drinking and quit gambling. Hell, the night I spent with Rita, all we did was talk. I swear. I slept on her sofa. I've taken over the running of Bonne

Chance, my plantation. I'm honestly trying to live up to James's expectations, whatever they were."

"Pshaw, you've been as righteous as a Baptist preacher, boy. And if you don't mind my saying so, just as boring. I think I liked you better when you were a hell-raiser."

Reese saw the twinkle in the wrinkled brown eyes and laughed lightly. "Yeah, so did I. Being noble is damned hard work."

The judge grinned and nodded his balding head. "So you're not out to seduce Miss Bentley, or steal her fortune to pay off your debts. Say I believe you. What are we gonna do about the fop?"

Remembering how he used to call James the same thing, a hint of sadness drifted over Reese. It had been a term of affection between them. But despite the fact that he looked so much like James, Reese felt nothing but contempt for Albert Bentley.

"I want what's best for Patience, your honor. If I thought that meant sending her with Bentley, I'd do it in a minute." It would tear his heart out, rip his soul apart, but he would do it. "I think she should stay here."

"I agree," Carson said frankly. "I'm a pretty good judge of character, and I see a lot less to concern me in yours than I do in the baron's." He drawled the last word, making it sound like an insult. "But the fact remains, he's the girl's uncle. I'd like to nip this whole matter in the bud right now."

"Nothing would make me happier."

"Good, then we're agreed. You'll marry her."

"I'll what?"

"Marry her. It's the only way to end Bentley's claim. Once you're married, he'll have nothing more to say about it."

"I can't," Reese told him, squarely meeting the judge's gaze.

"Why not? You haven't done something foolish like getting yourself engaged to that Mallory chit, have you?"

"No, it's nothing like that. Bentley told you, I'm deeply in debt. There's a very real possibility that I'll lose Bonne Chance. I don't think that's what James had in mind for his daughter when he sent her to me."

"Horse hockey. Her father trusted you to do what was best for the girl. You said yourself, you've made an effort to straighten out. So you've made some mistakes. So have we all. Live with it. Go on, and don't make the same ones again. If you still don't feel like you're good enough for her, go out and do something worthy.

"But hear this," he said solemnly, leaning in closer. "If you don't marry her now, Bentley stands a very good chance of getting his hands on Patience and her money."

Reese's mind spun with confusing thoughts and feelings. How could he marry Patience when he had nothing but a tainted past and a bankrupt plantation to offer her? What kind of future would he be sentencing her to? Certainly not the kind she'd have as the niece of a baron.

But how could he let her go? She didn't want to go with Bentley—she'd said so. She'd also said she loved him, something he hadn't had adequate time or privacy to thoroughly think through. He'd admitted he loved her, something he'd known and agonized over for weeks.

But to marry her. That was forever—at least it would be for him. If his parents had given him one thing in his life, it was to show him the true meaning of love and marriage. They'd shared everything, every moment. They'd lived, and died, for one another. And that's the way it would be if—when—he married.

"Get on with it, boy. No time for sitting on the fence."

Reese thought about what the judge had said. He wasn't worthy of Patience now. But maybe he could be. He'd changed in the past months. With a little work, he could be a man her father would have been proud to call his son-in-law.

A warmth spread through Reese's veins. He could almost hear James laughing at the irony. It was the sort of twist of fate his old friend would have appreciated.

"All right," he finally said, nodding his head with more exuberance than he truly felt. "If," he added sternly, "Patience agrees."

"Of course, of course," Carson said, going to the door. "I wasn't planning a shotgun wedding, you know."

Reese had to chuckle at the man's demeanor. You wouldn't know to look at Carson that he'd just decided the fate of a room full of people. Or that he was about to face a thwarted English baron.

"Ya'll get back in here," the judge said, motioning to all the occupants of the anteroom. "Jonas,

Sullivan, ya'll better come, too."

The secretary and the assistant looked at one another and shrugged, apparently accustomed to the old man's odd ways. Five confused and curious faces gathered in the judge's chambers. Carson went behind his desk again and shuffled papers around until he found a small black book.

"It seems we're going to have a wedding," he announced, thumbing the pages for the right section. "Ah, here it is," he trumpeted.

"What the devil are you talking about?" Bentley demanded. He stiffened hostilely, his chest puffed out with outrage.

"Ashburn here confessed to a slight indiscretion with your niece, Bentley," Carson told him offhandedly. "And I'm sure you'll agree that the only proper thing to do about it is for him to wed her."

"I certainly would not agree!" Albert bellowed. "She belongs with me. I'm entitled."

The judge's head snapped up, and his soft brown eyes hardened with fury. "That's a mighty strange way to put it, Bentley. If I didn't know better, I'd wonder if you were talking about your niece or her money."

"I—of course I'm talking about Patience. You can't mean to go through with this travesty."

"Miss Bentley," the judge said, smiling kindly at Patience, "do you have any objections to marrying Ashburn?"

Patience blinked dazedly. "Reese?" she called, her voice small and unsure.

"I'd be honored if you'd have me, Patience."

"I won't stand for this outrage!" Bentley shouted.

"Then I'll toss your butt out," the judge told him. "Now shut up or I'll hold you in contempt of these proceedings. Miss Bentley?"

Patience nodded quickly, her eyes never leaving Reese. What was he thinking? Was he angry? Had the judge forced him to marry her? What, exactly, had he told Judge Carson about what had gone on between them?

All the unanswered questions should have put a damper on her joy, but they couldn't. For whatever reason, Reese had agreed to marry her. Right here, right now. Today would be her wedding day. Tonight, her wedding night.

She should be worried about what she was wearing or how her hair looked. But she didn't care. All that mattered was that she would soon be Reese's wife.

"Bentley, you and Miss Mallory can serve as witnesses."

"I'll do no such thing," Albert hissed. "You can't get away with this. My barrister will see to that."

He slammed out the door without giving Patience or the other occupants of the room a second glance.

Carson hurrumphed and scratched his shiny pate. "Just as I thought. Ah, well, Sullivan, you'll do just as well. Get up here."

"Yes, sir," the little man chirped, stepping forward with enthusiasm.

"Miss Mallory, you don't have any objections to this marriage, or know of any reason why it shouldn't take place, do you?"

Reese and Patience turned simultaneously to see Rita standing by the chamber door. Her eyes were damp, her lips dry. Her pearly complexion looked pallid.

She stared at Reese for an interminable moment, then smiled. He took a step toward her, holding out his hand.

At Rita's smile, a synchronous sigh of relief swept the room. Placing a congratulatory kiss on Reese's cheek, she came forward to stand next to Patience.

"No, your honor. I don't have any objections."

"Thank God. Then let's get this over with before Bentley has the whole damned Chancery Court down on our heads."

The group shared a brief, light moment as the judge looked over his book.

"Let's see now," he began, flipping pages.

Reese moved closer to Patience and took her cold hand in his. She glanced up earnestly, a thousand questions in her clear blue eyes.

Reese had no answers for her. Although he felt right about what he was doing, he still felt woefully inadequate for someone like her.

In the end, he simply turned silently toward the judge without uttering the words she seemed to need to hear.

Chapter Twenty-one

Judge Carson shuffled them all out as soon as the ceremony concluded. Rita congratulated them and then had Reese hail a cab for her. By mid-morning, Reese and Patience were standing on the steps of the courthouse once more—this time as husband and wife.

"I'll hire a carriage and we can be back at Bonne Chance this afternoon," he told her stiffly. "There's a small restaurant on the corner. You can wait there while I make the arrangements." He took her arm and started along the bricked sidewalk.

Patience made no response. She didn't know what she'd expected. She hadn't had time to actually think about how their first day as a married couple would proceed. But she was sure that if she'd thought about it, she wouldn't have imagined it beginning this way.

Wordlessly, they strolled toward the restaurant. Inside, Reese deposited her at the first table they came to. Tossing some bills onto the table, he told her brusquely, "Order whatever you want. I'll be back."

She watched, openmouthed, as he turned and went back through the door.

Reese crossed the street and hurried toward the livery. His mind whirled with everything that had happened. Dear God, he was married! Married to Patience Bentley.

The enormity of it all left him dazed. He hadn't planned it this way. Oh, he'd thought a lot lately about what it would be like to call Patience wife. But none of his imagery had gone quite the way the actual event had.

What must she be thinking? Was she horrified at what she'd done? Wondering what kind of husband he'd make? Certainly she'd be worried about what he'd expect of her now that they were wed.

She'd said she loved him. But she was such an innocent, she must be frightened and confused. He sped his pace in an effort to get back to her as soon as possible.

Then he paused. Already he couldn't wait to see her again, hold her, touch her. He'd ached for her these last torturous weeks with a need that surpassed anything he'd ever felt—knowing, assuming, he would never fulfill that craving. How in hell would he ever keep his hands off her now that she was his?

Judge Carson's words rang in his ears, blocking out every other thought.

He had to prove his worth before he could truly make Patience his wife in every sense of the word. And to do that, he had two very important tasks before him.

First, he had to save Bonne Chance—their home now—from Symmons. And he had to do it on his own, without a cent of James's money. To do that, Reese had realized earlier that he'd have to mortgage the plantation. Though it grieved him to do it, he knew it was the only way.

Second, and most important, he had to make up to James for what happened at the docks that fateful night. He had to do the very least he could for his friend. And that meant finding James's killers and seeing justice done.

Then, and only then, could he consider himself deserving.

But what would he tell her in the meantime? Would she understand why his honor must take precedence over his passion, his love?

No. She'd try to tell him it didn't matter. And if she ever found out his plans to find James's killer, she'd interfere for sure. If she tried to talk him out of his decisions, would he be strong enough to refuse her?

He knew the answer to that. There'd be no way he could ignore such a temptation. He'd just have to avoid her, stay as far away as he could get until he was ready to take that final step.

It might take a while, but he resolved to make Patience a good husband. And then he intended to make her his wife in every way. The sooner the better.

He quickly made the arrangements for the carriage and driver to take them home. Stopping at the restaurant, he went in to collect Patience. Her frosty glance stopped him in the doorway, and she rose from the table and passed him without a word, making her way to the carriage ahead of him.

Reese frowned. He'd expected apprehension, maybe even pique that he'd made her stay at the restaurant. But she looked ready to explode as she swept by him.

Were her actions only irritation at being left alone? Or was she already regretting her choice, which had actually been no choice at all?

Despite his concern, he knew better than to try to second-guess Patience. She'd kept him off balance since the first moment they met. He wouldn't know why she was upset until she was ready to talk about it.

The ride home passed in a blur of scattered small talk and uncomfortable silences. He tried to draw Patience out, but the more he talked, the quieter she became. The ire he'd detected at the restaurant waned, only to be replaced with a strange sort of melancholy.

Reese wanted to tell her how happy he was that Albert Bentley hadn't been able to take her away. He longed to divulge his pleasure at the unexpected outcome of their encounter with Bentley.

When she offered to marry him in order to save the plantation, he'd immediately refused. But nothing could have made him deny himself the honor of her hand after he'd heard her announce her love for him. With love, he felt certain everything else would somehow work itself out in time.

And he did love her, he thought, glancing sideways at her profile. But if he opened his feelings to her now, he wouldn't stop with telling her how he felt. He knew he'd end up showing her as well. And she deserved better. She deserved the best.

His gaze traveled to the creamy expanse of her neck, where he longed to place his lips tenderly, then lower, to her breasts and her hands clasped in her lap. He noticed her bare ring finger, and regretted not having had his mother's wedding ring when they'd said their vows.

That omission could—would—easily be corrected as soon as they reached the plantation. He wanted to see the familiar gem glowing on her hand. He wanted an outward sign of his good fortune in winning such a prize. He needed the world to know she was his, or would be soon.

His body immediately responded to the brief rumination. He was as eager and erratic as a summer storm. He was thankful he'd be leaving immediately for Mobile, so he wouldn't be tempted to give in to the hunger that ate at him even now. For it would surely take a physical separation to keep him from making love to his beautiful wife.

The carriage pulled up in front of the main house, and Reese opened the door and leaped to the ground before it came to a complete stop. Grasping Patience around the waist, he lifted her out.

The driver waved and flicked the reins, turning

the carriage back toward town.

"I see you didn't bring your kinfolk back with you."

Patience and Reese turned to see Ma Jewel standing on the veranda, wringing her hands in her apron. She held her lined mouth rigid, trying not to let her anxiety show. But her dark eyes gleamed with worry.

Reese placed his large hand on the small of Patience's back, and she trudged up the steps. Her legs felt leaden, her heart heavy.

The emotional turmoil of the day suddenly sapped what was left of her strength. Reese's indifference stung, and her uncle's bitter rejection hurt terribly. And Albert's appearance, so like her father's, had reminded her of her loss.

Now that she was home, she found to her dismay that she couldn't hold her feelings in check another minute.

"Oh, Ma," she whispered. "It was horrible. My uncle didn't care anything about me. He never even spoke directly to me. I don't know why he came all this way, but I can only assume it was for the money." She longed to tell the woman of her marriage to Reese, and its disappointing end, but not with him standing behind her.

"Shhh," Ma soothed her, pulling Patience to her ample bosom. "Don't you fret now. Ma's here. You're home, and there ain't nothin' to worry 'bout now."

She clutched Patience in her maternal embrace and rocked to and fro, clucking her tongue. "Wha-d'ya do, Misser Reese? Poke the old varmint in the nose and send him back across the ocean with his ears burnin'?"

Tears filled Patience's eyes, and Ma dug a crumpled blue hanky out of her pocket.

"Let's go into the house, Ma. There's a lot to tell, but first I think Patience needs to rest. She's had a very upsetting day."

"That's right," Ma said, her arm going around Patience's shoulders. "You just come on along with Ma and I'll fix everythin' right up."

Patience felt foolish, breaking down that way. But her nerves were stretched beyond the limit. First the pandemonium in the judge's chambers, then being left alone for nearly a half hour in the restaurant. And now he hadn't even mentioned their marriage to Ma.

Her whole body was engulfed in tides of weariness and bone-deep despair. The joy she'd felt during the first moments after she became Reese's wife had faded like fog beneath the July sun when he made no tender overtures toward her.

She couldn't know what he was thinking and didn't have an inkling of how he felt. Was he angry? Regretful? Did he feel a fraction of the love she felt for him?

Reese hadn't said he loved her, hadn't even commented on her declaration of love for him. He'd said nothing to ease her mind and her soul. Only that he'd be honored if she'd be his wife.

She'd thrilled briefly at that crumb of sentiment until she realized it was very possibly for her uncle's benefit alone.

Again she wondered why Reese had agreed to

the marriage. Why had he told the judge "a slight indiscretion" had been committed? Was it only to keep her out of Albert Bentley's clutches? Or was it guilt because of the torrid embrace they'd shared?

The encounter had burned hotter than a Southern summer night, even now sending pebbles of hot gooseflesh along her arms. She remembered his lips on hers, his hands memorizing her curves. The trembling passion still shook her with its explosive force.

But they'd stopped before anything unalterable had happened. Reese could have proclaimed his innocence without being dishonest.

But he hadn't.

Letting Ma lead her to the bottom of the stairs, she turned back to catch one last, long look at Reese. The signs of strain and fatigue were evident beneath his eyes and along the lines of his mouth. His gaze caught hers, and the frown lines on his brow eased slightly.

He'd married her, for whatever reasons, she reminded herself. If he seemed distant, she would have to try to understand. As chaotic as the day had been for her, he'd also been buffeted by the waves of providence sweeping them both along. Maybe, hopefully, that was all that was bothering him.

Reese took three steps toward her and stopped. Staring into her upturned face, he forced a weak smile. "Rest, Patience. I'll see you in a bit." He bowed forward and placed a gentle kiss on her lips. His hand came up to caress her cheek, and she tipped her head to feel his rough palm against her flushed skin.

"That's right," Ma cooed, helping her up the wide, sweeping staircase. "Ma's gonna take good care of you."

Reese wanted to be the one to help her up the stairs. He longed to unfasten the buttons marching up her straight spine, exposing soft, gauzy underthings and warm, pink flesh. His lips ached to taste her skin, her mouth.

Lord, he was in for a difficult time. They hadn't been home for five minutes and he was already as randy as a stallion.

For the first time in months, he went into the parlor and poured himself a drink. His body throbbing with need, he decided to make it a double.

But as he lifted the glass to his lips, he stopped. The amber liquid glowed in the crystal tumbler, tempting him. The smooth, warm scent of alcohol beckoned him. But the memory of Patience's trusting face as she told the judge she loved him made him set it aside.

He was tired. She'd released her exhaustion in an outpouring of emotion upon their arrival, but he had enjoyed no such luxury. His weariness would have to wait to be appeased. There was work to do if he aimed to stop Samuel's plan to claim Bonne Chance.

And, God help him, he meant to stop the bastard. One way or another. For good this time. Because now he had someone who counted on him to look after her and protect her. He had someone to share this place with, the way his parents had meant for it to be shared. And he'd be damned if Symmons was going to take that away from him.

Patience awoke, momentarily disoriented. She pressed her fingertips to her temple as the memory of recent events rushed pell-mell through her sleep-drugged mind.

She felt sluggish and her head hurt, as though she'd slept a long time.

Shooting a startled glance at the window, she flung aside the covers of her bed. Rushing to the draperies, she yanked them aside and gasped. It was morning!

Rubbing her eyes, she stared frantically out at the copper glory of the rising sun. Already the slaves were filing into the fields for the day's chores.

"I slept through my wedding night," she moaned, feeling a cold sickness in her stomach. Why hadn't Reese come to her as he'd promised? Where had he spent the night?

Surely he'd told Ma of their marriage by now. Dear Lord, what would she think when she realized he hadn't slept with her on their wedding night?

Mortified, she didn't want to dress and go down to breakfast. She didn't want to face him—or the others. Shame burned her cheeks. Sorrow welled in her chest.

First her father, now Reese. No one, it seemed, wanted to stay with her for long. Was she unlovable?

"What's the matter with me?" she asked the reflection in the mirror. Sad, plaintive eyes stared back at her. She frowned and rubbed her cheek. Self-pity didn't become her.

Twisting her mouth derisively, she shucked off the helpless feelings. Languor made her vulnerable, but she reminded herself that she was a strong, self-assured woman. She would face Reese Ashburn across the breakfast table and simply ask him why he hadn't come to her room. Candid, forthright openness had always worked for her in the past.

Stripping off her gown, she quickly washed with lilac soap. She dressed in a soft blue day dress of watered silk and pinned her hair up in a loose topknot.

Feeling more herself, her spirit returned with vigor. Perhaps he'd been as tired as she had. Possibly he'd gone to his own room to rest and, just maybe, he'd also fallen into a deep sleep. They had both been exhausted. It was a logical explanation.

Unfortunately, she couldn't quite make herself believe it. Men had urges which would overrule mere exhaustion. Trudy had told her about *that* when Carl Garrard had been courting her. She'd also told her what a woman could expect on her wedding night, and how best to endure it without complaint.

Of course, Patience hadn't been afraid Reese would hurt her, or even make her uncomfortable. In fact, she'd rather looked forward to learning the secrets a man and woman shared.

So why hadn't her husband been equally eager to teach them to her?

"There's only one way to find out," she told her reflection. She pulled open the door and headed for the dining room.

"Gone? What do you mean, gone?"

Ma collected a dirty plate and a cup, half full of coffee, from the table. Patience could see that Reese had come and gone already. His rumpled napkin lay beside his place at the table; crumbs lightly dusted the tablecloth in a circle where his plate had rested.

"Got up with the chickens this mornin'. Said he had business in town. Didn't know when he'd be back. But he tole me the good news, and I cain't tell you how happy I am. Didn't think I'd ever see that boy settle down." She smiled a toothy grin and patted Patience's hand. "You've made this old heart sing, you have."

Slumping into her chair, Patience shook her head. "I don't understand," she whispered. Ma clattered Reese's silver onto a tray. "Why didn't he wake me last night?"

"What was that, honey?"

Patience glanced up and met the woman's questioning eyes. She hadn't meant to make the query aloud, and she was thankful at least that Ma hadn't heard it.

"Nothing," she murmured.

"You'll be hungry. I'll fix you a heapin' plate."

"No," she said, her tone listless. "I don't want anything, Ma."

"You gotta' eat. You're a married woman now," Ma said with a knowing wink. "And if I know Misser Reese, you'll be needin' your strength."

She chuckled as she ambled through the door to the warming kitchen.

So Ma didn't know Reese hadn't come to her room last night. Patience didn't how it was possible, but she was thankful for that small blessing at least.

However, knowing her husband had left her without a word, it was meager comfort indeed.

Chapter Twenty-two

Reese pulled open the glass double doors of the Mobile City Bank. To the left was a high, polished-oak counter with small windows. To the right was Darius Woolsey's office.

Regretting the way he'd acted at their last meeting, Reese had decided to give Woolsey his business. Besides, he'd always used City Bank in the past. If he had to mortgage Bonne Chance, he wanted to feel as reassured as he possibly could that whoever he dealt with wouldn't turn around and sell the mortgage to Symmons.

The manager looked up and caught sight of Reese through the open door of his office. His face blanched and he scooted back in his chair.

Reese made his way across the lobby and poked his head into the room.

"Got a minute, Woolsey?"

"I—I'm busy right now, Reese. All this paperwork to finish."

"This won't take long," Reese said, going in and shutting the door behind him. "I've come to see about that loan we discussed."

"The loan? I don't understand. You still want to borrow money?"

"Yeah, I do. Is there a problem?"

"No, not at all. It's just—never mind."

"So, about the money . . ."

"Sure, sure thing, Reese. Just let me get the clerk to draw up the agreement. I'll be right back."

He skittered around his desk and disappeared out the door, returning a few minutes later with a document. He filled in the top blank with Reese's name, then went down a few lines and entered the amount.

"That's right, isn't it?" he asked, turning the page around so Reese could see what he'd written.

"Yes, that's the correct amount." His eyes scanned the document. It seemed straightforward.

"What about the mortgage? Isn't there a form for that, too?"

"Mortgage? No, no need for that. Just sign at the bottom." He pushed the paper toward Reese. "Right there."

Reese picked up the page, a frown furrowing his brow. "I don't understand, Woolsey. You said I'd have to mortgage Bonne Chance in order to get the loan."

"That won't be necessary now. Go ahead, sign."

Sweat beaded on Woolsey's forehead. The man

nervously licked his lips as his trembling hands fumbled around the desk for a pen.

"What the hell is going on, Woolsey? Why are you willing to let me have an unsecured loan now? What about the board of directors?"

"No problem there, Reese. They know all about—"

He stopped short, a flush creeping from under his stiff collar. He gulped, and his Adam's apple bobbed grotesquely.

"About what?"

"Well, I—we heard about you and Bentley's daughter," Woolsey told him. "It's been all over town that you married the girl yesterday in Judge Carson's office." He found the pen he'd been searching for and snatched it up triumphantly. "I think it's wonderful."

"What's wonderful?"

"That you took my advice. Smart move. Of course, I don't see why you need a loan now, but with all her money backing you . . ."

Reese's hand tightened around the document, crumpling it into a ball. "Is that what this is all about? Now that I'm married to Patience Bentley, my name on a sheet of paper is worth more?"

"Well, sure, Reese. I mean, all that money," he repeated. "The only thing I don't understand is why you still *want* the loan. You certainly don't need it now."

Rising slowly to his feet, Reese leaned over the desk. Woolsey swallowed hard and backed away, his eyes wide with fright.

"I'll tell you why, you little weasel. Because I'm

more of a man than that. I didn't marry Patience for her money. I won't use it to pay off my debts, and I won't use it to secure a loan from this bank."

"Well, I just assumed—I mean, why else would you marry the chit? Everyone knows she's—"

Reese gripped the gray pinstriped cravat tied carefully at the man's throat and raised his hand, lifting Woolsey out of his seat.

"I told you before, if I ever heard you say anything derogatory about Patience I'd break your face."

"Now wait a minute, Reese . . ."

"Do you know why my fist isn't already dancing over your teeth?"

"No-no."

"Because I've changed, Woolsey. I'm a new man. I don't let my impulses rule my life anymore."

The man nodded briskly, his hands grabbing frantically for his shirt front.

"And because I want you to tell everyone who's been talking about my wife how much it annoys me. Do you understand, Woolsey?"

The banker opened his mouth, but nothing came out except a small squeak.

"And you can forget the loan. If I can't get it on my own, I won't get it at all. Do I make myself clear?"

Once more the man nodded. Reese released him and he slumped into his chair, tugging at the ruined cravat.

Tossing the document onto the pile of papers littering the banker's desk, Reese turned to go. A crowd had gathered outside the door of Woolsey's office, and he had to wind his way through the throng of curious onlookers.

As he reached the door of the bank, Woolsey rushed to his feet. Standing safely in the doorway of his office, he shook his finger at Reese.

"You haven't changed, Ashburn," the man called. "You're still gutter trash. You can marry anybody you like. It's not going to make any difference."

Reese turned away, tugging the heavy glass door open. Behind him he could still hear Woolsey.

"You hear me? You're nothing but a ruffian, Ashburn."

Reese ignored the man's taunts and the startled stares from the other customers entering the bank.

He refused to answer the call of his temper telling him to go back and finish the man. He *had* changed. Someday he'd prove it to the whole damned town.

But first he had to prove it to Patience. And to himself.

Patience moped about the house for two days. She tried to spark an interest in the infirmary, but Mag had everything under control. Ma didn't need her help in the house, and the account ledgers were up to date.

Ran had all the slaves working in the fields. The blossoms of the cotton plants had fallen off, and the bolls were just beginning to appear. Brightly colored red leaves replaced the green seed leaves.

Everyone had something to do. Everyone except her.

"You still laggin' about?" Ma asked, replacing the stubby white tapers in the candlesticks on the mantel with fresh, unburned ones.

"I'm not lagging," Patience told her defensively. "I'm enjoying a bit of free time, that's all."

"Yep, I reckon you've earned it. Still, if you was to get bored, I'm sure we could find something for you to do."

Patience whirled, her eyes bright. "Like what?"

"Well," the old woman said, dusting the brass candlestick with the apron tied around her waist, "let me see. You ain't moved yer belongings into Misser Reese's room yet."

Her mouth twisted and she continued to swat at the candlestick, but Patience could see the whites of her eyes as she cut them sideways, waiting for a reaction.

"Move? Into Reese's bedroom? Ma, I couldn't do that."

"Why not? You married to him, ain't you?"

"Yes, of course," Patience said casually, hoping the blush creeping over her cheeks wasn't obvious. "But—well, ladies don't . . ."

"What don't ladies do?"

"You know—sleep. In the same room with their husbands." She'd expected Reese to come to her room on their wedding night, but Trudy told her men did their business and then left. She was adamant about their not staying.

"What you talkin' 'bout, child?"

"Effluvium."

"Say a'gin?"

Patience felt the crimson stain on her face all the way to her hairline. She glanced around in embarrassment and leaned close to Ma. "Effluvium."

Ma shook her head, and Patience huffed a frustrated sigh.

"You know, Ma. Vapors."

"Vapors?" The black eyes widened, and her mouth made a tight little O.

"Men and women exude vapors when they sleep. It isn't healthy to occupy the same room, intermingling them."

Ma jerked back, her eyes like wide saucers in her face. "Who told you that nonsense, child?"

"It isn't nonsense, Ma. Trudy, the woman who took care of me, explained it all. She said that's why ladies and gentlemen don't share bedchambers."

Ma stared at Patience for a long minute, then her chins began to quiver. Patience frowned. The quiver turned to jiggles, and Patience reached out and touched her arm.

"Are you all right, Ma?"

Suddenly the old slave burst into laughter. She chortled so loudly that Patience jumped back a full foot. Ma doubled over, her hands gripping her bulky middle.

"Child, you do have some fanciful ideas," she said, between chuckles.

"Ma, this is not funny. I'm very serious. Please stop laughing," Patience said, her ire growing with her humiliation.

"Oh, me," Ma said, dabbing her eyes with her

apron. "You best sit a spell and let ole Ma straighten you out."

"That isn't necessary, Ma," she told the slave. "I had this discussion with Trudy when I was seventeen."

"Oh, yes indeedy, it is necessary," Ma told her, patting her arm. "You cain't be tellin' Misser Reese you ain't gonna share his bed 'cause he might fart."

"Ma!"

"Sit, girl," Ma ordered. "We gonna have us a chat. It's my place, I reckon, since you ain't got no mama, and this Trudy, whoever that fool is, has twisted your head around good."

"My head is just fine, Ma. I really don't think this is a good idea."

"You hopin' he'll just stay all night in the study again when he comes back?"

The black eyes were still tinted with merriment, but a serious look had come over Ma's face. Patience tightened her mouth.

"You knew?"

"'Course I knew. I run this place. Don't nothin' go on I don't know 'bout. But," she said, leading Patience to the sofa. "It was just 'cause you were so wore out. He went up to check on you more'n once. Said you were sleeping so sound he didn't want to disturb you."

"I did wonder why he didn't come to me that night."

"Well, don't you worry. Misser Reese was jus' bein' thoughtful. But," she added, her gray eyebrows rising, "you don't want him being thoughtful when he comes back, do you?"

Fighting her embarrassment, Patience slowly shook her head.

"That's a girl. Now you listen to ole Ma. I'm gonna tell you how it is."

An hour later, Patience stood beside her bed, her clothes laid out in piles across the spread. Her mind whirled with all the things Ma had said. Some of them Patience still wasn't sure she believed.

She was a free-thinker, an educated woman with modern ideas. But if Ma had told her the truth, she certainly didn't know much about being married.

In the end, Ma had convinced her that she should move into Reese's room. The sooner, the better.

Reese rode toward home, astonished at the sense of fulfillment he felt. He'd left the bank enraged and bewildered. He'd known at that moment that if he went to the other bankers in town, he'd meet with the same reaction. Even if he got one to agree to carry a mortgage on Bonne Chance, it would only be a gesture.

Everyone knew he'd married Patience, and they knew their money would be secure now if they extended him a loan.

No matter which way he turned, it seemed he couldn't solve this problem without Patience—or James's—money.

Then he'd remembered something from his financial discussions with Patience. She'd been surprised, and encouraged, that at least Cooper had not borrowed from the factor against the future crop.

Reese knew that was a common practice, but no one on Bonne Chance had ever considered it, mainly because, in the past, there'd been no need.

After dismissing Cooper, he'd threatened to bypass the factor, certain the man had been padding his profits. He'd even gone so far as to discuss with James's shipping manager the possibility of shipping direct without using the broker.

Instead, after the disaster at the bank, he'd gone to see Willis Powell, the factor Bonne Chance had used for years.

Now he remembered the gist of that conversation with a measure of pride. It might not have been the solution he'd hoped for, but he'd managed to save Bonne Chance without touching a cent of James's money or relying on his wife's assets. He'd accomplished something entirely on his own. And it filled him with a gratification he'd never known. Pride in an achievement. Quiet observance of a personal victory.

Powell had been surprised to see him, even a bit apprehensive. But Reese had dredged up his manners and greeted the man with courtesy and respect. He hadn't mentioned the past overcharges, instead approaching the broker as the new manager of Bonne Chance.

Apparently, Powell counted heavily on the money he made from Reese's crop each year, and he was more than willing to renegotiate terms based on current rates and interest when Reese made it clear that he had researched such facts.

Without blinking, Powell had signed a bank note for the amount Reese needed to pay Samuel. Powell said most of the plantation owners he dealt with borrowed heavily all year, barely making enough on their crop to pay off what they owed.

Reese would be able to pay off his loan and still have enough to cover his other debts. If, in the future, he decided to try bypassing Powell, he could go that avenue once Bonne Chance was out of debt.

All in all, he was returning to the plantation feeling successful and optimistic. He'd cleared this obstacle on his own. If others should occur, he knew he'd be able to handle them now.

Finally, after years of feeling useless and superfluous, he felt valuable, as though he truly had something worthwhile to offer both Patience and Bonne Chance.

Worthwhile. The word meant so much more to him now than at any time in the past. It meant feeling as though Bonne Chance belonged to him—as though he'd worked for it, and could enjoy its benefits without feeling they'd been handed to him.

But most important, it meant he was one step closer to being the man Patience deserved to call husband.

He'd missed her more in the past two days than he ever remembered missing anyone. Not even James's sudden departure from his life had left this kind of void. Longing ripped through him when he pictured her lying, sound asleep, in her bed. Hunger gnawed his insides every time he recalled the fact that she was now his, if only in name.

Soon, though, he'd make her his wife in every sense of the word. He wouldn't be satisfied to stand looking down on her sleeping form. He'd climb in beside her and touch her closed eyelids, her softly parted lips. He wouldn't leave her to dream alone while he tossed and turned on the sofa in his study. He'd hold her so close that even their dreams would unite.

Yes, he intended to love Patience with every ounce of emotion he now held in. His body ached for her; his lips craved the taste of her mouth.

It would be hell keeping his hands off her until he fulfilled the obligation he'd assigned himself. But abstain he would, until he found, and brought to justice, James's killers. Then, and only then, would he do what his heart so desired and make love to his wife.

Chapter Twenty-three

With a long, exhausted sigh, Reese closed the door to his bedchamber. He needed to clean up and change clothes before going down to supper. He hadn't seen Patience yet and was thankful he'd have time to wash the dirt of the road off before facing her.

Shucking his shirt, he poured tepid water from the pitcher into the basin and scrubbed his face, neck, and arms. It felt so good that he unfastened the buttons on his trousers and ran a damp cloth over his chest and stomach.

His skin puckered and pebbled with gooseflesh in the slight breeze from the open French doors. Beneath the mat of wiry hair, his chest tingled. Closing his eyes, he could almost imagine Patience's cool fingers lightly skimming his skin.

His loins tightened and he leaned his head back,

enjoying the sensations. As his body responded to the intimate daydream, he longed to make it a reality.

Carried away by his response, he didn't hear the door open. Patience's startled gasp yanked him from the fantasy, and he whirled to see her standing, wide-eyed, in the doorway.

"What the devil are you doing in here?"

He turned toward the washstand, trying to hide the evidence of his arousal. He fumbled with the towel until he could gain control.

"I—I didn't know you were back. I just came up to change for supper."

"Fine, go change," he said roughly, wishing she'd leave before she realized how weak his resolve was at that moment. He couldn't have her yet. He couldn't tell her how much he wanted her for fear she'd dissuade him from his determination or try to interfere with his plan for finding her father's killer.

"I—I can't," she whispered.

"Why not?"

Gripping the towel in front of his loosened trousers, he looked over his shoulder at her scarlet face. Her beauty struck him like a blow, and he slowly faced her.

Dear God, she was the most perfect woman he'd ever seen. Even in her work garb, with a smudge of dirt on one cheek, the sight of her made his heart turn over. Like some primitive beast, his mind cried out with victory that she was his. His wife, his love, his life.

He wanted her so badly that the ache had become a permanent part of him. It was always there, in the pit of his stomach, burning like an ulcer. He crushed the towel in his fierce grasp.

Her gaze had moved to his chest, and he looked down to see a single drop of water slowly sliding over the ridges of his chest and abdomen. She licked her lips and he groaned. He could almost feel the tip of that small pink tongue lathing the moisture from his skin.

"My—uh, clothes are in there," she told him, forcing her glance back up to his face. She pointed behind him.

Stupidly he turned to stare at the chiffonier. A frown furrowed his brow, and for a split second he thought he must have come into the wrong room by mistake. Instantly he rejected the idea. This had always been his room. He could find it with his eyes closed.

He scanned the dark paneled walls, the forest-green velvet coverlet and drapes. The heavy oak furnishings had always held his belongings; the bed had welcomed him back each time he returned.

With a trickle of foreboding, he slowly stepped over to the dresser. Pulling out a drawer, he sucked in a harsh breath. His hand instinctively went to the soft, silky underthings, and he clutched them in his fist, watching as the dainty ribbons snaked over his rough, tanned hands.

He longed to lift them to his nose and inhale the sweet scent of Patience he knew he'd find there. He wanted to bury his face in their satiny warmth. If he'd been alone, he would have savored the pleasure, knowing it was as close as he could get for the time being.

Frustration made his words harsh as he turned to her, the filmy article still locked in his grasp. "What is the meaning of this?"

She stepped into the room, her blue eyes enormous as she watched him mangle her chemise. "I moved my belongings in here while you were gone," she said, thinking surely he must have guessed something so obvious. But he just stood there, dumbfounded.

"We're married now, and I just assumed . . ."

Her words trailed off as he stared at her. She felt her embarrassment creep over her cheeks, staining them a deep crimson. She'd been right. She never should have listened to Ma Jewel. Ladies clearly did not sleep in the same room with gentlemen.

"I'm sorry, I thought—that is, I'll move back into my own room right away," she stammered, reaching for the chemise.

He didn't release it, and she tugged harder. Still he continued to hold it, and finally she let go before their tugging ripped the fragile garment.

"No," he said, his tone not at all convincing. "No, that's all right. I was just surprised."

She started toward the dresser, her hands pulling anxiously at the neat piles of lingerie. "I'll get them out of your way . . ."

His hands came out and clasped hers, stilling their nervous movements. She could feel the heat from his bare chest seep into her back as he leaned in close behind her.

"Stop," he told her, his voice low and soothing now. "It's all right."

"But . . ."

"But nothing." God, he'd made a mess of things. Why hadn't he considered that she'd make the first move if he didn't? And how was he going to avoid her, and keep his desire in check, with her so near? Still, he could see she'd been hurt by his indifference, and he couldn't embarrass her further by insisting she move out.

"I've never been married before, Patience. You'll have to bear with me if I do or say things without thinking."

"I shouldn't have . . ."

"Yes, you should have," he said firmly. "You had every right. Now stop fiddling with those things and leave them where they are. I'll just get my shirt, and you can have the room to yourself. I'll send Gay up with fresh water."

"But this is your room." She whirled around, putting them a hair's width apart. Her soft, sweet breath fanned his neck, sending shivers of desire rocketing through him. Her small hands came up instinctively and rested on his bare chest. He flinched from the icy-hot needles of awareness that shot out from her touch. She immediately withdrew her fingers, and he ached to grab her hands and hold them against him once more.

"My shirt," he murmured, trying to find the presence of mind to step away from her before he cast his good intentions to the wind.

"You shouldn't have to leave," she told him, the look in her eyes stirring the smoldering embers of his passion. It sounded so sweetly like an invitation that he nearly groaned.

"I'll have the water sent up right away," he told her, forcing himself to take a step back. He opened two more drawers before finding a clean shirt. Snatching it up, he backed toward the door.

"I'll see you at supper," she called, her tone forlorn and small in the huge, dark, masculine interior of his room.

Reese strode out of the chamber before his hunger for her overcame the last of his good sense. He paused on the landing, slumping against the wall. A ragged sigh escaped him, and he felt sweat dot his brow and upper lip. His stomach cramped with the effort it took to deny his need.

He'd never wanted a woman so badly that it caused him physical pain to walk away. He'd never loved a woman so much that he'd deny his own pleasure out of a sense of honor.

"James, you blackguard," he whispered beneath his breath. "You're repaying me, all right. In ways you never imagined."

He pulled his shirt on and went to find Gay and Ma Jewel.

Patience stared out the doors leading from Reese's room to the balcony overlooking the fields. He'd done it again.

Somehow, for the past week, he'd managed to avoid meeting her in their room. Every evening he worked in his study until late, then slept on the short sofa there. In the morning, he waited for her to rise and go down to breakfast; then he went up to his room, where he washed and dressed for the day.

Meals had been consumed in a quiet, strained atmosphere. She longed to ask what was wrong. Why didn't he come to her? Why did he avoid her as much as possible? Why hadn't he made love to her?

The boldness of her thoughts surprised her. She knew so little of the ways of men, but she longed for something more between them and assumed it could only be found in that mystical joining she'd heard whispered about.

But Reese seemed determined not to take that monumental step. Was he still angry with her for offering him money to save Bonne Chance? He'd certainly proven beyond a doubt his ability to triumph on his own in financial situations.

Did he resent having had to marry her in order to thwart her uncle? Reese could have concealed the fact that they'd kissed, and she'd probably be on her way to England by now.

The fact remained, they *were* married. For better or worse. For richer, for poorer. The words took on new meaning when she said them now. Their message rang clear to her heart.

For all time, Reese would be her husband—no matter that they continued to disagree on the issue of slavery, and despite the fact that he was still quiet, withdrawn at times, while she remained outspoken and frank. He persisted in hiding his feelings. She felt as if hers were emblazoned across her face every time she looked at him.

Her hand stilled on the thick velvet of the

drapes. The delicate lace curtains on the windows blew against her arms, raising prickles of sensation along her sun-warmed skin.

She and Reese were joined together forever. She knew by the talk she'd heard when she first arrived that her husband was a virile man. His success with women was practically legendary. His fondness for feminine companionship was renowned.

The sharp sting of jealousy pricked her. She loved Reese. She couldn't bear to think of him with another woman. She didn't want to consider that he might be finding that companionship elsewhere. He was her husband. She wanted to be his wife.

That's why she'd done what Ma suggested and moved into his room, despite her uncertainty and misgivings. But she'd slept alone, in his bed, for seven long, lonely nights.

What was she doing wrong? What wasn't she doing right? She remembered some of the advice Ma had freely doled out—suggestions Patience had found shocking and, for the most part, remarkable.

Even now, the memory brought a bright flush to her cheeks and made her heart hammer in her chest. Could she do the things Ma proposed? More important, if it meant winning her husband's affections, could she not?

Reese bent over the ledger on his desk, the rows of figures a blur before him. His mind wasn't on the accounts. Why he'd even tried to concentrate on them was beyond him. Every night he locked himself away from Patience, trying to fight the force of his desire for his wife.

God, sometimes he felt he'd go insane with wanting her. Countless times he'd started for his bedchamber, telling himself he was being ridiculous. No man in his right mind would deny himself the love of his own wife.

But he always stopped himself before he reached her. He always remembered his vow before it was too late. Whether she would have agreed with him or not, Reese had convinced himself James's daughter deserved a husband who was worthy of her.

Paying Samuel the money he owed had gone a long way toward redeeming some of his past wrongs. But Reese was still haunted by the memory of James's death. Only by finding his killers and bringing them to justice could he wipe that final stain from his character.

It would take a lot longer to prove to people he had changed, but that last act of retribution would at least make him feel as though he'd somehow repaid James—and Patience—for that awful night. Then, and only then, would he be able to make love to her without the shadow of his guilt casting a pall over them.

The plantation was temporarily stable, and he felt secure leaving it in Ran's hands for a brief time. He should have gone straight to Mobile after paying Samuel and begun his search for the murderers. But he'd missed Patience so much that he'd been drawn back to Bonne Chance like a man in a trance. All he could think of was seeing her face, hearing her voice.

He'd put off leaving for a week, but he couldn't put it off any longer. The sooner he went to Mobile, the sooner he could begin his search. The longer he waited, the colder the trail would become.

He'd leave first thing in the morning, he decided, closing the ledger and replacing it in the top drawer of his desk. His willpower wouldn't last much longer if he stayed here, knowing his wife slept upstairs, in his bed, each night.

He checked the clock on the fireplace mantel. It was late enough. She'd be asleep.

He made his way up the stairs, the way he did each night. At the door of his bedroom, he chastised himself for acting like such a silly, besotted fool. But he couldn't resist one look, one small peek at her as she slept. Each night, he waited for her to fall asleep and then stole into his own room like a thief in the night and peered longingly at his wife.

It was the absurd action of a man who, for the first time in his life, found himself hopelessly, desperately in love—and who, for the first time, found he could not have the woman he so desired.

The door creaked familiarly as he pushed it forward on its hinges. His gaze swung to the bed and the rumpled covers piled atop the mattress.

He eased the door closed, then walked on silent feet toward the small slice of moonlight filtering across the bed. Leaning over, he castigated himself for behaving like an idiot. Why did he torture himself this way each night? Why couldn't he stay away?

"Reese?"

He jumped at the sound of her voice, cursing hotly as he whirled around. Behind him, in the shadows of the room, he saw her move. She took another step, and he could see her figure outlined in the pool of moonlight. She wore a white satin nightgown, gathered and tied at the neckline and wrists. The hem fell to the tops of her bare feet, and her small, white toes peeked out from beneath.

"Jesus, you nearly scared the life out of me."

"Did you want me?" she asked, her words, her tone filled with a double entendre.

Reese's breath lodged in his throat and he struggled to make his words sound normal. "What were you doing back there?"

"I was waiting for you," she said, taking another step toward him.

"But why . . . ?"

"I've been awake a few times when you came into the room. I pretended to be asleep, hoping you'd come to me and wake me—hoping, just maybe, you'd join me."

"Patience, you don't know what you're saying."

"Yes, I do. Oh, I may not know every detail of what goes on between a man and a woman, but I understand the basics. I understand enough to be hurt when my own husband doesn't want to share that part of marriage with me."

"Patience, it isn't like that. I swear . . ."

"Then why haven't you come to me, even once,

since we've been married? Why have you avoided me until I dared to hide in our bedroom and confront you under the cover of darkness so you wouldn't see how ashamed I feel?"

"Oh, God, Patience . . ."

"What is it, Reese? Am I too short? Too young? Is my hair the wrong color? I've heard about your exploits with women, Reese. And even if I allow that some of the talk might be exaggeration, I know you're a man with physical needs—needs that you aren't satisfying at home."

"Don't," he said, crossing the room and clutching her shoulders in his hands. "Don't even think that," he told her roughly. As he touched her, all the emotions he'd held in check came pouring out. He shook with need. His body flooded with unfulfilled passion.

Before he could stop himself, he crushed her mouth beneath his. His tongue traced the fullness of her lips, then explored the recesses of her mouth. He gathered her so close, she had to stand on her toes, and still he didn't release her.

"Do you see," he murmured, his lips touching her ear, sending frissons of desire through her. "Do you see how much I want you?"

"No," she said, shaking her head, trying to clear her frazzled thoughts. "No, you don't."

He growled deep in his throat and grabbed her hand. Drawing it down to the fastenings of his trousers, he pressed it against his arousal until he wanted to groan with the painful pleasure of her touch. "Feel how badly I want you. I'm dying from it. You're all I think about, all I dream about."

"Then make love to me," she told him boldly. "Make me your wife. Tonight."

"I can't," he said, releasing her so fast she reeled dizzily.

"Why? I want you to. You claim to want it." She was thankful for the dark, certain her cheeks were flaming with humiliation. But she'd never backed down from anything in her life when she felt strongly that it was something worth fighting for. And her marriage was certainly worth fighting for.

She stiffened her spine and thought about the things Ma had told her. *Men didn't want a shrinking violet in their bed. They might want a lady on their arm, but they want more than that between the sheets.* Patience ignored the rush of embarrassment that told her to send him away before she further disgraced herself.

"I realize our marriage wasn't exactly conventional. And I know I made a mistake offering you money, although I don't really know why that was wrong."

"Stop it, Patience. It isn't your fault. It isn't anything you've done, or not done. This is something I have to work out myself. Alone."

"No," she said, coming up behind him. She touched his arm, and he clenched his fists to keep from taking her in his arms once more. "No, you don't have to do anything alone anymore. That's what I'm trying to tell you. I want this to be a real marriage. I want to be your wife, your partner." She ran her fingertips along the hard, muscled flesh of his forearm and felt him tremble.

"I want to be your lover," she told him.

Reese turned to gaze at her and saw the fire of passion in the deep blue flames of her eyes. His arms went around her, and she tipped her mouth toward his. She watched as his lips lowered toward hers, and he knew he was hopelessly, irreversibly caught in her spell.

Chapter Twenty-four

Reese lowered his head to the curve of her neck, gently nudging aside the fabric of her nightgown. His mouth caressed her throat, her shoulder. When the gown stopped his progress, he bent down and took the ribbon between his teeth, untying it.

The soft fabric slid over her shoulder and down her arm. His lips followed it across the smooth, exposed flesh.

"Is this what you want, Patience?" he asked, his voice jagged beneath the passion.

"Yes," she whispered, tracing the lines of his back with eager fingers.

His lips lowered to the swell of her breasts, and he touched each one in turn with the tip of his tongue. She smelled wonderful, just the way he'd imagined hundreds of times. She felt so right, so perfect in his arms. Her soft little gasps of surprise drove him mad with desire.

She arched in his embrace, thrusting the peaks of her breasts against his chest. He felt her nipples harden as desire wracked her, and his manhood sprang immediately to full life.

All thoughts of honor and worth flew from his mind as she moaned his name on a breathy sigh. The gown slid down to her waist and he leaned back, watching the white roundness of her perfect shape highlighted in the glow of moonlight.

His lips touched each precious nipple with tantalizing possessiveness. He lathed and loved first one, then the other, as her heart pounded a rhythm into his brain.

As his hands skimmed her waist and hips, taking the gown down to the floor, he continued to study her. Never had he seen a woman so beautiful, so perfect. Every inch of her aroused and enflamed his desire. As his hands caressed her thighs, her knees buckled and she sank into his waiting arms.

He lifted her and laid her carefully on the bed and then began to shed his own clothes. She didn't try to cover herself, or hide her body from his view. Not once did she turn her face away or refuse to meet his hungry gaze.

She watched him boldly, seductively. She waited, seemingly as eager and impatient as he. When he was naked, he stood, awaiting her response. Again she amazed him when she reached out and took his hand, pulling him down onto the bed with her.

His hands sought her pleasure points, determined to show her the true wonder of lovemaking. His tongue returned to tantalize the buds of her breasts, which had swollen to their fullest. His body cried out for the sweet softness of her core, but he held back.

Patience caressed the hard tendons of his shoulders, explored the ridges of his back, hips, buttocks. Her nails raked hot paths of pleasure over his skin, sending him to the edge of his control.

As he moved to partially cover her body with his, she instinctively parted her legs, and he slipped into the welcoming cradle of her thighs. Their bodies fused together with one involuntary spasm, and he cried out as she accepted his fullness with a lusty sigh.

"Dear God," he groaned, shaking with sweet agony. He tried to hold back the floodtide of emotions, but they burst forth and he showered hot, desperate kisses along her cheek and jaw as he rocked against her.

Patience bent her knees, sliding her feet toward her buttocks and lifting her body closer to his, searching, seeking the ultimate fulfillment.

Reese clutched her tightly and called her name over and over. He took great, gulping breaths and fought to keep his passion in check until he felt the shudders move over her. Her eyes opened wide, and she met his pleased gaze with startled realization. As the tremors shook her, he let go his own response and together they soared in exquisite harmony with one another.

For nearly a quarter of an hour, no sound broke

the stillness of the room except the labored breaths they expelled. Reese couldn't speak, couldn't voice the words and feelings careening through his mind and heart.

God, he'd never felt so alive, so complete. So guilty, so regretful.

Why had he come into the room at all, knowing how fragile his control was around her? How could he have let this happen, when he'd just renewed his vow not to touch her until he was worthy? Why had he given in to the hunger she aroused in him when he'd decided to leave her again in the morning?

The soft sound of her low, even breathing admonished him. She slept trustingly in his arms, the peaceful sleep of a satisfied lover. He longed to remain where he was, content to hold her and revel in the fact that she was truly, wholely his. But how could he do that when he still didn't feel he deserved her love or trust?

And he knew those feelings would soon be tested, perhaps beyond their limits. Because he couldn't tell her his plans for finding her father's killer. She'd interfere, try to stop him. He looked at her sweet, alluring face and knew it wouldn't be hard for her to convince him to stay with her and forget his objective now. His only hope was to be gone before she awoke.

But when Patience found he'd deserted her once more, would her love survive the pain of feeling betrayed?

Damn Reese Ashburn! Patience thought, raking her hand over the top of the dresser and upsetting all the items carefully laid out there. Pins, combs, cufflinks rained to the floor in the fury of her rage.

How could he leave her like that? Not one word, not one moment of his time. Just missing saddlebags and an empty drawer where his clothes had been.

And a ring box on the pillow where his head had rested.

Wherever he'd gone, he obviously planned to stay a while.

She felt like a prostitute, paid and abandoned. And why not? That was the way she'd acted! Why, oh why, had she listened to Ma Jewel?

When she thought how she'd practically begged Reese to make love to her, her face blazed with shame. She'd been brazen, wanton—and totally lacking in experience, making her performance all the more ridiculous.

Her seduction certainly hadn't bought her his undying devotion. Why had she thought she could captivate Reese? Her unsophisticated actions no doubt amused him, but she had no hope of enticing a man with the experience and worldliness Reese possessed.

He was used to the talented touch of seasoned seductresses. He was probably laughing all the way to Mobile. That thought filled her with a wretchedness she'd never known before. She slumped dejectedly into a chair and plopped her head on her hands. She felt bereft and desolate. Her fingers reached into the pocket of her dressing gown, and she withdrew the black velvet ring box.

A ring given at the time of their marriage would have meant something special to her. Receiving such a beautiful gift would have made a wonderful memory if he'd chosen to give it to her at any other time, in any other way. But left on an otherwise empty pillow, after their first night of passion, it felt like remuneration.

The tiny hinges creaked as she opened the box. A dazzling emerald, surrounded by perfectly faceted diamonds, winked up at her. He was certainly a generous benefactor, she had to give him that. If he treated all his women this well, it was no wonder Bonne Chance had been on the verge of bankruptcy when she'd first arrived.

Just the thought that he might have given such a gift to another woman instantly rekindled her anger, and she shut the tiny lid with a snap. A single hot tear streaked down her cheek.

The unexpected knock at the bedroom door had her hoping, absurdly, that Reese had returned. She swiped at the lone symbol of her anguish. "Come in," she called, hoping the tears she fought back didn't cloud her voice.

Ma bustled in, a stack of fresh-laundered linens in her arms. "Thought you'd like me to change the bed this mornin'," she said with a mischievous grin. She stripped the soiled sheets from the bed without so much as a raised eyebrow and bundled them into a pile, tying a single knot on top.

The first clean sheet popped loudly as Ma snapped it into place. Patience started and dropped the ring box. The little velvet case rolled across the floor and settled on its side at the edge of the forest-green rug beside the bed.

"What's this?" Ma said, bending at the waist to collect the box.

Patience darted from her chair and made a grab for the box. Ma held it out of reach, pretending to study the black velvet.

"Ma, give that to me," Patience demanded.

"Oh, I jest love pretty baubles," she told Patience with glee. "You don't mind if I have a quick peek, do you?"

"Yes, Ma . . ."

Her words trailed off as the tiny hinges protested. The old slave's gasp had her searching the box to see what had caused such a reaction.

"What is it?"

Ma turned to her, tears glistening at the edges of her onyx eyes. For the first time since Patience had known her, she looked completely nonplussed.

"That boy sure must love you, child," she whispered, slipping the ring from its slot. She held it out and, taking Patience's hand, slipped it on her finger.

"No, Ma, don't . . ." Patience began, trying to pull her hand away. "It's just a reminder of something I want to forget."

"It's more'n that, honey," she told Patience, holding her hand so she couldn't remove the ring.

Patience huffed and stopped fighting Ma's grip. "What are you talking about?"

"You know how Reese was when you first got here?"

Patience nodded.

"He never stayed put for any time. He was always lookin' for somethin', but never findin' it."

"You aren't making any sense, Ma. What has Reese's past got to do with this ring?"

"His ma and pa loved each other very much—so much, they sometimes made that boy feel like an outsider. He's spent the better part of his adult life lookin' for somewhere he could belong."

"Yes, I noticed that loneliness in him right off," Patience admitted. "It was one of the things that made me . . ."

She stopped, biting her lip to keep back that damning admission. But apparently Ma didn't need the words. Her eyes told Patience she understood.

"I ain't seen that ring in nigh on sixteen years. Not since Reese's ma died. His pa followed right behind, and Reese's been on his own ever since. But he used to stare at that ring for hours, and I knowed what he was thinkin'."

Patience touched the cold stones circling her finger. She rubbed the warm gold of the band. "What, Ma? What was he thinking?"

"That one day he'd find someone he could love as much as his pa loved his ma."

Suddenly the stones grew warm against her skin. The fire of the emerald seemed to glow a brilliant green in the morning sunshine. She looked at the ring, the only thing Reese had left her after their first night together. And she knew words weren't necessary. He'd told her how he felt with this one self-revealing gesture.

* * *

Rita Mallory opened her front door with a wry grin. "Honeymoon over already?" she teased, laughing at Reese's black scowl.

"Can I come in?"

She waved her hand inward. "You did pay for the place." Her casual air couldn't quite hide the pain in her eyes, and Reese knew the quips were for his benefit, to cover whatever real emotions she might be feeling. Over the years she'd gotten good at masking sentiment behind insouciance.

"It's your house, Rita. If you'd rather I went somewhere else . . ."

"Don't be ridiculous. Come in."

He dropped his saddlebags on the floor. She went to the cabinet in the corner and lifted a whiskey bottle in his direction. He shook his head sharply.

"I need a place to stay for a while."

"Wifey toss you out already?" she asked, her tone sharper than her words warranted. "She must be smarter than she looked."

"Cut the sarcasm. I know you liked Patience the moment you met her. Damn women, the way you all stick together."

"Well, we're members of a sisterhood of sorts, I suppose you could say. But you're right. I do like her. She has mettle. So if you've been a bad boy I'm afraid you'll find little sympathy on my doorstep."

"I'm not looking for a shoulder to cry on," he told her, eyeing her gaping red robe. She smiled and pulled the lapels of the garment together. "Or comfort of any kind," he added meaningfully. "I've come to Mobile for a specific purpose, and I need to use this place as part of a subterfuge."

"Oh, this sounds intriguing. Why don't you tell me all about it while I brew you tea."

"Make it coffee. And you'd better make it strong. It's going to be a long night."

Two hours and two pots of coffee later, he settled back on the sofa. Rita's eyes had gone from teasing to terrified.

"You can't do this, Reese. My God, do you realize how dangerous your plan is? These men are killers!"

"Yes, James's killers. Murderers, who have so far gotten away with their crime. I'm about to change that."

"But to try and trap them—you'll wind up just like James. No, you've got to reconsider. There must be another way."

"Do you think they're going to just stroll into the sheriff's office and turn themselves in? It's been months. No clue has turned up. No suspect has been arrested. I can't let it go any longer."

"Why? Why do you have to do this now? Things are starting to look up for you. You've managed to save Bonne Chance. You've got Ran running things smoothly. You're married now, to a beautiful, respectable woman. People are beginning to think maybe you have changed for the better."

"Then we'll just have to convince them they're wrong."

"By pretending you've moved back in with me?

By drinking and gambling your way back into another kettle of trouble?"

"I won't really be drunk, so there isn't any danger of my being caught unawares. As far as gambling goes, it serves my purpose just as well to win as to lose. If I'm on a winning streak, I'm likely to accept another game of high stakes without a thought to the consequences."

"Uh-huh, and what about Patience? Does she know what you're up to? What is she going to think when she hears you've moved back in here with me?"

"I'll explain it all to her after I've done what I came here to do. Until then, I can't help what she thinks or hears."

"God, you're a cold bastard. That girl is your wife. You know what she'll think?"

"I also know what she'd do if she found out I'm going after the men who killed her father. She'd be right here, in the thick of things, poking her button nose into a dangerous situation."

"Ah, hah! You admit it's dangerous?"

"Dammit, Rita," he barked, rising from the sofa to pace the floor. "I was there when James was killed. I know exactly what these men are capable of. I'm not fooling myself that it won't be dangerous. That's why I'm not about to let Patience get involved. Even if it means she'll be upset for a time."

"Upset? I suspect she'll be more than that. She'll be after your hide—and mine—before this is through."

"Look, do you think I like lying to Patience? I

hate it, but I'll do whatever I have to do to protect her. I love her, Rita," he said, all the feelings he couldn't show Patience now spilling forth freely.

She touched his shoulder. "I know, Reese. And I'm glad you found someone like Patience to share your love with. I just want you to be alive to enjoy it."

Reese trusted Rita. He knew her better than anyone else, for they'd always been more than lovers. They'd been friends. He was thankful to see that, at least, hadn't changed.

"I love her more than I thought I could ever love anyone. Every minute I'm away from her, I miss her and long to be with her again. But I can't be with her, not the way I want to, until I settle the matter of her father's death."

She nodded, chewing the corner of her lip thoughtfully. "Well, then I guess you'd better get some sleep. I have a feeling you're going to need it when you hit the taverns tonight."

He laughed dryly and went to collect his belongings. "I've become something of a homebody, Rita girl. It might take me a while to get back into that boisterous routine."

"Shall I make up the sofa?" she smirked, fanning the collar of her robe. "Or will you be sharing with me?"

He threw back his head and laughed at her saucy joke. "I'll take the sofa," he told her firmly. "You might think my wife is all sweetness and decorum, but I've seen her temper."

Chapter Twenty-five

As Patience entered the infirmary, eyes were lowered and voices stopped in mid-sentence.

"Mag, is everything all right?"

"Just fine, miss. We've had a run of scrapes and cuts this morning, but nothing serious."

Ran nodded to Mag and ducked out of the clinic, tipping his hat to Patience. She noticed he didn't meet her gaze.

Glancing back toward Mag, she caught one of the workers staring at her, a sympathetic expression on his face. His eyes met hers and he scampered for the door. "Thanks, Mag, see ya," he mumbled as he raced by.

"What's the matter with everyone today?" Patience asked, shaking her head in bewilderment. If she didn't know better, she'd swear everybody was trying to avoid her.

"I don't know what you mean," Mag told her with a shrug. She went back to rolling bandages, two of the smaller children on stools helping her.

Patience frowned, wondering for a moment if something were going on. Then she saw a stack of linens that needed to be folded and she went to work, trying to put thoughts of Reese and the slaves' peculiar actions out of her mind.

At dinner, Gay spilled Patience's water and dropped a chicken leg on the table beside her plate. When Patience tried to question the girl about her nervousness, the slave burst into tears and ran from the room.

Even Ma Jewel seemed unusually short-tempered and acerbic. She chastised Gay for the mishaps and then for her reaction, even though Patience tried to make light of the whole episode.

Finally, Patience had had enough. She slapped her napkin down beside her plate and, pushing away from the table, she stood.

"Would someone please tell me what is going on around here? Did somebody die? Is someone ill? Why are you all acting so strange?"

"Nothin' but a careless mishap," Ma declared with vinegar in her voice. "Silly girl ought'a know how to pour water in a glass by now."

"It was an accident, Ma. Gay is usually very careful. Besides, I've told you before, I can pour my own water and serve myself. I don't need to be waited on."

The front bell rang and Ma looked at Patience, her hands on her hips. "Don't suppose you need no one to answer the door, neither."

"No, I certainly do not," Patience said. "Why don't you take Gay into the kitchen and find out what's bothering her. If you can't calm her down, give her the day off or something."

Ma waddled into the warming kitchen, muttering all the while beneath her breath. Patience rolled her eyes heavenward and went to answer the door.

"Virginia!" Patience fought to hide her surprise. "Won't you come in?"

"I'm sorry to bother you," the woman said apologetically. "But I wonder if we could talk."

Patience raised an eyebrow, wondering what Samuel Symmons's daughter could possibly want to see her about. But she nodded and, with a smile, said, "Certainly. Come into the parlor. Can I get you anything? Coffee, or perhaps lemonade? It's awfully hot out today, isn't it?"

She knew she was babbling, but couldn't seem to stop. A feeling of foreboding swept over her. This day had started out strange, and it was quickly progressing to bizarre. After Reese bested Samuel in his bid for Bonne Chance, Patience had assumed she would never see any of the Symmonses again. Obviously, she'd been wrong.

"Yes, it is," Virginia said, taking a seat on the gold brocade sofa. Patience sat opposite her.

"So, lemonade then?"

"What?" the woman blinked and then her expression cleared and she quickly shook her head. "Oh, no, thank you. I wouldn't care for anything."

"Well, then, did you want to discuss something specific, or just chat?"

"I know you don't consider my family close friends, and I want you to know I don't blame you for that. Father can be awful when he's thwarted, and Reese defeated him soundly this time. Not that Father didn't deserve the licking." She shook her head disappointedly. "I still can't believe he tried to take Bonne Chance away from Reese."

"You knew what your father was up to?" Patience's spine stiffened and she felt her ire grow.

"Oh, no," Virginia rushed to assure her. "I had no idea until Reese stormed out of our house that day. I told Father what he was doing was despicable, but he's become obsessed with uniting his property with the land Reese owns."

"I gathered as much, but why are you telling me all this now? Reese raised the money to buy back his markers and Bonne Chance is on its way to being solidly secure once more."

Virginia dropped her gaze, and Patience was suddenly reminded of the other odd behavior which had seemed to follow her since early morning.

"Has something happened that I should know about, Virginia? Something to do with Reese?"

"He's in Mobile, you know." She didn't look up, and her hands continued to twist around a handkerchief in her lap.

Patience took the opportunity to compose herself, forcing a lightness into her tone. "Of course. He's there on business."

Virginia looked up at Patience through the thick veil of her lashes, and her mouth turned down in a frown. "Did Reese ever tell you that my father planned for us to be married?"

Cold water thrown in her face couldn't have surprised Patience more. Her mask of indifference fell away. "What? When?"

"Oh, it was a long time ago, when we were children. The Ashburns were still alive then, and so was my mother. We all spent a lot of time together. My father had the idea that if he could unite the families, he could unite the plantations. With him in control, of course. But even then, Reese managed to impede his plans."

"How?"

She laughed lightly and finally glanced up, directly into Patience's wide, startled eyes.

"He didn't love me," she announced.

Patience rose from her seat and paced to the fireplace. Her palms were coated with a layer of nervous perspiration, and she spread them on the cool marble of the mantel.

"Virginia, why are you telling me all this?" She suspected it wasn't a friendly reminiscing.

"I want you to understand why I'm about to tell you something I'd rather not."

"Which is?"

"Reese has always been very nice to me. We grew up together, and I consider him one of my closest friends. That was the main reason neither of us could ever consider marrying the other. And he knew I wanted to attend college, something my father refused to even consider. Father believes too much knowledge is unladylike."

Patience nodded, not trusting her voice. She didn't know where the conversation was heading, but she knew with a certainty she couldn't explain that she was not going to like what Virginia had to say.

"I've gotten off the point," Virginia apologized with a slight smile. "I just wanted you to understand that you did something the rest of us could never do, Patience. You reached Reese, and you changed him. For a time he was like a different person, responsible and settled. He seemed content."

"For a time?"

Virginia glanced sideways and cleared her throat. "Everyone is gossiping, Patience. I've never been ashamed to admit that I love to listen to gossip. But this is one time I wish I hadn't heard the talk."

"I don't put much stock in rumors, Virginia."

"Nor do I," the woman hastened to admit. "But—well, I wanted you to know."

"Know what?"

"I don't know what happened between you and Reese, and it's none of my business. But you need to know that he's fallen back into his old ways, Patience."

"What are you talking about?" The apprehension blossomed into outright dread. Patience had felt something was amiss, even before the whispers, the looks. She'd suspected trouble before Virginia uttered the words she'd feared.

"He's gambling heavily again, and drinking. And . . ." She hesitated, fingering the lace handkerchief.

"And what?"

"Nothing," she said, jumping to her feet. "I just wanted you to know what folks were saying. I hope it's all false, Patience. I really do. But maybe you should go and see for yourself."

She pressed Patience's hand between hers and then rushed for the door. Patience had a sinking suspicion what fact Virginia Symmons had been unable to repeat. She'd carefully avoided the issue of where Reese had been staying during his recent spree in Mobile.

Unfortunately, Patience had a pretty good idea. She heard the door slam shut behind Virginia and sank onto the sofa. All the doubts and self-recriminations she'd struggled with for the past five days rushed over her once more.

After they'd made love, Reese had fled for Mobile. Back to the wild lifestyle he'd led before her arrival.

Back to the mistress whose talents he obviously preferred.

That night Patience chose to sleep in her old room. The feminine surroundings were oddly comforting after the cold, masculine atmosphere of Reese's room.

She lay awake, her mind whirling with all she'd heard that day. Was it true? Had Reese reverted to his old ways after all the strides he'd made? Had he left her bed to return to Rita Mallory's?

Was the ring on her finger just an obligatory gesture? Or had he been trying to tell her what he couldn't say with words?

"Or am I fooling myself because I don't want to

admit I've been forsaken?"

She toyed with the ring, sliding it on and off her finger like picking the petals of a daisy. *He's true to me; he's betraying me.*

She didn't want to believe Virginia's fears could be true. But why would he go to Mobile, so soon after returning? Had business called? Or had his former life, and his former love, beckoned?

She knew of nothing regarding the plantation that would demand his attention. But, she reminded herself, Reese usually played his cards close to his chest.

The question remained, were those cards metaphorical or literal?

Reese was her husband. She'd given him her love, her body, her very soul. Didn't she owe him her trust and her faith as well? Didn't she at least owe him the benefit of the doubt? She couldn't jump to conclusions based on rumor and innuendo.

Slipping the ring back on her finger, she jumped from the bed. Tossing some clothes into her valise, she began to make plans.

She trusted Reese, and she always would. Unless she witnessed such debauchery with her own eyes.

"You look too convincing," Rita told Reese as she stood by the sofa surveying his appearance. "If I didn't know better, I'd swear I could smell the whiskey from here."

"You can. I dabbed a little here and there for effect."

"Well, don't expect the French perfume companies to beat down your door for the secret," she warned, wrinkling her nose in disgust. "Or the women either."

"The only person I'm interested in attracting is a killer."

A shiver raked Rita's spine; her eyes grew fearful and wary. "Reese, I really don't think this is a good idea. I wish you'd let the sheriff handle it."

"I've let him handle things for months, and nothing has happened. These robberies are still going on all over the docks—the only difference is no one else has been killed. But even that is just a matter of time. Someone else will eventually try to fight these thugs, and they'll die for it. I have to do this."

His shirt was dingy, his trousers wrinkled and stained. He'd let his beard grow the five days he'd been staying at her house,. and a heavy black shadow covered his jaw. His usually slicked-back hair was loose and over-long, hanging around his face in disarray.

"What makes you think whoever killed James will make another play for you? You haunted the docks for three months after James's death and no one bothered you."

"Hell, I could have tripped over the bastards after James died and I probably wouldn't have noticed, I was so soused. This time I won't be drunk or unaware. It may not be me they go after, but I'll be there just the same. I'm ready for them now." He tucked a single-shot percussion pistol into the waistband of his trousers. His father had taught him to shoot as a boy, but he'd never thought he'd need the skill for protection. He realized, not for the first time, that he'd been foolish and naive for a long time.

"What if they recognize you? They could kill you just to be sure you don't identify them."

"If they were going to recognize me, they've had plenty of opportunities before now. It's been six months, and I'm sure they've run through a host of pigeons since then."

"Maybe, but I imagine they remember the one they killed—and the one that got away."

Reese touched her cheek and smiled grimly. "Don't worry. I have a feeling the bastards never gave me, or James, another thought. But they will, Rita girl. Before I'm finished, they will."

Chapter Twenty-six

Patience heard the wheels of the hired carriage as it pulled away behind her, deserting her on the steps of Rita Mallory's house.

She bolstered her courage, raised her hand, and knocked. She waited, valise in hand. The outside of the cottage was tidy. A small flower bed bloomed by the porch, adding a touch of color to the gray stone structure.

The door swung open, and Rita's eyebrows climbed toward her hairline. She wore a purple silk gown and a sardonic expression.

Her gaze locked on the valise Patience carried. Her mouth twisted derisively. Leaning out, she scanned the front of the house closely.

"What are you looking for?" Patience asked, following her glance.

"I thought perhaps someone had hung an inn

sign on my house. I've had more traffic through here than all of Queen's Row on a Saturday night."

"So he has been here?"

"Reese? Yeah, he's been here. In and out like this was his private hostel."

Seeing the look of pained disappointment cross Patience's face, Rita slowly shook her head. "It isn't what you're thinking."

Patience tipped her chin up and squared her jaw. "How do you know what I'm thinking?"

Rita quirked a single brow, and the corner of her mouth turned up in a mock smile. "Because that's what I'd be thinking if I were you. You'd better come in and let me explain."

Patience lifted her case and entered the cottage, her head held high.

"Would you like some tea?"

She turned to face Rita, surprise widening her eyes. "Yes, I'd love some."

"Don't look so shocked," Rita told her, going to the fireplace and swinging a kettle of water over the glowing embers. "What did you expect me to offer you, rot gut?"

"No, of course not," Patience rushed to assure her, certain she'd insulted the woman. She relaxed and dropped her valise by the floral velvet sofa. "I'm sorry, I suppose I'm a bit on the defensive."

Rita shrugged, pouring tea leaves into the kettle from a tin canister on the mantel. "Understandable."

Silence fell over the room until the kettle lid began to zing with steam. Rita poured the brew through cheesecloth into a ceramic pot. More servicable than decorative, the pot seemed to fit with Rita Mallory's surroundings.

The room held the basic furnishings—sofa, rocker, desk, a plain woven rug. Two rooms made up the front of the cottage. Through a narrow doorway, Patience could see a small bedroom. A white chenille spread with pink tea roses covered the bed.

Her mind painted a picture of Rita Mallory and Reese, lying together on that bed, locked in a passionate embrace. Jealousy suffused her. A knife of pain ripped through her heart.

Rita saw where her gaze had landed. "Don't think about that," she said, her voice impersonal and detached. "That was business. Old business."

"Business? How can you . . . ?"

"Don't try to understand someone like me, Patience. And don't try to understand my relationship with Reese. There are some things you're better off not knowing about."

"He's my husband now. If he's still . . . seeing you . . ."

"He's been sleeping on my sofa. *Seeing* me is all he's doing."

"Why?"

Rita shook her head. "His choice, not mine," she admitted with a nonchalant shrug that didn't quite cover her pained expression.

Patience fought the surge of relief she felt at Rita's admission, but did not comment, not wanting to hurt the woman any more than she already had.

"I meant, why is he here at all? What's going on, Rita?"

Sipping her tea, Rita studied Patience over the rim of her cup. She puckered her lips and blew the steam away from the brew. Again, she shrugged. "You'll have to ask him."

"You know, don't you? He must have told you why he was in town when he asked to stay."

"Men confide in women like me all the time, Patience. It doesn't mean anything."

"In this case, I think it does," Patience said. "You helped him before, with Judge Carson. You helped me, too. You and Reese are—were—more than—"

"Business acquaintances? Yes, we were." She set her tea aside and released a weary sigh. "We are. Friends."

"Then please tell me what's going on. Why did he come to Mobile?" Her face instantly flooded with color, and she sipped her tea to cover her embarrassment. "Did he tell you anything about—us?"

"Look, Patience," the woman said quickly, holding up her hand. "Reese hasn't betrayed your trust in him, with words or deeds. He doesn't talk to me about your private life. I know he loves you, and that's all he's said. Please, just go home. When he's ready, he'll explain everything to you."

"But is he drinking again, gambling? He hasn't done any of that in months. He seemed so happy at Bonne Chance. I thought we were beginning to share something special."

Rita glanced down into her cup, and Patience immediately regretted her emotional outburst. She'd embarrassed herself *and* Rita. She swallowed hard and fought for calm.

"I'm sorry. I know this puts you in a very bad spot. I wouldn't ask you if it weren't so important. Please, Rita, help me."

The redhead pursed her full lips and studied Patience for a long minute. "Settle down. I'll put another pot of tea on and we'll talk." She stood and refilled the kettle.

Patience removed the jacket of her navy-blue traveling suit, folding it and laying it over the back of the sofa. She fluffed the wrinkles out of her crisp white shirtwaist and smoothed her skirt around her. Unpinning her wide-brimmed bonnet, she laid it aside.

When she looked up, Rita was watching her with amusement.

"What?"

"A real lady. In my house, asking for my help. Who would have thought that?"

"You're a real lady, Rita. More important, you're a good friend to Reese and to me."

"Yeah, that's really where my true talent lies," Rita said with a smirk. "Friendliness."

She burst into baudy chuckles, and Patience couldn't help but join in. She'd sounded so priggish, so trite. But at least they'd managed to find a measure of humor in this bizarre situation.

"To understand what Reese is doing," Rita started, burrowing into the corner of the sofa opposite Patience, "you have to understand how he felt about your father. And about James's death," she added, tucking her feet beneath her as she settled in.

"He and my father were very close. I know that. Father talked about Reese every time he visited me." She bit her lip and glanced up at Rita, chagrined. "That was one of the reasons I wanted so badly to hate Reese when I first arrived. I'd been terribly jealous of him for years."

Rita nodded and refilled Patience's cup. "Well, if your father had had a son, he couldn't have loved him more than he loved Reese. They were inseparable. And when James died—was killed," she amended, "Reese fell apart. For months I waited to hear that he'd been found dead too. It was only when he was called home because of you that he rallied himself somewhat."

"Yes, I remember the way he looked that first day. Cuts and bruises all over his face. I still thought he was the most handsome man I'd ever seen."

"I meant what I said, Patience. Reese loves you. I didn't know he could love anybody that way, after so many years of building walls around his feelings. But you got through, somehow. What he is now is because of that love."

"But what is he doing here, Rita? You have to tell me—I have to know."

Rita shook her head. "He didn't want you to find out."

"I've come all the way from Bonne Chance to find out. I won't give up until I know the whole story. If you don't tell me, I'll just find someone else who will."

Finally, Rita nodded with a resigned sigh. "All right, I'll tell you."

* * *

When she'd finished repeating Reese's plan, Rita met Patience's terrified gaze. She placed her hand over Patience's trembling one and squeezed.

"He has to do this, Patience. Before he can put aside his guilt over James's death and find happiness with you, he has to feel he's made up to your father for failing him."

"That's ridiculous," Patience cried, snatching her hand from Rita's grasp and jumping to her feet. "My father had memorized the inside of every Boston saloon before Reese was ever born. Even when mother was alive, he'd sometimes stay out all night. I remember her pacing the floor when I was barely old enough to walk, waiting for him to come home."

She strode to the fireplace and back, yanking impatiently at her skirts when they wrapped around her feet.

"Reese didn't influence my father's behavior. If anything, Father no doubt led Reese down the path of debauchery. Why do you think my father was disinherited and sent to America in the first place? He tried to drink away the family fortune by the time he was twenty-one."

"Reese suggested the tavern they went to that night. He blames himself for James's death and doesn't feel like you can have a life together until he settles the score."

"Settles the score! My father was viciously attacked by robbers out to steal his money. They would have done the same whether Reese had been with him or not."

"I'm not saying I agree with Reese," Rita hastened to tell a frantic Patience. "I'm just repeating your husband's reasoning."

Huffing, Patience planted her hands on her hips. She tapped her toe for a second, then shook her head. "I knew I married a reputed drunk and rakehell, but I didn't know I married I blockhead. Of all the asinine . . ."

She stopped, a flush creeping over her cheeks. Patience pressed her fingers to her lips. "I'm sorry, but I don't think I've ever been so mad."

"Men'll do that to a girl. Try not to worry. Reese has been taking care of himself for a long time. I'm sure he'll be fine."

"Uum," Patience mumbled, tapping her fingernail against her lip.

"Right now," Rita said, pushing to her feet, "it's getting late. I'm going to change and get ready for bed. You can share with me tonight," she told her, nodding toward the bedroom, "and have it out with Reese when he comes back in the morning."

"Oh, thank you. I will," she muttered, her mind whirling with all Rita had told her. She had no intention of waiting until morning to give Reese Ashburn a rather large piece of her mind. Of all the idiotic things she'd ever heard of, his scheme had to top the list. And that was exactly what she intended to tell him as soon as she found him. And then they were going home to put all this foolishness behind them once and for all.

She waited until Rita had entered the bedroom, then snatched up her jacket and slipped quietly out the door.

* * *

Reese eyed the wealthy patron over his whiskey glass. The man had been throwing money about for nearly two hours. A pompous peacock, he ignored the whores in favor of the cards and booze.

The fop caught Reese's eye, but the man who entered the Hog's Head tavern after the peacock snagged Reese's full attention.

The rough wool jacket, the stringy black hair—it could be one of the attackers. It could also be some poor chap looking for a cheap drink.

But Reese didn't think so. He eyed the slovenly fellow, who eyed the peacock. Tension grew at the base of Reese's neck, knotting muscles and raising the short hairs on his nape. His palms were damp with anticipation, and they left smears on the thick glass he clutched tightly.

He'd been considering rejoining the game, but now he decided to wait and watch. If the man was one of the attackers, Reese didn't want to scare him off. He wanted the bastard to make a move so he could finish this.

He missed Bonne Chance. God, he missed Patience. He wanted to go home and put this whole wretched incident behind him. He'd never forget James, but for the first time he saw a future for himself. A future with Patience. And he wanted a chance to experience that eventuality.

One night of making love to his wife had only whetted his appetite for more—more of her love, more of her fierce passion. Hell, he even missed her sassy diatribes.

He wanted to share everything with her—his

hopes, his worries, his successes. All the things he'd experienced since she blew into his life like a hurricane.

But first he had to put an end to the guilt that gnawed his guts whenever he looked at Patience and saw, even fleetingly, her father in her eyes.

Suddenly Reese's spine stiffened. A surge of excitement coursed through him, and his heartbeat pounded loudly in his ears.

The grubby man moved to a table closer to the dandy. Their backs nearly touched now. Except to glance back rudely when the younger fellow's chair screeched against the planked floor, the foppish man didn't acknowledge the other's presence. He continued to play, calling for more whiskey and laughing raucously.

Reese wanted to move closer, to hear any words that might be exchanged between the two. But again, he didn't want to call attention to himself. So he sat in the corner and nursed his whiskey.

Earlier he'd joined in the game for a time, pretending to lose heavily. He'd groused loudly about the other players and the cards. He'd pretended to go off alone to sulk in the hopes he'd look like an easy mark for someone offering a new game with new blood.

So far no one had approached him. As he saw the black wool coat lean closer toward the natty gray dinner jacket, he thought he understood why. Tonight he wasn't the target.

The peacock's head tipped to one side as though he were catching the thread of a conversation, and the pulsing knot of trepidation in Reese's stomach tightened. The whiskey soured in his gut.

Then the man nodded, and Reese had no more time to think about what he was doing or consider his choices. The bloke in the wool coat tossed a coin onto the table and sauntered out of the tavern. The fop gathered a pile of winnings, stuffed them into his pockets, and made for the door.

Reese jumped to his feet, digging his own money out. He didn't bother to count the amount, instead dumping a handful of coins beside his half-empty glass. He whirled to follow the men—and ran headlong into a serving wench.

"Excuse me," he mumbled, stepping to the side to dodge her. She took a step in the same direction, mirroring his movement. He bobbed, and again she stepped in front of him.

Chuckling, she flashed him a buck-toothed grin. "Why don't we just dance and get it over with."

Reese took her shoulders and set her roughly to the side. She cursed him lewdly and made a rude gesture as he rushed past her, nearly upsetting her tray.

He burst through the door, scanning the bricked street along the waterfront. Blood raced wildly through his veins. The rapid-fire pounding of his heart nearly deafened him as it pulsated behind his ears.

He took a deep breath, sucking in the smells of dank wood and dead fish. Salt spray whipped his cheeks as the bay breeze blew, announcing another summer storm.

His frantic gaze searched the shadows of ship moorings and fish barrels. One lone whore strolled along the docks, her dress soiled and ragged, her walk marred by a pathetic limp.

Not sure which direction the men had taken, he hurried to the corner. Nothing.

The whore noticed him and was making her way across the street. Reese pulled a crumpled bill from his pocket and waved it at her. She hobbled eagerly toward him.

"What'cha got there, fancy Dan?"

"A V-spot. If," he said, holding the bill away, "you saw two men come by here."

"A slick and a soaplock? I seen 'em." She eyed the five-dollar bill greedily and licked her dry, cracked lips.

"Where'd they go?"

"'Round the corner and into that alley yonder," she told him, pointing in the direction opposite to the way he'd originally gone. He slammed the money into her palm and thanked her as he raced after the men, hoping it wasn't too late.

Another alley, another trap. A crazy mixture of hope and fear gripped him. His breath felt trapped in his lungs. Flames of foreboding burned through his chest.

He had to put an end to the shame and remorse he felt over James's death. More than anything, he wanted to see justice served. His determination overrode his apprehension as he sped toward the alley.

Skidding to a halt at the dark, narrow opening, he peered around the corner and saw the shadows of the two men approaching the opposite end of the passageway. He opened his mouth to call out a warning, then realized he could be signing the peacock's death warrant if he alerted the thief.

Silently he darted along the brick structure, pressing close to the wall to hide his approach. The men had slowed their pace, and they seemed to be conversing in whispered tones.

Perspiration popped out on Reese's brow and dripped into his eyes, stinging them. A chill black silence surrounded him and he saw, like ghastly etchings, images of the attack on him and James.

His breath came in short gasps as he forced the memory aside. He couldn't think about that now, couldn't let it affect what he had to do. If he didn't make a move soon, the scene might very well repeat itself.

He was only a few steps behind the men now. The peacock seemed to be in a hurry, stepping ahead of the other man as they reached the end of the alley. Reese pulled the pistol from his waistband and rushed forward. Praying he wasn't making a mistake, he slammed it down on the shiny black head.

The man crumpled to the ground in a heap, a weak groan the only sound in the eerie quiet of the back street.

The peacock whirled, his hand snaking toward his coat pocket and then dropping to his side when he saw Reese.

"What do you want?"

"Don't be afraid," Reese told him, holding his hands out. He realized he still held the gun and he tucked it back into its place. "I'm certain this man was about to rob you."

His heavy jowls shook as the man glanced at the form lying on the ground at Reese's feet. "Oh, my word. Do you mean the game was just a ploy to get me alone so he could assault me?"

"I don't know if he meant to harm you, but I'm sure he would have taken your money. In fact," he puffed, still trying to catch his breath and slow his speeding heart rate, "he may have accomplices nearby."

"I think you may be right," the peacock said, a chilling note of authority drifting into the voice that, only a moment ago, had sounded weak and effeminate.

Ominous foreboding sent an icy finger of dread along Reese's spine. He saw the man on the ground shift, rolling to his knees. Reaching for his pistol, he heard the unmistakable sound of a hammer being cocked.

"I wouldn't if I were you," the dandy said, the warning in his words distinct.

Reese slowly raised his head—and felt his heart plummet to his feet. The peacock lifted his hand, and the faint glow of the moon lit briefly on the steel barrel of a nasty-looking pocket pistol.

"Just a little stomacher," the man told him. "But I don't think I'm likely to miss at this distance."

"You're making a mistake," Reese said, his fingers inching toward his waist.

The man made a derisive noise in his throat and lifted the gun closer to Reese. "I don't think so."

The man on the ground cursed soundly and pushed to his feet. He wiped a trickle of blood from his head with the back of his hand, then brought it down fast and landed an unexpected blow to Reese's jaw.

"You son of a bitch. You cracked my skull."

Reese staggered from the punch, then righted himself. He stepped toward the peacock.

"He's a thief and a murderer," he told the man, stepping between the thief and his prey. "I'm trying to save your blasted neck."

"Well now, that's mighty nice of you, Mr. Ashburn. Considering I'm counting on collecting a handsome reward for putting yours in a noose."

The man's words, as well as his use of Reese's name, registered at the same moment that the man cuffed the base of Reese's head with the pistol.

Reese belatedly realized, as he slumped to the ground, that he'd been set up again.

The carriage pulled to a stop in front of a rundown, shabby building directly on the waterfront. Patience peered at the structure, her small nose crinkling in dismay.

"You want me to wait, lady?"

She glanced up at the driver and nodded nervously. "Yes—yes, please wait," she said, climbing down from the conveyance. She picked her skirt up as her feet sank into a puddle of sludge at the edge of the street.

This couldn't possibly be the place Rita had told her Reese intended to go tonight. No one in his right mind would set foot in such a wretched establishment.

Of course, she reminded herself, Reese wasn't in a sound state of mind right now. Otherwise he'd never have devised such a foolish plan.

Cautiously, she stepped toward the tavern. Sounds of revelry filtered through the thin walls and she took another tentative step.

Suddenly she heard the carriage pulling away, and she whirled, running after the rig.

"Wait, stop!" she called frantically, trotting behind the spinning wheels. In a second it was out of sight and she slumped in dismay.

"Hello, Patience."

With a startled shriek, she spun back toward the tavern. Her heart slammed into her throat and then slowly, torturously, settled back in her chest.

"Oh, my goodness, am I glad to see you." Actually, she could think of a hundred people she'd rather see, but right now she was in no mood to quibble.

"I'm charmed. But what are you doing in such a nasty place alone? And where is your husband?"

Abruptly, Patience's relief dissipated. She cast a glance over her shoulder where her carriage had gone. She'd asked the man to stay. Why would he leave her that way?

"Can I give you a lift somewhere?"

"No, thank you," she said, stepping back. She eyed the distance to the door of the tavern.

"You'll never make it," the man told her, inching closer. His hand came up and clasped her wrist. She opened her mouth to scream, and a strong-smelling rag was thrust against her face.

Blackness engulfed her and still she fought, kicking and clawing at the arms that held her. She gasped for air. The noxious odor burned a trail through her nostrils, and she fainted.

Chapter Twenty-seven

Reese climbed his way out of a thick fog of pain and confusion. He lifted his hand, touching the goose egg on the back of his neck. His leaden arm fell to his side.

Sounds drifted in and out of focus—angry words, heated arguments. He tried to make out what was being said but couldn't for the blood pounding in his ears.

Rolling to his knees, he tried to stand. Dizziness swept over him, and he toppled to the side. The voices continued to roll in and out like waves lapping the shore.

A woman. No, a man. Several men. Arguing, yelling. He wondered if he'd gotten drunk and couldn't remember. Was this the hangover that would finally kill him?

He remembered the lump at the base of his

skull, and flashes of memory rushed back at him. He'd been clubbed—by the pompass peacock he'd been trying to help.

The blow must have cracked his skull. He thought he heard—was that Patience and—Samuel?

Staggering to his feet, the haze finally lifted and he took in his surroundings. Crates and barrels lined the walls. The voices came from the back of the warehouse, the refracted light from two oil lamps positioned to his left.

"You're a fool and a failure. Nothing you've tried has succeeded, and this won't either."

What was Patience doing here! And why was she giving Samuel the sharp side of her tongue? How had they gotten into what he could only assume was Samuel's waterfront warehouse?

His head cleared fast, and he stopped himself before he could go rushing into the open. He'd been set up, only to wake in the company of his worst enemy. A man he didn't trust. A man who, it would seem, had somehow gotten his hands on Patience.

The sound of an open palm meeting flesh sent his reason fleeing. Patience's involuntary cry cut through him like a razor.

Forgetting caution, he ran for the end of the warehouse. The first man he came to turned at the sound of Reese's footsteps. It was the thief in the wool coat.

Reese lunged, landing atop the man and flattening him. Before the thug could react, Reese landed a solid punch on the man's jaw and watched his head loll to the side.

"Very nice," Samuel said, clapping his hands as he stepped into the open. Patience whirled to see Reese struggling to his feet.

"Reese!"

Samuel grabbed her arm and yanked her back to his side when she would have run toward her husband. She tried to shake off his hold, but couldn't.

"We've been waiting for you to join us, Ashburn. So glad my friend there didn't crush your head."

Reese glanced sideways and saw the man who'd hit him, divested of the expensive jacket and vest. His shirt sleeves were rolled to the elbow, and Reese could see a scar along his forearm.

Again, scenes from the night he and James were attacked came rushing back. He saw the blood, the knife. He remembered the hand holding the weapon, twisting it. He saw again the hairy wrist, the scar.

"You son of a bitch," he snarled, making a lunge for Samuel.

The remaining thug stepped forward, a knife suddenly appearing in his hand. He poked the tip of the blade into Reese's throat and Reese froze midstep. The man laughed, then casually used the tip of the blade to pick his fingernails as Samuel chuckled.

"What's the matter, Ashburn? Lost some of your piss and vinegar?"

"I should have known you were behind what happened."

"Thieves roam the waterfront at will. It was a simple matter to make it look like a robbery gone awry."

"Yes, I can see that now. A perfect setup. What I don't understand is, why? Why James?"

"Not James," Samuel said with a sneer. He flashed a cutting look at the man to Reese's right, and the thug studied his shoes. "You, Ashburn. You were the target. Only you've got more lives than a frigging alley cat. That wasn't the first time I'd tried to end your miserable, useless life."

"For Bonne Chance?"

"Of course for Bonne Chance. You still don't understand, do you? You were a worthless wastrel. You never gave a damn about that plantation. Yet you were the only thing keeping me from what I wanted."

"Because I wouldn't sell."

"No, you wouldn't sell. You didn't want the place, and you didn't care a whit if it fell to ruin as long as it didn't affect your whoring and gambling. But you wouldn't let me have it, either."

"So you decided to kill me? And then what? Buy the place cheap?"

"I knew killing you was the only way I'd ever get it. You would never give it up willingly." He shrugged. "So I tried that first. But after these imbeciles messed up the attack, I knew I'd have to bide my time. I couldn't risk another accident too soon. Even that dimwit of a sheriff would have gotten suspicious. But then you played right into my hands. Buying your markers up was like taking candy from a baby, if you'll pardon the cliché."

"Only I won again," Reese said, eyeing Patience. The imprint of Samuel's hand was still clearly visible on her cheek, and rage temporarily clouded his thoughts. All he could think about was getting his hands on the bastard and ripping his heart out.

His lips thinned and his nostrils flared, but otherwise he didn't show any sign of the fury thundering through him.

"No!" Samuel barked. "You didn't win. You only delayed the inevitable. I'll still have Bonne Chance. This stupid, witless ploy of yours to find James's killer was the break I needed. You made sure everyone knew you'd gone back to your old ways. Once again, you played right into my hands. All I had to do was lure you out with a familiar scenario and then arrange a little accident. No questions. No suspicious sheriff. It's the perfect plan."

Samuel was right, Reese realized. He'd been a fool. Again. Only now the stakes were higher. He looked at Patience. She was staring at him, fear coloring her blue eyes. He longed to go to her, to tell her how much he loved her, how sorry he was he'd messed up again and involved her.

Suddenly she cocked her lips in a half-smile. Her eyes flashed, and he wanted to groan aloud. She was getting another idea. He recognized the signs, and it sent a cold chill down his spine.

Before he could warn her with a look, she stomped her heel into the instep of Samuel's foot. The man roared with rage and raised his hand to slap her again. The thug stepped in front of Reese, his knife poised.

"Go ahead," his wife challenged, tipping her cheek toward Samuel. "Slap me silly. It won't change the fact that we beat you, Samuel. Reese and I—we've won. And you don't even know it."

Samuel lowered his hand. A snarl twisted his mouth. "What are you talking about?"

Reese inched closer, and the knife snagged a button on the front of his shirt. The button pinged to the floor and rolled away, and Reese was forced to step back.

"You'll never get your hands on Bonne Chance, Samuel," Patience proudly announced. "You're forgetting that Reese is no longer the only Ashburn left. I'm his wife, and Bonne Chance goes to me if anything happens to Reese."

Reese closed his eyes and stifled a groan. "Shut up, Patience," he warned through clenched teeth.

"And for your information, Samuel," she proceeded, totally ignoring Reese's admonition, "I'm already carrying the next Ashburn heir."

Shock, pride, and stark terror rocked Reese. His mouth fell open, and his stomach churned with dread. She was lying, she had to be. They'd only made love that once, and it hadn't even been a week since that glorious night. She couldn't know if she were pregnant already.

"For God's sake, Patience, shut up," he hissed.

Didn't she understand the depths of Samuel's corruption? He'd think nothing of killing her, pregnant or not, if she stood between him and Bonne Chance. Yet she was purposely focusing all his hatred and rancor on her.

Understanding dawned instantly. Reese longed

to throttle her, even as he admired her courage.

His gaze fell to the knife pressed against his abdomen. He still didn't know how Patience had gotten into the middle of this predicament, but it was his mess and his responsibility to get them out of it. Alive.

Patience continued to harangue Samuel, and the two got into a bitter argument when Samuel admitted he'd sent for her uncle to stop any chance of Reese marrying her to get his hands on her money.

Curling his hands at his sides, Reese waited until the man with the knife glanced over to watch the spectacle. Then, with a single, sudden arc, he grabbed the hand holding the knife and whirled, shoving it into the man's chest.

The man's agonized scream rent the air, and Samuel whipped around to face Reese. The thief slumped to his knees, the embedded knife still in his chest.

"No!" Samuel screamed, taking a hurried step toward Reese.

Patience quickly glanced between Reese and Samuel. She saw the frenzied hatred on the older man's face as he reached for the pistol tucked into his waistband. She hurled herself at Samuel, landing on his back. She clutched handfuls of hair as he twisted and bucked, trying to throw her off. His gun skidded across the floor and under a crate.

"Patience!" Reese called, rushing forward.

He darted left, then right. But Samuel continued to rage like a wild bear, thrashing first one way, then the other. Patience held on for dear life, scratching and clawing at his face and eyes. She kicked with her heels.

With a fierce howl, Samuel grabbed her hands and slung her over. He lifted her like a rag doll and tossed her backwards into a crate. Wood splintered, and the crate crashed to pieces.

Reese yelled her name and charged Samuel, a red haze of fury and fear all he could see. He grabbed the man's shoulder and spun him around, landing a solid punch to his meaty jaw.

Samuel staggered back, but kept his balance. He came at Reese, his fist raised. But Reese blocked the punch and sent him to the floor with a hard right.

Turning, Reese tried to see Patience amid the pile of boards that used to be the crate. He took a step toward her and heard a sucking noise from behind.

Whipping around, he saw Samuel leaning over the dead man. His foot was levered against the man's stomach as he wrenched the knife from his chest.

Reese crouched, inching away from where Patience had fallen. He watched as Samuel tracked his movements. Like a predator, the man descended. He lunged and parried, smiling when Reese jerked back, barely missing a vicious swipe with the knife.

"Give it up, Ashburn. I'm going to kill you this time. I swear it. And then I'm going to kill that bitch you married."

"You can try," Reese taunted him, circling first one way and then the other.

Patience's still form was directly behind Samuel now. Reese risked a fleeting glance in her direction and swallowed the bitter taste of fear that threatened to choke him. She hadn't moved.

"You're a cur, Ashburn. You don't deserve Bonne Chance."

"Maybe not," Reese agreed, dodging another thrust. "But I mean to keep it just the same."

His taunt succeeded in making Samuel angrier, and the man swung the knife, catching Reese's upper arm.

Reese grunted, clapping his hand over the wound. Immediately blood seeped through his fingers, spreading onto his white shirt.

"Ah, hah," Samuel cried out with glee. "You're a whelp, Ashburn. A weakling."

"And you're a dead man," Reese said chillingly through clenched teeth.

Too late, Samuel saw Reese's plan. He'd backed him into a corner. Crates and barrels surrounded him. He couldn't retreat, couldn't sidestep.

Reese ripped the dangling sleeve from his shirt and advanced, wrapping it around his hand. In desperation Samuel lunged, and Reese caught the knife blade with his swaddled hand.

The blade cut through the cloth almost immediately, and he felt the sting as it sliced his palm. But he had the advantage and he rushed Samuel, forcing the knife against the man's throat. They slammed into a stack of crates and went down in a tangled heap.

Recovering quickly, Reese leaned back and balled his fist, determined to finish Samuel off.

As he looked down, his hand stopped in mid-air, and his stomach roiled. A bloody gash cut from Samuel's right ear to the center of his throat where the force of the fall had driven the knife blade into his neck. His eyes were wide, a look of astonishment caught in the dead gaze.

Reese sat back on his haunches and fought the wave of revulsion that engulfed him. He took several deep breaths and pushed to his feet. Staggering, he made his way across the warehouse to Patience.

Kneeling beside her, he lifted her head onto his lap. Her golden curls fell in disarray around her heart-shaped face, and he brushed them gently off her cheeks and forehead.

"Patience," he whispered, smoothing the strands back. "Darling, can you hear me?"

Rocking forward, he pressed his lips to her temple. "Patience," he called, over and over.

Blood ran from his arm onto the front of her white blouse as he gathered her in his embrace.

"Come on, darling, wake up," he said, trying to lift her into his grasp. He got his feet beneath him, and her head slumped back against his chest.

He hefted her into his arms and slowly pushed to his feet. Tears filled his eyes.

Reese couldn't remember the last time he'd cried. Not when James died, though he'd felt the pain of it to his very soul. Not even when his parents died. He'd been conscious of his elevated position then as the new master and didn't want to appear weak.

Now, all he could think of as he carried her out

of the warehouse was never again hearing Patience's voice haranguing him. Never seeing her startling blue eyes flash with indignation.

He'd only taken a few steps when she peered up at him and, arching one brow, said sharply, "Don't drop me."

He almost did as relief made him go weak in the knees. He lowered her to her feet, steadying her gently.

"Are you all right?"

He eased her over to a barrel on the dock and she sat shakily.

"Yes, I think so."

Her hands surveyed for damage and she paused, stricken when she came to the stain of blood on her chest.

"Mine, not yours," he told her.

She released a short, sharp gasp. "Oh, well, that makes me feel much better," she told him sarcastically, her eyes scanning him closely.

"I'm all right. Really," he added, when she noticed the missing sleeve, the dried blood on his arm.

"Samuel?"

He shook his head. "I'm sorry. I never meant to put you in danger."

"It wasn't your fault."

Her eyes met his, and she gripped his hand. "None of this was your fault, Reese. Not Samuel's obsession, not my father's death. That's what I came to tell you."

She held her hand to his cheek, and he covered it with his bandaged one. "I love you, Patience. I wanted you to have someone worthy of you. Someone your father would have approved of."

"And that's exactly what I've got," she told him. "I loved your loyalty to my father, your integrity when it came to saving Bonne Chance on your own. I'm humbled by your honor, thinking you had to prove you were worthy of me."

He clutched her to his chest and thought he'd never let her go. For a long minute he didn't move, didn't breathe for fear the whole scene would go up in a puff of smoke like an illusion.

Gaining control over his emotions once more, he straightened. "Let's get you back to Rita's," he said, lifting her to her feet. "I'll send for the doctor and the sheriff."

His arm went around her, and he supported her as they walked into the pale glow of early morning.

"So I'm damn near perfect, huh?"

A grin snaked across Reese's face, and Patience playfully poked his ribs as they lay in bed together, safely back at Bonne Chance at last.

The past hours had been a harrowing experience for her as they'd had to relate all the events leading to the final altercation in the warehouse.

She'd explained to Reese how she'd come to be in Mobile and how Samuel, watching to make sure the attack on Reese went as planned, saw her and decided to use her to get to her husband.

But now it was over and they were locked in each other's arms following a wonderful session of lovemaking—the first of many, Reese informed her.

"Don't get cocky," she told him. "You've got a long way to go before you'll be the perfect husband."

"But you said you I was loyal, honorable, and the best possible husband you could have."

"Yes," she admitted, dragging a ragged breath into her lungs as his hand skimmed her hip and thigh. "But there's still this little issue of slavery. And then there's Ran's position as overseer." She pushed his hand aside and rolled to face him. "He deserves to be acknowledged for the work he does. And what about . . ."

Reese grabbed her and placed a long, silencing kiss on her lips. Should he tell her that he'd already decided to give Mag her freedom papers for a wedding present? Or that he'd decided to make Ran overseer despite the furor it would cause? She deserved to know he'd been strongly considering her views these last few weeks.

He pulled away, and she opened her mouth to speak. Reese kissed her again.

"I'm beat," he said, when they finally parted. "And the only thing I want to debate is whether you want to eat before or after we make love again. So let's save this particular battle for tomorrow."

She grinned and leaned down, pressing a quick peck on his cheek. "All right. But be warned, I don't plan to give up."

He threw back his head and laughed. "I never thought you would, darling," he said, rolling her beneath him. "Not for a minute."

"Reese," she whispered.

"Yes, darling."

"After. Definitely after."